Over My D
Murder at E

A Bebe Bollinger Mystery

by

Christoph Fischer

Dedicated

To My Friends in the Eurovision Community:
Sid Hellyar, Valdemar Gomes, Gijsbert Groenveld,
Ertug Miras, Ofer Hamburger, Mickael Dennis and
Russell Davies

www.christophfischerbooks.com

Table of Contents

Prologue: Malmö; Sweden (May 2013)

Bebe couldn't keep up with all that was going on around her on the media balcony. A team of paramedics were busy working on the victim lying only a few metres away: their actions spoke volumes. Bebe had seen enough of her fans fainting in over-heated concert halls to know that this patient would not be resuscitated any time soon. As if to confirm her fears, the paramedics exchanged a look and shook their heads. A chill ran down her spine. The dart made it clear that this was a premeditated murder, and put all the dubious events and 'accidents' that had gone on in the run-up to the contest into a sinister context.

The security guards were quick to respond. They cleared the balcony, ushering the journalists and TV crews to a conference room on the mezzanine level.

"You may continue your coverage for now," they were told by a suited man with a headset and clipboard. "When the police arrive they'll decide what happens next. To make sure they can carry out their investigation, we have strict instructions to keep you all here for questioning."

A TV audience of over one billion people was watching the contest – the British TV viewers waiting for Bebe to chat to them in less than a minute – while a murderer was still on the loose. What were the organisers and the police thinking? Would they strike again, and if so, who would be their next victim? Was the dart maybe meant for Bebe? Was she safe? What could she do to prevent the murderer from striking again and ruining her moment in the Eurovision sunlight?

Leonard took her softly by the wrist.

"We're on in ten seconds," he said, looking into her eyes. "Forget about the guy and focus on the show. Security and the police have this covered, you're not in danger. Just be professional. Can you do that for me?"

Bebe gulped and nodded. Her thoughts went to the dead presenter and she regretted her earlier irritation with him. The poor man. She took a deep breath, glanced to the stage to remind herself what a big deal the next few minutes were for her career and what she had to do now. This light on the camera turned to red and she was on...

Chapter 1: Cardiff; (March 2013, six weeks earlier)

Bebe Bollinger struggled to squeeze her oversized suitcase into the boot of her Porsche Boxster. The car had been an impulse buy. It was everything *she* wanted to be: Stunning, energetic, fast and unstoppable. For a showbiz star with lots of luggage, the car, unfortunately, had minor downsides. It was a pity how practicality rarely matched with style, she mused. How did other celebrities manage so well?

Having lived several months on a cruise ship as the entertainment, she had accumulated a huge collection of outfits and memorabilia… as everyone in her shoes would have, Bebe was sure. She hadn't begun her journey with as many belongings, however…

"On a cruise nobody will blame you if you wear the same outfit a few times," her hairdresser friend Bertie had assured her when she had packed for the trip. "You can't be expected to have 30 or more outfits with you."

Bebe had seen the logic in this and let him persuade her to limit her luggage. Once on the cruise, though, she quickly realised how wrong Bertie had been. Of course, he had never been on a cruise, so what did he know? The people on board didn't seem to miss a trick, and while they had been most receptive to her musical performances, the lack of compliments towards her attire had Bebe soon max out her credit card on the ship's boutique and on several shopping sprees whenever the boat stopped in a port. She had accumulated a huge selection of new exotic dresses that got the desired recognition from her audience. What her bank manager would have to say about this was something different entirely. The credit card bills to come wouldn't be pleasant to deal with.

The car had been a stretch financially, too, and an impulse-buy after signing a new record deal the previous year. It wasn't as if her 'Best of Bebe Bollinger CD' had been a mega success, nor had her subsequent tour across Europe ever completely sold out. Nevertheless, thanks to a formidable duet with Will Young on his new album she had landed enough TV appearances and collected sufficient royalties to solidify her finances. The humiliation of last year, when she was passed over for the Eurovision gig in Azerbaijan, was far behind her now. Thank God.

She managed to close the boot, although probably at the expense of one stubborn hat box; maybe that was a good thing anyway. One of the friends she had made on the cruise, a particularly young and handsome gay man from Denmark, Tom, had advised her to 'lose all of her headwear'.

"Darling you have such beautiful hair," he had said. "Your magic doesn't come only from your voice." Who cared if he was just being nice, if it was a compliment she would take it.

In her heyday, mean people had referred to Bebe's facial expression as a mad stare, so the memory of Tom's compliment still gave her goose bumps. With a big smile, she switched on the engine to brave the drive home from the ferry terminal car park in Cardiff to West Wales.

The motorway was as busy as ever and demanded her full concentration. Bebe regretted not having spent money for a taxi to the ferry before she'd set out on her trip. The reasoning behind this had been fear of her daughter Helena, who knew few boundaries, and who might have taken the opportunity to 'test-drive' her mother's new car while Bebe was at sea. The little minx was capable of break-ins and God knew what. Even with the house being watched by the neighbours and a reliable house sitter, when it came to Helena it was better to be safe than sorry.

Driving along the M4, Bebe suddenly wished for company – someone to whom she could tell stories from her cruise. She pulled over to the hard shoulder and plugged in her phone and hands-free set. She was struggling with the rather complicated technology the new car offered her. While she had mastered some fairly complex new sound-mixing equipment for her musical career, Bebe felt hopelessly outwitted when it came to cars. The number of times she had inadvertently set off odd features she didn't even know existed was frightening. These modern motors were nothing but scary, however great they looked.

The temperature was mild for March, unlike the same time the previous year when the country had seen a blizzard of unprecedented proportions – and the body of a woman had been found under the snow in Bebe's little hamlet. Bebe was forced to solve the case to save a scandal around her. She was glad that dramatic episode of her life was over and done with, although in the end, the event had reinvigorated her career and she had made a good friend in Beth, the police detective assigned to the case. In fact, Beth was the current house sitter and the first person Bebe had to call.

"How is everything in Llangurrey?" she asked. "You know I've been worried sick about Helena doing something to the house."

Beth let out a deep and reassuring laugh. "Helena may behave like a wild child with you, but she's scared stiff of me. She hasn't been round once."

"Phew. Now what else has been happening while I was away?" Bebe asked, hoping that Beth hadn't been sitting in the house all those months doing nothing. The girl needed to go out and find a new love, not stay indoors, indulge in her ridiculous chanting and brood over her broken heart.

As if she had read the intention behind the question, Beth replied: "I've developed the perfect channel-hopping routine through the crime fiction programmes on your satellite subscription. That's as exciting as it gets for me these days."

Bebe desperately wanted to encourage her friend to at least intensify her job search, but her efforts in that regard had too often fallen on deaf ears. And it was questionable if a career in crime solving and private investigation was necessarily right for Beth. Without Bebe's help, last year's murder case in the hamlet, which had been assigned to then police officer Beth, might still be unsolved.

"On a different note," Beth said, perking up, "you'll never guess who volunteered to enter Eurovision for the UK this year!"

That got Bebe excited. The Europe-wide song contest was frowned upon as cheesy and trivial by many, but it had an alleged one billion TV audience, enough to make it interesting to adventurous, or desperate, singers to go for it all the same. After last year's debacle for the UK's representative Engelbert Humperdink, however, Bebe couldn't quite imagine anyone would volunteer for the job. Bebe had almost made it to Eurovision herself the previous year, if only as a backup singer and had counted her blessings when the act she didn't join had flopped. She still wondered if Engelbert's disaster at Eurovision had been his fault, as everyone had assumed. The poor result on the score board had also been blamed on UK politics and the country's unpopularity in Europe, the placing within the show and many other reasons.

"Who?" she asked. "Someone famous? Someone I should know?"

"Oh yes," Beth said. "You know her very well."

Now Bebe's mind went around in circles, trying to picture famous singers that might be interested, but she had to dismiss all of them. Almost all of them. "It's Bonnie Tyler," Beth said, "and her song was written by Desmond Child. It's far from being a hopeless case from what I can tell."

Bebe was flabbergasted. "Have you heard the song yet?" she asked.

"Yes. As you can imagine, it's not my cup of tea," Beth said, "but then again, you know my eclectic tastes. Little Eurovision stuff would please me."

Bebe's head was spinning. Had she been hasty and made a false judgement about the song contest? If Bonnie was prepared to do it the year after the UK had come last but one – after a superstar of Engelbert's calibre had bombed – then maybe, just maybe there was potential in the show, and Bonnie had caught on to it. Bebe was suddenly no longer sure she had been right in telling her agent never again to bring up the word 'Eurovision' in her presence. Her fingers started to tap nervously against the steering wheel. Desmond Child! Admittedly, the man wrote mainly rock, far more suited to Bonnie than to Bebe, but every song could be rearranged to suit different singers. Bebe and her pianist Maurice had jazzed up several of Child's songs which had been well received at her concerts. 'Poison' in Bebe's husky voice had resonated particularly well on the cruise ship.

"Has the cat got your tongue?" Beth asked into the silence that had slipped into the conversation. "Maybe I shouldn't have told you this while you're driving."

"It's a bit of a shock, that's for sure. Maybe I better get off the phone," Bebe said, realising that she had again come too close to the car in front of her in all this excitement. "I'll see you shortly chez moi. Put the kettle on."

Bebe thought back to one late-night conversation she had had on the boat with that handsome young Danish boy, Tom. He was a hardcore fan and had followed news from the national selections whenever he could find an internet connection. He had told her that, after a poor showing for his home country the year before, Denmark stood a good chance of winning at Eurovision. His enthusiasm was belatedly contagious.

With so much to think about, time passed quickly. Bebe soon found herself navigating the many roundabouts around Carmarthen in West Wales and it wasn't long before she got to the turnoff to Llangurrey. The mile-long stretch from the main road to her hamlet was a narrow single lane with various passing points. It felt good to be home, despite the sky filled with grey, angry-looking clouds. The moody colours of the scenery and the dramatic clouds made her feel alive. As good as feeling the warmth of the sun on her skin had been, she was glad to be back in her part of the world, and she sensed exciting changes ahead.

She opened the car boot and began struggling with the suitcase, wrestling mightily to free it from the small space.

When Bebe let herself into the house Beth was on the phone to her oddly named lesbian ex-lover Fred, who currently was also Bebe's agent and manager.

"Bebe just walked in the door, Fred," Beth said in a sour tone. "Why don't you ask her yourself?"

With that she handed Bebe the phone and walked off, shaking her head angrily. What a disappointing homecoming. Bebe had expected flowers, drinks and a big fuss from the moment her Porsche pulled into the parking space. And now there was a conversation waiting for her about work, before she'd even unpacked? Ah, the price of fame, she sighed internally.

"Darling Fred, I don't like the sound of that conversation," Bebe said, laughing nervously. "What's going on?"

"Bebe, sweetie," Fred purred into the receiver, "so glad you're back home. I've got a few offers which Beth doesn't think are good enough for you, but you know she wants only the very best for you. I'm offering the very best we can do right now, not what we might be hoping for in a few years' time. Haven't I got you to good places and made a success of it?"

Bebe tried to catch Beth's eyes but she had turned away and was looking out of the window, one foot tapping.

"You're brilliant at putting a good spin on things," Bebe said, "but you better spit out what you want me to do. And it better be good, I'm dead tired and not in the mood for third-rate programmes. You should know that much about me by now."

"Okay," Fred said, almost singing in the most enthusiastic voice imaginable. "They want you to go on Top Gear."

Bebe shook her head.

"You of all people should know that I'm a terrible driver," she uttered. "Besides, that audience isn't remotely the kind of people who would buy my music."

"It's all about media coverage," Fred replied. "Do you know how many people are forced to watch that tedious car show because their spouses are fans? Those people will love you. You could take that Clarkson on as well and give him a piece of your mind. When you sit on that sofa... wham! You tell him what an arrogant man he is and bang, you're an instant hero. Composers are more likely to give you a good song if you're notorious. If you're being just nice to your audiences in those piano bars they won't even hear about you."

The woman has a point. But Top Gear?

"Fred, I'll ring you back when I've had a moment to reflect on this," she said. "I've literally walked in the door and I want to take my shoes off, have a drink and a bath and unpack. Until then I'm going to be of no use to you."

She hung up and returned the phone to Beth.

"I told her it was a stupid idea," Beth said. "That woman never gave anything on my opinion." Only now did Bebe take in how well her friend looked: Smooth skin, no dark bags under her eyes, silky longer hair and a few pounds less around the hip.

They hugged warmly, then settled in the kitchen to make a cup of tea.

"You look in good shape," Bebe said.

Beth seemed to perk up.

"There's something positively radiant about you," Bebe added.

"Thanks. Your Wii sports has a lot to do with this, and my laziness to get out of the house stopped me buying snacks."

"You're still not smoking?"

Beth seemed to beam with pride: "Nope, still clean."

Bebe nodded, pleased. "Great, so the only thing left for you to do is finding a girlfriend and a new job, once you made up your mind which direction you would like to go in," she said.

"Even for an ex-copper it's hard to get a job in the areas I'm interested in."

"Who wouldn't want to hire someone like you and your experience? I think you're not putting the effort in because of the mean bastard you last had as your boss. Your next boss could be nice."

Beth shrugged, unimpressed, and turned away. She typed on the laptop in front of her and with a big smile she turned the screen for Bebe to see: A YouTube video of Bonnie Tyler was playing. The subtitles stated: 'UK Eurovision entry'. Bebe watched, fully entranced.

It was a slow song, neither in the tradition of the Jim Steinman years of Bonnie's career nor like her earlier work. Bebe quite liked it. She had always adored Bonnie: A true Welsh woman with a big heart, with little pretence and a great voice. She was one of the few 'competitors' that Bebe genuinely wished well. Bonnie's voice had held up brilliantly through the years. It made Bebe wonder why on earth Celine Dion and Maria Carey had managed to march right into the music scene and take away all the good songs that really should have gone to established singers, such as Bonnie and even maybe Bebe herself. If only she hadn't burnt her bridges to go to that competition herself.

Chapter 2

Beth went back to London, leaving Bebe alone to sort out her affairs. When she wasn't recording new material in her basement sound studio, Bebe was following up on mail from some of her growing band of fans and trying to get creative with her expense claims to cover the cost of some of her cruise wardrobe. When all that became too much, she found herself searching the media for the public's response to Bonnie's song, which was consistently positive. Bebe's finances weren't half as bad as she had thought. Payments for several of her TV appearances had come through late, which compensated for the extravagant purchases she had made abroad. The situation was so good it tempted her to make a trip to London to meet her agent.

"That's excellent news," Fred cheered when she heard of Bebe's plans. "I've got a few chat shows interested in you. I was beginning to rip out my hair that you wouldn't return my calls. These are genuinely big opportunities."

Bebe rolled her eyes.

"I'll believe that when I see it," she said. "You agents are all the same, trying to sell us some mediocre mid-morning show as the sure way to a commercial breakthrough. Or unsuitable stuff like Top Gear."

"I've cancelled that since you didn't seem to be up for it," Fred said. "But I've pulled a few strings, smoothed a few people and got you the very best you so rightfully demand."

Bebe tried hard not to laugh. "What have you got then?" she asked.

"The Peter Beatle Show … Past Midnight … Good Morning … and … Ladies' Time," Fred said slowly, clearly savouring the moment.

"Wow," Bebe replied and felt like fainting. "If that's true, you deserve a big pay rise."

"Absolutely," Fred agreed. "I'll arrange those appearances and email you the schedule. Just don't make any plans until this is done."

"I promise."

The excitement was simply too much to bear for Bebe. She sat down on the chair by her piano and suddenly she knew just the song for the occasion: 'Maybe This Time' from Cabaret. She knew the tune well and had just started to play it on the piano when the doorbell rang. She wasn't expecting anyone, so she ignored the call at first. When the ringing intensified, followed by banging on her front door, she reluctantly got up and opened it.

In front of her stood her daughter Helena.

"You're back," Helena called out cheerfully and tried to hug her mother.

Bebe stepped back and crossed her arms over her chest. It never failed to amaze her how this girl could behave as if nothing had ever happened. Bebe had forbidden Helena to come to the house after she had turned up last winter with a male underwear model and had vandalised the place. The girl only came to her when she needed something... pretending to care. Bebe wasn't going to fall for this again.

"What do you want?" she asked.

"Can a daughter not simply check in with her mother?"

Helena's broad smile and sparkly eyes got Bebe worried. It was a sure sign a plan was afoot. After 25 years of being a mother, she could count the occasions on one hand when Helena had been genuinely nice without an ulterior motive.

"A daughter can." Bebe said. "You – well, I'm not so sure. Just cut to the chase and save us both some time."

Helena tried to step inside but Bebe blocked her way.

"It must be money," she guessed. "How much do you want this time, and what is it for?"

"Just a couple of grand to go on holiday," Helena said, twirling a finger in her currently purple hair like a shy school girl. Bebe gasped.

"Nothing else then? How about a new car? An apartment?"

Helena stopped playing with her hair and looked hurt.

"You've had a really successful year and you've been on a few months holiday on that cruise," she said. "It's only fair you let your daughter have some fun, too. It's been ages since I last had a holiday."

Bebe grinned. "I'll do you a deal," she said. "If you can stick with one job and one man for an entire year, I will treat you both to a holiday in the sunshine. That is, if the man isn't married to someone else."

Helena let her head sink, probably forcing tears to appeal to her mother's soft side.

"What's another year to wait for a holiday?" Bebe said, ignoring her daughter's manufactured sadness. "Achieve something, and then reap the rewards. Don't go on holiday to escape your boredom, go on holiday because you need a rest. Then you'll enjoy it so much more."

With that she let the door slam in her daughter's face and went upstairs to pack for her trip to London.

While Bebe was still agonising over which of the dresses she had bought would best suit the TV shows, Fred called and informed her that the first appearance would be the next morning.

"You didn't waste any time," Bebe observed. "Good job!"

"And bring a change of clothes," Fred said.

"Darling, you know I always bring a selection," Bebe replied. "But I thought Peter Beatle was a radio show?"

"There'll be some filming," Fred said.

"Of people talking on the radio?" Bebe asked.

"Haven't you heard of Peter's fashion segment?" Fred asked. "It's one of his most popular features."

"Never," Bebe admitted.

"Well," Fred said. "Some of it gets shown on their website and streamed via Twitter. You'll be fine, all you need is to show good humour."

"I should have known there was a catch," Bebe said under her breath.

"Don't worry," Fred soothed. "Peter is a bit of a fashion icon. He and his team will take your dresses apart, but they do so in a very funny manner. I know it doesn't sound very tempting, but it's well received and people who appear on it generally get a lot of kudos for it. And it's the younger generation who listens, which is exactly where you want to get known."

Bebe ignored the 'get known' part, however insulting it sounded. She surely was known already, only mildly forgotten. Bebe sighed.

"I guess it would be too late to cancel," she said. "I'll be there tomorrow… with a change of clothes and the best spirit I can muster."

Bebe went straight back to packing and then climbed into the Boxster and drove to a London hotel, where Fred had booked her a room. Once settled in, she went online to find out more about the 'funny fashion segment' on Peter's show but soon got distracted by an article concerning Eurovision:

Czech Eurovision performer Daniela almost killed by falling spotlight read the headline. She clicked on the article. It was a sensationalist piece that made a huge fuss about a technical error at some European gig. Apparently, a spotlight at a Eurovision party in Amsterdam had inexplicably come unhinged and missed the singer by a hair's breadth. The article argued that some parts of the Eurovision fan community were hostile trolls, deemed capable of anything, which made one wonder if it had been an accident at all.

Fascinated, she looked at Daniela's Wikipedia page and website and listened to the song on YouTube, which led her to more videos of the contestants. She found herself watching Bonnie's video again and eventually Bebe was so tired, she only wanted to go to bed. Whatever Peter Beatle's show was about, she would be fine. She was sure of it.

Chapter 3

The next morning an assistant producer led her through the radio station's corridors. Bebe had chosen to wear a blue velvet dress that was warm enough in these cool April temperatures but one that she could easily take off when prompted to get changed for the fashion show.

The assistant producer pointed at one of the chairs, handed Bebe a headset and then left her alone in the room.

Bebe put on the headset and inspected her surroundings. It was filled with cameras and microphones and looked like the diary room on Big Brother, except it lacked comfortable seating. The bar stools without a back to lean on were a terrible choice. Bebe also preferred radio interviews where she could fully see the host. Here, there wasn't even a glass screen to the DJ booth.

"Welcome," she heard a deep voice through her headset.

"Hello," Bebe said into the microphone nearest to her. "Is that Peter?"

"Your microphone isn't switched on yet," the voice said and laughed.

"Are we expecting more guests?" Bebe asked, pointing at the empty chair. When she didn't get an answer, she assumed the microphone was still switched off. "Just as well," she said to herself. "I just hope it's not some godforsaken has-been and I'm part of an oldie-but-goldie programme."

"What makes you say that?" the voice asked.

Damn! What could she say now?

"So," she said and cleared her throat, "is there another guest?"

"Of course," the voice replied. "Tonia Carmichael."

The name did ring a bell, but she couldn't put it into context.

She was damned if she should admit to her ignorance, so she said: "Nice."

Bonnie's song 'Believe in Me' had just started to play in the background when Tonia arrived a minute later, ushered in by the same assistant producer. Tonia was a beautiful woman, slightly younger than Bebe, with dark hair and a figure Bebe would die for. The face looked familiar but Bebe still couldn't remember where she had seen her before. Tonia sat down next to her after awkwardly shaking Bebe's hand. Bebe thought maybe the woman didn't know who she was, either. A harrowing thought…

Tonia put on the headset quickly and took a sip from one of the many bottles of water around. Tonia also, seemed to find the bar stool uncomfortable. She fidgeted nervously, trying to find a position that didn't feel odd.

"Are you ready?" the deep voice said.

They both nodded.

A few seconds later the song faded.

"Welcome to my fashion spot where I interview people who think they have fashion sense but who are probably mistaken," Beatle said.

Bebe immediately looked at Tonia, who was wearing a tight red dress, guessing it was probably not a cheap outfit, based on the silky shine and the soft material. Beatle introduced Bebe as singing 'legend' and Tonia as TV personality without giving any more details.

"As always, I advise viewers to go to our website and look at the dresses while we chat away and tweet us your opinions on their frocks, #fashionbeatle. I'll give you a few minutes to check them out. In the meantime, here's Coldplay."

Bebe didn't like the sound of this one little bit. She saw Tonia nervously fiddling with her dress, adjusting it to look perfect. Bebe wanted to warn her that this was all being filmed, too, and would make matters worse. While the outfit probably made her look like a million dollars standing in front of a mirror, sitting down it wasn't quite so well fitting, Bebe noticed. Was that the purpose of these dreadful chairs? When the song was finished Beatle's voice came on the radio.

"Welcome Bebe and Tonia and thanks for playing along. Please tell us about your background in fashion," he asked his guests.

"I daren't say it now," Tonia replied and giggled. "I started designing my own clothes when I was sixteen. I've stopped doing that now, but I've worked on a few TV shows as fashion advisor."

"And what about you, Bebe?" Beatle asked.

"I'm no expert," she replied. "I wear what I like and hope for the best."

"A brave statement," Beatle said. "Let's see what the audience has had to say about your dresses. They didn't take long to make a judgement," he said. "For those who didn't check the website: Tonia is sporting a designer label, a sassy red number by what could well be Dolce & Gabbana, clearly out to impress us."

Bebe could see a smile on Tonia's face.

"Unfortunately, Tonia chose to accessorize excessively," Peter continued. "Look at the number of jewellery items. The dangling pendants and bracelets are reminiscent of Madonna in the Eighties, and not in a good way. I applaud Bebe for going with a simple blue velvet number and only minimalist jewellery. Not a very expensive or contemporary look but timeless."

Tonia looked hurt, despite braving a smile.

"Bebe, you've been in the business for a while," Beatle said. "Give her some advice on what to wear next, while we're playing the Kaiser Chiefs.

The assistant producer came in and signed for them to take off the headsets and follow him to the room next door. Tonia put on a grey trouser suit, very similar to Bebe's second outfit.

"You can't wear that," Tonia insisted when she noticed. "We look like clones."

"Darling, we'll be slaughtered by Peter and the audience, whatever we wear," Bebe replied. "It doesn't matter, we just have to brave his criticism and laugh along."

"I hate that... " Tonia said, and referred to him with shocking rudeness.

Bebe was so surprised that she let out a quick nervous giggle.

"Just look at his poster for the show in the lobby," Bebe tried to calm Tonia down. "He's no one to judge us. 'Fashion guru' Peter Beatle is wearing denim all over. And it's obvious he's older than he tries to look. The highlights don't fool me and that face oozes Botox. One thing, though – when you go back in there, don't adjust your dress as you did earlier. It made you look insecure. And don't touch your crotch; everything you do in there is on camera."

Tonia nodded slowly, as if this was difficult to take in. The assistant producer rushed them back into the sound studio where they could hear Peter chatting away to his audience.

"Now I've lured Bebe into a false sense of security," he said. "Winning the first round she got careless and thought her grey trouser suit would find your approval. Reading your comments on Twitter it's clear that neither of the women impressed you."

Bebe shrugged and smiled in the camera next to her. She was furious at Fred for not properly preparing her for this show but she wouldn't let that show.

"Tonia copied her in desperation to avoid a second defeat, but this time you're both looking a bit too smart for what suits you." Before Bebe had time to reply she heard her voice over the loudspeaker: "Don't touch your crotch."

Tonia and Bebe looked at each other in panic. Their conversation had been recorded? Tonia's rude name for Peter was played next, followed by Bebe's giggles. "Don't touch your crotch" was played yet again, along with the word and the giggle. And again.

"A little fashion advice Bebe dished out earlier to Tonia," Peter said and giggled himself.

Bebe was mortified and almost missed her cue when Peter asked her – as if nothing had happened – about her 'Best of Bebe Bollinger CD' and the comeback.

"I had a fantastic time on tour," she said, trying to get her bearings back. "Of course, I get judged on my outfits there, too, and my fans were just as harsh as you."

Beatle played the clips again.

Bebe tried to think of something funny and innocent to say to rescue the situation but her mood was spoiled. Tonia sat slumped in her chair like a broken doll, while Beatle did all the talking for them. He told the audience about Bebe's hobby as crime solver and revealed that Tonia had once performed as part of a group at Eurovision. Bebe wanted to ask Tonia more about this, but Beatle played the rude clip yet again and suddenly, in a moment of resigning herself to the inevitable disaster this show had become for her, Bebe started to giggle and then she simply couldn't stop laughing. It got so bad, she couldn't say a word and had to hold her stomach. It had been a long time since she had been so out of control.

"That word really got Bebe going," Beatle said. "Look at the clip on our player if you can. One minute Bebe looks like she's going to walk out on us over our rudeness and next she cracks up and shows what a dirty minx she is."

Beatle had taken it too far now, but Bebe still couldn't stop laughing and she could only hope people wouldn't judge her for this awkward moment. In a showbiz career that had lasted decades not once had Bebe lost her control this badly.

The show continued for a while longer, and, once recovered, Bebe had no problems chatting about the fashion advice she had received on the cruise. By contrast, Tonia was quieter and soon seemed tired of the show.

When it was over Bebe gave Tonia a consoling hug. Then she hung back, hoping to get an off-the-record chinwag with Beatle to get his take on Eurovision and Bonnie Tyler. But there was no time to chat. Once the fashion segment of the show was done, he played her duet with Will, the musical style of which probably was a stretch for him on this show.

Then she was immediately ushered out of the studio and told to get changed quickly in the 'ladies' and to leave her visitor's pass at reception. Fred had left a message saying she would meet Bebe afterwards at a very fine restaurant in Soho. At least that was promising. Not all agents would spend for their clients like that. Fred was a vast improvement on the last few, and not just in that regard.

Outside, the cold wind blowing around her reminded Bebe of her career. There were obstacles at every corner, but she felt confident she could overcome everything thrown in her way. It had been a while since her last visit to the hot spot for London's elite, and lunch with Fred always promised to be considerably more fun than the Peter Beatle Show.

"Darling, you're trending on Twitter," Fred said, when Bebe sat down by their table and held out her mobile phone.

"What do you mean?"

Bebe grabbed the phone and stared at the screen. There was a little clip of Bebe giggling hysterically, while Tonia said, "I hate that …."

"Peter posted this on Twitter," Fred said. "It's a teaser clip and meant to bring a larger audience to the show. With this clip trending there's bound to be record figures of an audience, let alone the streaming figures on the Internet."

"I wish it was something a little more sophisticated," Bebe said. "I don't want to be ungrateful, but wouldn't it be nicer if my duet with Will was viewed or bought this often?"

"Naturally," Fred agreed. "But enough of that Will Young duet, darling. That paid the rent for a while, but we both know that can't be the only thing you want to be known for. The sooner we move on to the next thing instead of milking it, the better for your image. I advise you strongly not to keep mentioning it in interviews. It makes you look desperate."

Bebe was indignant at the tone but she had to whole-heartedly agree. She was more than a one-trick-pony and she had to prove it.

"Then what do you suggest I do next?" Bebe asked. Fred turned around to reveal an ice-bucket with an open bottle of Bollinger champagne.

"Celebrate," she said and poured Bebe a glass. "Let your hair down, be yourself and let the world see you're having fun. People love someone in a good mood."

"But I'm a serious artist," Bebe said. "I can't throw decades of hard labour down the drain for a short-lived impression of being fun."

"Be serious on the stage as much as you like," Fred said. "But give your fans a human side, show the press that there is more to Bebe than they know. Let them see you laugh and wonder what's Bebe got to laugh about? What is there to know about her that we don't? We heard about her divorce, we know about her childhood, but look at her now: She's having a ball, and we want to find out exactly why." Bebe took a big sip of champagne. She hadn't eaten since early morning and felt a little faint. The alcohol would go straight to her head.

"You make it sound so incredibly easy," Bebe said. "Somehow, I can't see it work like that."

Fred topped her glass up. "Try it," Fred said. "Trust me."

Over the course of lunch Bebe got more specific briefings for the other shows, but the champagne did its thing and both women became very casual about it.

"Don't worry," Fred assured her in slurred speech, "I put everything you need to know in an email. When you get home, read through it and tomorrow will be a cake walk for you."

In her inebriated state Bebe was compelled to believe Fred. Hadn't she made this morning a success?

"God, is it five already?" Fred suddenly whistled through her teeth. "Time to go."

She got up and abruptly rushed out, leaving Bebe to compose herself and, as it turned out, to pick up the bill. Standing up showed her how tipsy she was. Without her fat prescription glasses, she found it hard to manoeuvre. She hoped that there were no photographers around, but she knew there could be.

She took a taxi back to her hotel and went through the schedule that indeed was in her email inbox. It all sounded simple enough. The Good Morning Show was hosted by people she already knew. The presenters were lovely people, not out to embarrass her but to fill the morning with pleasantries and harmless chit chat. There was next to nothing that she could say that would bomb.

Ladies' Time was also a very pleasant show where women liked to gossip and spill the dirt. There was nothing she had to worry about. The audience were women and gay men, her two prime record buyers. She would just have to be herself, maybe a little extra humble. And who didn't have a good time at the 'Past Midnight show'? The host was such a delight… a lovely, polite man. It was going to be a day to remember.

The phone in her purse began to ring. She didn't recognise the number.

"Hello darling," she heard a distressed voice in a familiar accent. "You won't believe what has happened."

"Tom," she called out, delighted that her Danish friend from the cruise was checking in with her. "How sweet of you to call. How are you?"

"Terrible," Tom said. "I just had to call you to tell you about Daniela, the Czech entry for Eurovision."

"Why?" Bebe asked. "I heard about the spotlight crash in Amsterdam."

"The papers say it was an accident, but I have a friend in the Dutch police who told me that they're investigating the incident, and the chosen unit is an elite team specialising in threats to celebrities."

"I see," Bebe said, although she didn't.

"Daniela's life is at risk," Tom said. "She refuses police protection. It could be a matter of life and death."

Bebe laughed. "Don't be so melodramatic, Tom," she said. "There's probably a very harmless explanation for this."

"I'm not being dramatic," Tom insisted. "I thought you'd be interested since you solved that murder case all by yourself last year?" That was bringing back a flush of memories Bebe had managed to suppress.

One night on the cruise ship she had gotten tipsy and told the story of the body in the snow. She painfully remembered how she had bragged about her skills as a detective. There was a reason why people told you not to drink. She had probably grossly exaggerated and given the impression of being a professional private detective. "Darling, that doesn't mean I smell a crime whenever something odd happens."

"Poor Daniela," Tom said. "She had a memorable stage show for the song and now she can't do it. That will cost her victory."

"Bebe, will you come to Malmö with me?" he asked after a short pause.

"What has Malmö to do with this?"

"Eurovision," Tom exclaimed. "I've got a press pass because of my Eurovision blog and I can get you one, too. You could be part of my team. Together we could keep an eye on Daniela. Don't tell me you wouldn't mind another go at crime solving."

Bebe laughed. "Darling," she said, smoothing her bob with her free hand. "It's not a proven crime. And as tempting as this would be under other circumstances, I'm currently working around the clock on TV appearances. I can't see how I could take off time for a detective gig which might not be a real case in the first place. If you ever have evidence of actual foul play I suggest you hand the information over to the police in Stockholm…"

"..Malmö!"

"…okay, Malmö, and be done with it."

"If Daniela gets killed next time, it will be on your conscience," Tom hissed. "I can't do this by myself. I need you."

She could tell he was being serious.

"If only I had the time," she said. It was true that she was interested in going, mostly to watch Bonnie's reception, to see what the show was all about and maybe to connect with some of her fans. Curiosity about Daniela and the mysterious accident played only a minor role.

Chapter 4

Beth called and asked her out for a nightcap at The Candy Bar, the go-to place for lesbians. Bebe, who by now had sobered up a little, decided to go for it.

The lights in the bar were set too low, and in the pinky-red colour scheme Beth was hard to locate. Some customers were deep in conversation, others on their own and either checking out the talent in not-so-subtle stares, or bent over their drinks, inebriated.

Bebe was frequently hit on in these places and loved the attention – whose ego couldn't do with it at the age of 60? – but if she was honest with herself, she preferred admiration without sexual undertones.

Beth was one of the figures hunched over the counter by the bar, sitting on an uncomfortable stool whose shape as an opening flower seemed a deliberate innuendo by the owners.

"How did it go?" she asked, pulling herself up from her slump. Judging from her eyes, Bebe gauged that Beth was more tired than bored. Beth's fingers drummed nervously on the counter and her feet tapped against the floor. In front of her stood several tequila shots.

"Marvellous," Bebe sang and plonked down on the stool next to her friend. She ordered a cocktail and told Beth all about the show and the dawn of her new naughty image. "What about you?" Bebe asked. "What's new?"

"Nothing but rejections and failed interviews," Beth said and downed another shot. "At first my unemployment was deliberate, due to lack of trying, but now I'm putting some serious effort into getting a job. And still zilch."

"Well, maybe I have just the job for you. On my cruise I spent a lot of time with a guy from Denmark, called Tom. Over a few cocktails I let it slip to him that you and I solved a murder case, and yesterday he asked me to come with him to Sweden as private eye for a threatened performer at Eurovision. I can't go, as much as I would love to. You, on the other hand, could go and gain from the experience."

"Darling, Eurovision is so not my scene," Beth said. "You told Fred never to mention that word again in your presence, and I shall ask the same of you. I can't bear it. It's cheesy, it's awful and it's pure camp garbage."

Bebe exaggeratedly looked around the pink room. "I can see that you can't stand cheesy and camp," she said, raising an eyebrow. "And I know you prefer techno to chanson, but do you know that last year a techno song won the show and brought the crown to Sweden?"

Beth grunted. "Still, in my experience as a police officer, threats to celebrities are very common and rarely lead to anything serious. Tell Tom to hire an extra pair of bodyguards instead of snooping around aimlessly amongst the thousands of stalkers. The police have more pressing matters to attend to."

"You could be one of those bodyguards," Bebe pointed out. "And you certainly have no other 'pressing matters to attend to'."

"I don't think I could bear it," Beth said, "and more importantly, I'm not convinced there's any substance to this 'threat'."

"You'd get paid to be there. Tom's not short of a few quid, as far as I can tell. He travelled First Class on that cruise, spent a fortune on satellite Internet connections and has no job other than his blog about Eurovision."

"Well, maybe," Beth said. "I shouldn't say no to a well-paid job abroad."

"Exactly, and think of all the beautiful blonde Scandinavian chicks," Bebe added. She turned around and scanned the room. "Anything here grab your fancy?" she asked.

Beth followed her gaze around the room and shook her head.

"It probably isn't helping that I still live with Fred. If only either of us could afford to buy the other out."

"Living with your ex is toxic," Bebe agreed. "All the more reason for a change of scenery. Imagine having access to Bonnie Tyler and her entourage," Bebe said.

Beth immediately perked up.

"Okay, I'll think about it."

Bebe got up to get another round from the bar.

"I don't think I've ever seen you in here before," the bartender said while mixing the drinks. She was a slick Tanita Tikaram lookalike in her thirties: dark, beautiful and of some fascinating mixed heritage. "But you do look familiar."

"I only come in here once in a blue moon to get this one out and about," she said, pointing over to Beth. "We've got to find her a date."

The bartender nodded knowingly. "What about you? Are you giving out dates?" she asked and stared provocatively deep into Bebe's eyes.

"I'm a career girl," Bebe said evasively, but felt herself flushing. "If you hear of any interested parties for my friend, make sure to mention it to us. I'd be very grateful."

She paid for her drinks and made her way across the room back to Beth, who turned out to be in deep conversation with another woman. Bebe didn't want to disturb them and headed back to the bar with the drinks.

"That was quick work," the bartender said. "You do look familiar, though. Are you friends with Susie or Fred?"

"Yes!" Bebe yelled over the noise at the bar. "Fred's my manager."

"Of course," the bartender said. "Bebe, the singer. I've listened to your album many times when hanging out with Fred. You look sexier in real life than on your 'Best of Bebe Bollinger CD' cover."

"Thanks for the flattery," Bebe said. "If things were different I should think myself lucky to be complimented by a beautiful young woman like yourself."

"I'm Jinx," the woman said and held out her hand. "I hope we'll see a lot of each other in the future."

Bebe took the hand to shake it but Jinx picked it up and kissed it slowly.

"You're a terrible flirt," Bebe said.

Then she turned away to see how Beth was getting on with that woman of hers. Pleased to see her friend score, Bebe left the bar and sent her a text.

I'll see you tomorrow x

Back at the hotel, she searched the internet for stories about Eurovision and found a few new articles and pictures of that poor Czech woman who apparently had injured her leg when she ran away from the falling spotlight. How Tom could see this as attempted murder was beyond her. But then, on closer examination of the images Bebe noticed that the woman looked positively ghastly in all photographs. Although the journalists all seemed to buy the angle of an accident, Bebe got an inexplicable feeling there was more to this than met the eye. Could it be that Tom was not being over-dramatic but right about this being a real case?

Chapter 5

The Good Morning Show the next day was just lovely. Bebe had feared her radio performance from yesterday would come up in conversation and taint the sugar-sweet atmosphere, but the theme of the show turned out to be her dear friend Andrew Lloyd Webber and a revived musical mania. The two presenters, a middle-aged man with a dark hairpiece and a voluptuous young starlet with an Irish accent, were incredibly kind to her and showed some clips from her best moments on stage.

"You really have such a wide range of talent," the man said. "Your husky jazz music and the more popular happy songs seem two different worlds."

"Do you think this duality has kept you from becoming a megastar?" the woman asked.

Bebe had remembered Fred's advice not to spend too much time talking about the past and so she replied: "Maybe. The good thing is that we can learn from the past and turn it to our favour. Since my 'Best of Bebe Bollinger CD' had such a warm reception I'm back in the studios, recording an album of new material from well-known composers. We'll be testing the market before settling on the exact nature of the arrangements."

"You must have a personal preference as to which end of the market you'd like to be settling in," the man with the hair piece asked her.

"That would be like choosing between your children," Bebe said.

"Well let's hear two more clips from Bebe's repertoire," the woman said, and the broadcasters obliged her by playing a clip of her song with Will Young and one of her oldest and most famous hits, 'Losing My Mind'.

For Bebe this couldn't have gone better, and she left the set positively beaming. Admittedly, this was not the most viewed channel, but someone might have seen it whose interest would be sparked.

"Thanks for stepping in at such short notice," the producer said to her afterwards in the foyer. "We didn't know what to do when Elaine Page pulled out of the show."

"Always a pleasure," she replied sweetly, although internally deflated that she had not been a first choice. Well, she told herself, Elaine's loss is my gain.

There was little time left before her next show. Bebe had to travel halfway across London. The receptionist at the TV studio made her feel as if she were hours late and soon Bebe understood why.

Ladies' Time was directed at women and for that reason had a focus on style and fashion. Bebe was offered a range of costumes instead of her own. At first it smacked like an insult, but when she saw the range of designer clothes available she forgot all about it.

"The labels throw their stuff at us," the woman in charge of Bebe's outfit said, sounding bored. She was tall and slim and blonde, no older than 30, covered in tattoos and piercings, wearing black heels, a black mini skirt and a white blouse. "Who do you want to be this morning?" she asked Bebe. "Lady Gaga or Joan Collins?"

"Neither, really," Bebe replied. "A bit of modern, a bit of class, nothing outrageous…"

"Joan Collins then," the assistant said with a sour face and disappeared in a vault of racks.

Bebe had a look at the dresses right by the woman's desk and picked a few that she thought would suit her.

"No, darling," the woman said when she returned with a selection of outfits. "Those are for the presenters. No offence, but we get paid to show those."

She held out a trouser suit with shoulder pads and a black skirt with a floral jacket.

Bebe chose the latter but before she got to wear the dress she was sent to make-up. She remembered the days when those moments were the opportunity for the producers to brief the guests and discuss the upcoming show. It seemed nowadays the element of surprise and spontaneity was more valued in these shows as nobody briefed or prepared her at all.

Her worries were swept away, however, when the hosts introduced Bebe as a jazz legend to a very enthusiastic crowd in the studio. The atmosphere was that of a hilarious party with some of the audience in tears. Bebe had no idea what had preceded her appearance, but she did appreciate the great vibes.

"You've come a long way," said one of the presenters, a woman far too young to be familiar with Bebe's early career first-hand. Despite a rather tarty appearance, the woman sounded very sharp and focused.

"I guess you can say that," Bebe replied. "But don't make me sound so old, please."

"Let's play a clip from your early career," the presenter said and pointed at a large screen behind them, where a crazy looking Bebe sang 'It's Him Who Will Be Sorry', one of her very first performances on TV when she had hardly learned to walk on stage without her heavy prescription classes, in the days before contacts.

The audience roared with laughter.

"Oh you stinker," Bebe said with put-on outrage to the presenter and smiled bravely, hoping this would go somewhere good.

Another presenter, a woman nearer to Bebe's age, then took over.

"When I saw you in those days I was convinced you were the incarnation of pure and innocent and that image stuck with you through your divorce. I think you were treated badly by that naughty manager who left you for a younger model, even when you were pregnant. I must say I never thought you could have a wild side."

"You make me sound so boring," Bebe protested. "Being a good girl doesn't mean there's nothing interesting about you. I just wanted the emphasis of my image to be on the music."

"Of course," the young woman replied. "What we mean is that the Sixties and Seventies were wild days where a bit of naughtiness might have enhanced your sales, but you resisted that urge."

"That wasn't a conscious decision…" Bebe began, but she was rudely interrupted by her own voice over the loudspeaker. She was mortified. That was the clip from yesterday's radio show. There was the sentence with the rude word and then Bebe's never ending hysterical laughter. Bebe could hardly bear turning around to the screen to see the actual clip from the camera recordings.

To her big surprise the audience's laughter didn't seem to be mocking her in any way. They enjoyed the clip and were laughing about the terrible word, sharing the same sense of naughty humour with Bebe. The irony amused Bebe, and her face, which had been frozen in fear just a few seconds ago, began to soften and turn into a smile.

"Until yesterday we were all fooled by you," the older host picked up the thread. "We've done some digging into your recent past and boy, did we get you wrong."

Bebe's stomach churned but she continued to smile bravely and turned to see what was happening on the screen behind her. There was a montage of recent pictures of Bebe: in the celebrity hotspot in Soho, opening the second bottle of Bollinger with Fred and looking very drunk; a picture of Bebe in the Candy Bar looking as if she was chatting up the bartender, a snapshot of Bebe in the cruise ship gym, looking rather sporty and fit, if not somewhat underdressed; Bebe sunbathing on the deck with another bottle of Bollinger and a newspaper headline from the local magazine crediting her with solving the gruesome murder last winter.

Bebe wanted to protest it wasn't her bottle on the ship but she never got a chance.

"You dark horse," the older of the two hosts said. "People, if you think you know Bebe Bollinger, then you're very mistaken. Forget about the perfectionist singer and meet the hoot that is Bebe."

A wave of applause roamed through the studio and the loudspeakers played a clip from Donna Summer's 'Bad Girl'.

There was only one thing to do. Bebe decided to join in, clasping her hands in front of her chest before opening her arms wide towards the audience as if to throw them a huge hug.

"Lady, I'm telling you, you better start changing your song repertoire," the young woman said. "We want to see a lot more of the wild Bebe. She's fab!"

The audience agreed. "Sing, sing, sing," they chanted, much to Bebe's delight.

"We've prepared a little surprise," the older presenter told the audience. "Bebe has recently been on a cruise ship and we invited her bar pianist Maurice here to accompany her singing 'Poison' by Alice Cooper."

Before she had a chance to protest that she hadn't agreed to any of this and hadn't even rehearsed she heard the familiar jazzy intro and saw that Maurice was already playing the piano on a spot not far from the presenter's table. How had she not noticed any of this?

The young host handed her a microphone and pushed her towards the stage. "Go!"

Bebe was too proud of how she had adapted the electric guitar sound into a piece that suited the piano. She played up the audience by raising her eyebrows and throwing in some naughty smiles throughout her performance. The reception was phenomenal.

The music stopped for a TV commercial break and Bebe and Maurice were quickly ushered off the stage.

"You naughty man," Bebe told her pianist off outside the studio. "You should have warned me."

"Bebe you're always best when unprepared," Maurice said. Although in his late seventies, the man was a brilliant musician. If only he would lose his habit of always sounding as though he was teaching a class of students: once a teacher, always a teacher.

"That was mortifying," Bebe insisted. "We did no check of the ear piece and the acoustics. I could have bombed terribly."

Maurice took her hand. "In all the years you've never missed one note," he said. "You've still got it."

"Are you going to be on 'The Past Midnight Show' as well?" she asked.

"No," he replied. "Only the one surprise."

On the way across London to her next and final show, Tom called Bebe again.

"I found out more about Daniela. Someone seriously went after her," he told her. "Despite clear police evidence, Daniela's still refusing police protection or bodyguards."

"How do you know all this?" Bebe asked, ever so suspicious of Tom's penchant for drama. Was he making this up?

"People contact my blog when they find out anything related to Eurovision. I now have a source who works directly for the Czech delegation," Tom said.

"It's up to Daniela," Bebe said, reluctant to get involved. "You can't force her to change her life. It's probably a stalker or a personal enemy. That's the price of fame."

"No, my friend swears that when Daniela walked off the stage in Amsterdam, one of the spotlights came down and almost hit her."

"I know. It was an accident," Bebe said. "We're past the times when spotlights could be manually dropped onto someone with a rope and yet, despite all health and safety regulations, sometimes one of those spotlights comes down. These things do happen."

"I know what I know," Tom said.

Bebe whistled through her teeth. "Okay, but don't you think it's a case for the police and not us?"

"Maybe," Tom said, "if they were doing something about it. I for one am going to Malmö to see if I can sort this out. Someone needs to get to the bottom of all this, and such a person should be a fan, accompanied by a detective undercover."

"Then you have to count me out, anyway," Bebe replied. "I'm not being big headed but I'm sure a few of the Eurovision fans will recognise me."

"But that's exactly the plan for our cover. We're both credible as TV presenter and assisting journalist, doing a show with you for my blog. It's ridiculously successful with sponsors now beginning to compete for my advertising space. You being a star fits perfectly well in that niche. Nobody there will suspect you're investigating another case. But being at Eurovision parties is exactly the sort of thing people would expect you to do. I can get access to all areas and together we can see what's going on."

Bebe laughed out loud. "Your persistence in this is admirable, but I've got to go now. I'm expected at my next show in just a few minutes."

Now she was up for the biggest wildcard of her TV tour: 'The Post-Midnight Show'. Alfie Armstrong, the host, was incredibly popular, and celebrities queued to get on his sofa. He was always up for jokes, good for surprises and weird angles, so she had to be prepared for anything. After the last two days she felt doubly cautious.

"You'll come in last," the assistant producer told Bebe during her fourth make-up session in one day.

"What's the theme for today's show?" Bebe asked, "And who else is going to be on?"

"Ewan McGregor is promoting his new film 'August: Osage County', Adele will chat about the Grammies and you'll judge Bonnie Tyler's Eurovision song."

Bebe frowned. Adele was talented, sweet and hard-working but Bebe was jealous of that woman. In her opinion, Adele was nothing but a younger version of Bebe. That Adele had made it so big with such a similar formula was grinding at her.

She watched the show on a monitor in the back. Ewan came across as lovely as ever and his movie looked a real piece of art, too. She tried in vain to get his contact details from his assistant for a possible duet, like the one he had released with Nicole Kidman after Moulin Rouge. The man had a wonderful voice but a tight team around him and Bebe doubted he would ever receive any of the business cards she had handed over to his staff.

When Adele came on stage, being applauded by everyone, Bebe could hardly watch. What wouldn't Bebe give for that level of success? God knows, she had the voice for the songs. Adele was a natural with people, down-to-earth and glamorous at the same time. Bebe had to be the only person in the studio not whole-heartedly in love with her. Even worse was that the young thing wrote her own songs, so Bebe couldn't blame composers giving their songs to Adele instead of Bebe.

"You're on in two minutes," the assistant producer told Bebe, gesturing for her to get up.

"Our next guest has a career spanning several decades," Alfie said. Bebe liked that he sounded truly excited. "Please welcome the one and only Bebe Bollinger!"

Bebe walked on stage, carefully eying the audience for the type of reception given her. It was warm, but nothing compared to this afternoon.

"Now Bebe tell us, how did you get that comeback of yours going? I mean, you've been quiet for a few years and then wham, you release a 'Best of Bebe Bollinger CD' and up and down the country there are tours, just as if you never had stopped. For me, that's sensational. What's the secret of your success?"

"Well, Alfie, I don't really know myself," Bebe said. "Show business can be fickle and sometimes it's just luck and timing."

"Go on," Alfie probed. "Tell us how you did it. Did you walk into the record labels office and say: 'Make me rich again,' or did they contact you?"

Bebe decided to go out on a limb. "To be perfectly honest, it was pure luck," she said. "I've been trying to get back into the limelight for years, but all the offers were for Big Brother and reality TV and I wasn't convinced that would help me."

The audience fell silent.

"Not that I have anything against those shows," she added hastily. "I wanted to make music."

The audience forgave her and relaxed.

"Well, I've been producing my own songs for years, but nothing generated serious business. Then, I was asked to replace Engelbert at Comic Relief, since he had decided to ditch it in favour of Eurovision. It was there I met some of the people responsible for my comeback. You might have heard the song I did with Will Young, and I'm now working on a few other projects."

"Don't you think Engelbert regrets his decision now?" Alfie asked.

"It's a shame he didn't fare better at Eurovision," Bebe said quickly. "I don't blame him for betting on it instead of the comedy gig, though. When I read the script for Comic Relief, I had to be dragged into the studio to do it. I thought it would flop big time and make me the laughing stock of the nation. And maybe it did, a little."

She giggled nervously. Was this self-depreciation working? She couldn't tell, but it was too late to change tact. "I would have rather gone to Eurovision than to Comic Relief, but for once, doing the opposite of what I thought was best, turned out to be my lucky star."

"Well done," Alfie said. "I saw that show and I thought you were fabulous."

Bebe turned. "Really?"

"Speaking of Eurovision," Alfie continued, "we had Bonnie Tyler scheduled for tonight's show but unfortunately Bonnie came down with a throat infection and can't be with us. So instead, we'll show you the clip of her Eurovision entry and then you get to tell us what you think of it."

While the video clip was playing Adele leant over to Bebe and whispered in her ear: "The make-up artist told me that Bonnie received a death threat and cancelled all her gigs this week. What do you make of that?"

"Blimey. I can't imagine how frightening that must have been for her," Bebe whispered back, while thinking what with those calls from Tom about the Czech singer, why shouldn't a similar mad man – or the same one – have a go at Bonnie? After all, these contests did attract a lot of nutters. The only question was – why did this madman target those two? No, she told herself. She mustn't get drawn into the drama and speculation.

"So, what do you think of the song?" Alfie asked Bebe when the video had finished playing. "Would you go to Eurovision with that song?"

Adele looked at Bebe with interest, making her feel particularly on the spot, and right there on national TV.

"Well, Alfie, I'm a different singer and the arrangement of the song as a rock ballad wouldn't work for me. I'm not entirely sure that it will win the contest for Bonnie, but a good staging, a rocking live performance and her star power should pull her well into the top half of the leader board."

"That doesn't sound very enthusiastic," Alfie stated. "As someone who recently launched a successful comeback, do you think this will do a lot of good for Bonnie's career, or is it a kiss of death, as it was for Engelbert?"

"Very harsh words," Bebe replied. "I think Bonnie doesn't need a vehicle like Eurovision for a comeback, just a strong album and a concert tour. Who wouldn't want to go and see her live? She's a legend and if she sets her mind on it fully, she'll succeed. Of that I'm sure. As for Eurovision, the show is changing and has become very unpredictable. Watch the bookmakers, they are usually rather spot on."

"What do you make of Eurovision, Bebe? Is it your cup of tea?"

"Some of it is," Bebe said. "I like that it's more diversified than it used to be. You know, it was either big ballads or cheesy pop. Now all genres feature, and nothing is guaranteed any more.

"Good girl," Alfie applauded her. "I hate it when people are so judgemental about it. It can be great fun and there are often some good songs in the show."

Bebe felt it was worth revealing a little more and showing some more warmth. "I've been invited by a friend to go to Malmö, and I'm very tempted."

"If you are, we need to do an interview together," Alfie said, "since I'll be over in Malmö, too. Make sure your people speak to mine. Even if it's just for a few beverages in the Euro Café."

"It's a date," Bebe said.

The next morning Bebe packed her bag, ready to return to Llangurrey. Around 4am Fred had sent her a text message, congratulating Bebe on her excellent performances but telling her that no new shows were in the immediate offing. So why not go home and they'd catch up some other time?

Bebe messaged her back, asking her to get in touch with Ewan McGregor and Adele's people about possible collaborations. At about the same time, Beth had texted Bebe that she was home safe. It made Bebe feel terribly old to realise that she never burned the midnight oil anymore.

On the drive back to Wales, her spirit sank, though. The whirlwind of four shows in two days had given her wings but those wings were starting to slow their beat and she was headed for a landing back to earth. The bleak reality was there were no planned studio sessions for a new album and no composers were asking Bebe to sing their songs. It made her realise nothing could be taken for granted in the music industry.

Once home, she picked up a few messages from Tom, urging her to call. Reluctantly, she dialled his number.

"I'm so glad you called," Tom answered in an excitable voice. "Have you decided to come to Malmö with me?"

"No," she said. "But I have a friend who might be interested in helping you out. She used to work for the police and helped me solve the murder case last year."

"That's not the same. You're the one who actually solved the case, and a celebrity who can go anywhere without arousing suspicion," Tom pleaded. "Have you ever received death threats?"

"No," she had to admit.

"I hear that someone also broke into Daniela's dressing room in Amsterdam and vandalised it," Tom said. "Do you still think she's being paranoid?"

"If the silly cow has nobody to watch her room while she's on stage, then I wonder if she has the right people around her, full stop; not whether she's in danger from some stalker."

"It doesn't count as stalking if there's a crashing spotlight involved," Tom said.

"I'm sure she's got it covered. My friend Beth will be happy to come along and help you if you want to do some investigating of your own. I hope to be working with Adele in the meantime, you won't blame me for choosing her over you, will you?"

"You better give me your friend's phone number then. And I hope she's good."

Chapter 6: Beth; Malmö

After speaking to Tom over the phone, Beth agreed to go to Malmö. The woman she had met in the Candy Bar no longer returned her phone calls, which had sent Beth into another emotional slump. The offer of a paid hotel and expenses seemed generous enough and it would do her good to get out of her comfort zone and do some actual work, even if it meant she would have to listen to dreadful cheesy music.

Before she flew to Eurovision, she did her homework on Daniela and Bonnie and read everything she could find on the internet about them and their Eurovision reception. She also researched their 'private' lives, or at least what was in the public domain. Daniela was nearer the height of her career than Bonnie, but both were bona fide stars who could draw in crowds and attention. While the Welsh singer's private life was very settled, Daniela's was more complex. Tom promised to fill in the missing gaps about that when they met in Malmö. If there was a criminal at work, Beth guessed he had chosen two of the more high-profile singers. None of what Beth had read, however, showed that either of the stars seemed particularly troubled by what may or may not have happened. Rumours that appeared on the fan websites about foul play were consistently denied by both artists and their teams. In Bonnie's case this was admittedly easier, since no incident had actually occurred.

Calling in a few favours, Beth had then found out from one of her former police colleagues that Bonnie had indeed recently received death threats, but they had not been taken too serious by the investigating officers. Bonnie's manager had reported them half-heartedly and they had been flagged because Daniela had received similar ones. Police investigated but couldn't find evidence of deliberate tampering. If Beth's police colleague, who claimed to have seen the original documents, judged that the whole thing was nothing, Beth was inclined to believe that, too. Yet the consistency of fan posts with conspiracy theories was impressive. One fan claimed to have seen the spotlight falling, another unverified eyewitness report stated it was a terror plot, while another swore an axe murderer had gone after Daniela backstage.

Only the last post stood out to Beth since it had been picked up by a popular Eurovision website as well. They reported the Czech singer had sought out a quiet corner to text her babysitter and suddenly saw a man coming towards her. The Czech delegation denied the story but the newspaper insisted on it being true, claiming sources close to Daniela. The singer had been lucky that her attacker had been inexperienced if not downright clumsy, which, on the other hand strengthened the case of those who said it was all a fabrication to get publicity.

No further official investigation had taken place. Just as well, her colleague had said, since a large group of paying fans had been granted VIP access backstage, and all those, plus the staff and the delegates from other countries, would have been too large a circle of suspects. In a nutshell: A spotlight had crashed close to Daniela but had missed her. Parts of the spotlight had broken loose and hit Daniela's foot after bouncing off the floor. Daniela tripped over and broke her foot.

The story had limited appeal for two reasons. One, Daniela played down the initial surge of media coverage, blamed the press for over-reacting and carried on as usual. And two, the song festival had only small hardcore fan base that would pay attention to the pre-event preparations. It seemed a far stretch for publicity.

The Eurovision fans already seemed more preoccupied over a different story to Daniela's injury: A planned lesbian kiss on stage by the Finnish singer.

"Daniela will soon regret she played the tough woman and passed on a chance for free publicity," Tom said when Beth spoke to him on the phone.

"Do you think this was a stunt?" Beth had asked.

"Officially this is a song contest," Tom replied, "but over the years it's become much more of a performance competition. The most outrageous props and costumes are being used to grab the judges' attention. Why shouldn't someone stage an attack to stand out from the rest of the crowd? It's show business!"

"I thought you were a big fan of Daniela?"

"I'm a fan of her music," Tom said, "but she's a bit too cool for my liking. Not as sweet and warm as let's say Bonnie, or that Finnish girl."

Even though Tom couldn't see it, Beth rolled her eyes. To her, Tom was a hit or miss source of information. One minute he had brilliant insight and detailed knowledge, the next he got carried away by the most absurd ideas.

"How do you envisage you and I get involved?" Beth asked, trying to get practical"

"Well, we got press passes," Tom said. "I'm the blogger, you're my assistant. We are here to meet and interview the stars. We'll mingle around the pre-Eurovision events, listen out for anything unusual and see what we can find out in the press conferences."

"Okay… but first you need to get as many facts about Daniela and her private life as you can. Not the public stuff, I've read all of that. Get me the juicy stuff from your unofficial sources. However, we must assume it is something to do with Eurovision in a wider context. An attacker could find Daniela anywhere, so the fact they chose Eurovision is significant."

Her flight took her to Copenhagen, the Danish capital 45km west of Malmo, separated from the town in Sweden by a fast and popular train journey across the Oresund Bridge. When she disembarked, Beth spotted a banner welcoming all visitors to the contest with a line taken from the Swedish entry: 'It's all about you'. She had heard that tagline before. On the train across the long bridge to Malmö the concentration of fans was noticeably higher than at the airport, some waving flags, and even wearing wigs or national costumes and some singing. She had seen references to Eurovision week – and even season – on the websites, but she had not expected it to be so true.

Her first press conference was that afternoon. Beth was one of the few 'journalists' singled out for a private audience with Daniela and her team. Most reporters had been limited to short general press conferences and they had to rely on luck to corner the individual participants after rehearsals or wherever they could find them for a one-on-one. Tom's blog appeared to have big street cred.

Daniela was meeting the journalists in a small meeting room at the business centre of her hotel, and by the time Beth had found the right street, dragging her suitcase behind her, she had only a few minutes before her appointment with the singer. No time to return a missed call from Bebe. Two security guards stopped Beth and searched her luggage before letting her through to a tiny, bland and windowless room painted yellow and brown. Daniela sat on a leather chair and rested her foot on a pouffe, staring at the ceiling and nodding distantly when her assistant introduced Beth.

"Don't get up," Beth said to Daniela. "And thanks so much for this opportunity," a line Tom had rehearsed with her in preparation.

"You're welcome," Daniela said, perking up in her seat, her eyes quickly scanning Beth before risking a shy smile. "You're British, aren't you? It's a great honour to be interviewed by you," she added. "I love so many British singers."

"Thank you," Beth replied, taking in the beauty of the star. Daniela had a slim athletic body, dark hair tied back to accentuate the perfect cheek bones and hypnotic hazel eyes. Beth struggled for the next line. She hated it when she found herself attracted to people she met in a working context. It was so unprofessional. Would it cloud her judgement? "I'm actually working for a Danish Eurovision blog. Maybe you heard of Tom Pillibi?"

Daniela's smile widened. "Who here hasn't?" she replied.

"So, what made you decide to perform at a song contest, when you are already an established star at home?"

"Last year, the Czech Republic didn't do well, so I offered my services," Daniela responded in a matter-of-fact tone. "I thought I had nothing to lose. Newcomers can be too nervous on stage and artists past their prime can fall short of expectations. I just wanted to be a good sport."

"Don't you want to win?"

"Of course I'd like to win," Daniela admitted. "But I'm doing it for the experience and, hopefully, a good placing in the final, which would be an improvement for my country."

"How is your foot recovering from the spotlight crash?" Beth asked.

Surprise washed over the singer's face. "My foot is fine," Daniela said after a short pause. "I'm a tough cookie."

"Who do you think was behind the attack?"

Daniela shrugged. "I have no comment on that."

"Oh come on Daniela. Someone is out to get you. Rumours are you received death threats. It would be devastating for the competition if that were to be true. How can you not be troubled by what happened?"

Daniela let out a bored sigh without replying.

"Could this be a disgruntled fan or a music rival?" Beth probed. "Your chances at this competition are rated very high."

"Betting odds are as changeable as the wind." Daniela said quickly. "I'd be fourth in line at the moment. The Danish girl should be taking more care, and the guy from Azerbaijan."

"Would it change your mind if I told you that other participants have also received death threats?"

Daniela laughed. She pulled herself up in her chair and sharply clapped her hands together. "No! Let's talk about something else." She tilted her head and stretched her arms above her head. "I want your followers to hear more about me and my music."

"How long have you been with your boyfriend?" Beth asked. "Are you planning on having a family soon?"

Daniela gave a startled look but recovered quickly. "I have two children already. I thought you might have read that somewhere before coming here. Currently, I have no steady partner," she added, "and I'm very happy with that."

"So there's no former lover who might bear you a grudge then?" Beth said.

"Maybe you've taken up enough of my time," Daniela said abruptly and the assistant, who had sat quietly in the corner got up immediately and walked towards Beth. "I've got a busy schedule this afternoon and to be frank, I don't think I'll get any useful publicity out of you."

Daniela picked up her phone and began to give it her full attention, completely blanking Beth.

"Err... thank you," Beth stammered. She pulled out a small business card with her phone number and gave it to Daniela. "In case you would like to hear more about those other death threats, or if you wanted to tell me more about the contest and its preparations, so I can relate it to the British audience."

Daniela took the card and shrugged without looking up or saying goodbye.

Chapter 7

Back in the hotel lobby a group of young men wearing Viking helmets whistled in unison. Their enthusiasm and the enjoyment were infectious and got Beth smiling. Despite being so coldly dismissed, Beth was still smitten with the Czech singer and was half day-dreaming when she received a call from Tom.

"You have an interview slot with the British delegation at 3pm here at the Olympus Hotel, on Baltzarsgatan. I'm waiting in the lobby for you. Get here as soon as possible, will you?" He hung up before giving her an opportunity to protest.

She still had all her luggage with her and worried she might lose her room at the hotel if she didn't check in on time, but she had no option. She should have been more organised and planned things through. Beth hated how investigations always took precedent over personal needs – it was why she had decided to leave the police force. That decision had not got her very far, she thought ruefully. As much as she had despised her ex-boss in the force, she knew that he had a point when he called her unprofessional, chaotic and not disciplined enough. As long as she solved cases, though, he didn't mind and was happy to cover up for her.

She had to hand it to Tom. His name really did count for something here if he could organise these interviews under such short notice. Who was he anyway? Royalty? When she reached the Olympus, Beth found him in the lobby, recognising him immediately from the holiday snapshots Bebe had shown her: Dark hair, striking facial features, a gym-shaped body and somewhat nervous energy.

He had spotted her instantly, too. "You are late," he scolded her.

"What a charming welcome," Beth replied coldly.

"I'm sorry, but I'm calling in a lot of favours for this. Where have you been? It can't have taken you that long from Daniela's hotel to here."

"That's quite enough," Beth snapped and dropped her suitcase next to him. "Make yourself useful and keep an eye on that for me, will you?" She was fuming.

Tom shot her an angry look, but he took the luggage off her hands.

"Okay, okay. Calm down. Anyway, this is the last round of pre-rehearsal interviews," he said. "It's the best shot at a lengthy interview before the mainstream press arrive and muscle in on the time available for us all. This may be your only chance to speak with Bonnie alone."

"Got it," she replied and grinned. "Remind me again, why am I doing this interview if you're already here?"

"I've got no experience as a police officer," Tom replied. "I want to solve this mystery but I get distracted by Eurovision stars, irrelevant trivia and all that stuff far too easily."

Bonnie Tyler waited in yet another bland conference room, smiling warmly at Beth from a large, dark blue leather sofa. A young man sat next to her with a lap desk; presumably he was her assistant. He didn't seem to belong at Eurovision, with his gothic look and worn Levis.

"So nice to meet you, Bonnie," Beth blurted out, immediately star struck. "You look stunning. Thank you so much for the opportunity." Beth actually meant it this time. Daniela may have been more her type physically and nearer her own age, but the former detective had always admired Bonnie. She had to force herself to focus and get on with the interview.

The singer smiled humbly and pointed at the leather chair opposite. "Come on, sit down, darling," she said with her trademark husky voice when Beth still stood there like a lump. "I've got to meet a lot of people and I want to spend as much time with each one of you as possible. This is all so exciting."

Beth sat down and opened her notebook. "How are you finding the Eurovision experience so far?" she asked the star.

"Oh, it's a lot of fun," Bonnie said, bubbling. "It's been a while since I've been to a festival like this. It's not the crowd I usually have around me, but the people are all so lovely. I feel very welcome and am enjoying it."

Beth knew from her experience with Daniela not to ask too soon about the death threats, so she continued to ask questions about the contest, and Bonnie had nothing but praise.

"How often have you been at Eurovision?" Bonnie asked Beth suddenly, something Beth wasn't prepared for.

"It's my second time," Beth lied and immediately regretted it.

"Where was the other?" Bonnie probed.

"Uh, Germany," Beth replied, hoping that the contest had indeed recently been there.

"Yeah, that was a good year," Bonnie said. "How did the organisation compare to this one?"

"I had no idea you were an actual fan of the competition," Beth replied, trying to steer the conversation away from herself and the German event she knew nothing about.

"Well, don't tell my fans," Bonnie joked. "I do have a soft spot for it and I'm chuffed to be here. Desmond is such a sweetheart to write me a song just for the occasion. How do you rate my chances?"

"I was going to ask you that very question," Beth said. "You're a bad interviewee."

Bonnie laughed. "Sorry," she said.

Beth beamed, more starstruck than ever. "Well I think it's marvellous you're doing this. It's brave and patriotic and I hope you'll do very well."

"Thanks darling," Bonnie said.

"I do have a question that might not have been asked," Beth said. "Rumours are that you received a death threat and that you cancelled a few live events because of it."

Bonnie shook her head firmly. "No sweetheart," she replied convincingly. "I had a throat infection, that's all."

"Do you think someone somewhere might bear you a grudge or see you as a threat to their career?"

"I suppose that's possible. I've been amazed at how seriously some people take this. My assistant Paul," she nodded at the young man who was furiously taking notes, "he's taking care of social media for me and he's shown me some nasty troll comments."

"But you still don't feel under threat?" Beth wondered.

"Not seriously, no. I've got people looking after me, the event has security and the town has. I'm never unguarded and if what happened to Daniela is related to me, then we're dealing with a complete amateur."

"So, you heard about her?" Beth asked, almost triumphantly. *So, people were still talking about it.*

"Do you think I should be worried?" Bonnie asked, not sounding particularly so.

"I used to be a detective in London," Beth told her. "I have a feeling in my bones that something about this doesn't add up and should be investigated. Can you think of any people in particular who were upset that you took on this project? Did the UK have anyone else lined up for participation instead of you?"

Bonnie laughed. "You really do sound like a detective."

"So?"

"Not that I know of," Bonnie replied. "We'd been talking since November and sealed the deal round about January."

"And in your private life," Beth asked, "any suspects?"

Bonnie shook her head. "Nothing I can think of. Professionally it's been so quiet there are no rivalries to mention."

"You never know," Beth said. "Here's my card if you ever would like me to investigate this for you."

Bonnie took the card. "That's very sweet of you. I might take you up on the offer if anything else happens. Paul, give her your card so she can contact you if she hears anything. Better safe than sorry."

Paul rolled his eyes but stopped his feverish writing and pulled out his wallet. "Here," he said and handed her a business card with a skull and bones on it.

"So, how did it go?" Tom asked her when she returned to the lobby.

"So, so," Beth admitted. "Daniela wouldn't talk about it at all and Bonnie played it down. No breakthrough, but I believe they're both more worried than they let on. Just a professional hunch."

They left the hotel and Tom led her through the inner city towards her accommodation. To her surprise, it was not quite what she had expected. The promised 'hotel' was the home of a Swedish gay couple in their twenties who owned a large modern penthouse, a stone's throw from Lilla Torg, a picturesque square around which Malmö's entire nightlife allegedly was throbbing. The door was wide open, allowing Beth and Tom to sneak in, past a group of smokers on their way to the balcony. Inside, the walls were covered with pictures of European events through the decades, and the owners had decorated the entire flat with bunting of European flags. Instead of the peace and quiet of a reserved Nordic culture and a lockable hotel room, Beth found the home swamped with Eurovision fans from all corners of the continent, discussing the entrants loudly and playing clips on their phones to each other. The owners, fans of Tom's blog, had responded to one of his posts asking for help with accommodation. Apparently, the city was fully booked out. The hosts were involved in a lively discussion in the living room and hardly paid attention to their guests. In the chaos of what looked like an impromptu party, Tom showed Beth to her room.

While he went to speak to the owners, Beth closed her door, sat down on the bed, put on her headphones and listened to the sounds of Tibetan gongs on her I-pod. Since her break-up with hedonistic Fred she had begun to live a healthier life, but her enthusiasm for it came and went, she couldn't trust it. At Bebe's house in Llangurrey, Beth had practiced Buddhist chanting and meditation and believed that the lack of it now was why her mind had lost some of its sharpness lately. During that time in Llangurrey Beth had eaten healthily, exercised, and read good books. She had even begun to like herself and forgot all about her continuous heartache. Once she had been back in that London flat, shared with her party-loving Fred, too many drinks and the occasional naughty cigarette had returned her to the life she didn't want anymore.

Despite the gongs of Tibet in her headphones, her mind stayed firmly fixed on the case and Eurovision. Did she really want to go back to solving murder cases and investigating human nastiness, or should she seek a different calling? She had seen the worst side of humanity as a police woman; moving into private investigation would expose her to more of the same. According to her teacher at the Buddhist centre, Beth needed inner peace and tranquillity. Yet that goal seemed often too illusive and unnatural. As her thoughts drifted all over the place, the noise from outside started to creep back into her consciousness. "Damn, damn, damn – peace will come, damn, damn, damn, peace will come" – a chant of a different kind grew louder and louder outside the door. She gave up and switched off the I-pod. There was no finding inner or outer peace here - that much was clear.

Still, she couldn't help smiling at the enthusiasm of these party people. When was the last time she'd been so completely consumed by an album or any music, really? Her favourite musicians, such as Paul Oakenfold and Benny Benassi, had peaked a few years ago and nobody had taken their place in Beth's heart. Calvin Harris wasn't half bad, but he didn't click with her in the same way. At least the crowd here had that excitement, and she envied them their passion deeply.

It dawned on her that this could work in her favour. These fans would know everything about the contest and might be able to provide her with the insider information she lacked. Tom had probably put her here on purpose. She got up and joined the party in the communal room, watching as the two chubby blond boys in their twenties who owned this place performed a remarkably good belly dance to Eastern European music, accompanied by clapping and cheering. Tom apparently had left already, so Beth sat down on an empty chair and watched the entertainers perform several well-rehearsed dance moves to songs in all kinds of European languages. She was impressed.

When at last the music stopped everyone sat down and Beth applauded as enthusiastically as she could.

"Tack," one of the blond boys said to Beth. "Vilka är dina favoriter i år?"

"Excuse me?" she asked, embarrassed that she didn't know as much as one word in a foreign language.

"What are your favourites this year? Which songs do you like the best?" he explained in impeccable English.

Beth hadn't really heard any apart from Bonnie's and Daniela's songs, so she named those two.

"You've got to be kidding me," came the instant reply. "You like those has-beens? You're not that old, are you?"

"I think they're great songs," Beth insisted, feeling on very dodgy ground. *Why hadn't she bothered to research the competition more thoroughly?* And where was Tom when she needed him?

"Those songs are boring," the other blond man chipped in. "They're both seasoned singers and should be able to come up with more original and up-to-date songs. I think it's an insult to us fans that they think their names are enough to win."

"And all the rumours about attacks on them," the first blond boy added. "Reeks of a publicity stunt."

"I'm not so sure," Beth replied.

"Me neither," said the second blond. "We're living in awful times, with stalkers and terrorists all over the place."

"Are people really angry at Bonnie and Daniela?" Beth asked.

"Ja," the first blond boy added. "Throwing a famous name at us and expecting us to vote for them is very poor form. Just look at the other acts! They pay star songwriters to write top songs, they invest in staging and costumes and then throw in the kitchen sink for their three minutes on stage. The UK and Czech Republic songs are weak. I hope they get trashed in the voting."

Her head sank as she realised she might just be out of her depth here. That stopped her hosts in their tracks.

"I'm Lars by the way, and that is Ola," the first boy said. They both looked remarkably alike. "Welcome to our home."

"Are you two twins?" she asked.

"A lot of people say that," Lars replied, "but no. We're a couple. We live in Stockholm for most of the year and are only here for the contest. It's nice to have it on home turf."

"Anyway," Ola interrupted. "We've got to get ready for tonight. Do you fancy coming along to the Euro Café? There's a large concert on and Bonnie Tyler's scheduled to play there tonight, too. She should have at least one genuine fan there."

"Sounds good to me," Beth replied. She had landed on her feet.

"Good," Lars said. "Meet you here in 45 minutes.

Chapter 8

Back in Wales, Bebe had been trying to reach Adele's agent, but to no avail. Of course, a superstar like Adele had enough people to guard her from the thousands of enquiries coming her way each day. Bebe was frustrated that a singer at the height of her fame had reached out to her, but she couldn't get through to the star to arrange the meeting both wanted. And this was despite the fact Bebe had been trending on Twitter and thousands were still viewing the YouTube clip of her laughing to that rude word. Had Adele not briefed her staff accordingly? If Bebe ever had 'clout' it was right now, wasn't it?

In the week following her show appearances, 'The Best of Bebe Bollinger' album climbed back up the charts, and Bebe had been on several radio shows where she had shown her fun side. "I do have a naughty side," was her rehearsed phrase. "Up to now, I've kept it to myself. I was afraid to offend sensitive fans."

A friend of Peter Beatle, a nightclub DJ from Manchester, mixed together some of the shows' lines with Bebe's laughter on a dance track that was getting a lot of views on YouTube and decent airplay on radio.

It had taken time for Bebe to accept this new image of herself, but if it went hand in hand with record sales, she could make her peace with it. Now all she needed was a new album and new songs.

"I'm working on it," Fred assured her when she called her about it. "You keep doing what you're doing, and I guarantee you there will be interest."

"There should be interest already," Bebe replied. "I was trending on Twitter…"

"Just be patient," Fred asked of her.

Frustrated, Bebe hung up and went outside. The sky was a dramatic grey, which, inspired her to put on her tweed jacket and tend to her small front garden. By the evening, Bebe felt as if she was going stir crazy.

Fred's words: 'Keep doing what you're doing' wouldn't get out of her head. What had she really been doing? Bebe asked herself. Nothing. Just a few TV appearances and chit chat. She wasn't touring any more, nor was she recording, and it was too soon to re-visit all the piano bars.

Suddenly, she had a moment of true insight: The only thing to do was to get herself back in the media. If they weren't coming to her, she had to go after them. And one way to do it was to follow Tom and Beth to Malmö and get herself in front of the Eurovision press. Those journalists already knew her and would probably jump at the story that Bebe was a Eurovision fan and had come to 'support' Bonnie and the UK, wouldn't they? This could also pave the way for a future Eurovision entry sung by her, if Bonnie did well this year. That looked increasingly likely, if you followed the bookmakers, which Bebe did.

She picked up her phone and called Beth.

"How is the investigation going?"

"We haven't had a breakthrough," Beth admitted. "The scene here is seriously weird. I doubt you'll ever see anything like it in your life anywhere else."

"Good weird?" Bebe asked.

"I'm not sure. People dress and behave outrageously. More your scene than mine, but who cares. I got to meet Bonnie Tyler. Have you ever met her in person?"

"Well, the odd chatshow and Top of the Pops a long time ago. We like each other but never hung out."

"Tom is a really big name here, by the way. I had no idea."

"Neither had I," Bebe admitted. "But are you having a good time, anyway?"

"I guess I actually do," Beth said. "Shame you're busy with Adele. You'd love it here, and people would love you."

"I'm glad to hear that. I've been toying with the idea of coming over for a few days if I can."

"That would be great," Beth said. "You could help us with the investigation, too. I don't think Tom is going to be of any use himself, and I'm tapping in the dark."

"Well, I wouldn't come to investigate crimes, darling. I'd come to check out the scene."

"Tom will be so disappointed."

"Then maybe I won't tell him."

Bebe hung up and went upstairs to start packing. It was fun to do that for the most glamorous and camp musical competition on Earth. Going through her walk-in wardrobe immediately put her in the prefect mood. If she read Beth's comments right, then an outfit that was outrageous and too much for UK TV was probably just about right for a day-event in Malmö. Too many of her old dresses had been sitting in her wardrobe for years without being worn; now it was time to bring them out.

Her flight was filled with Welsh Eurovision fans who couldn't miss Bebe in her leopard skin jacket and her black velvet dress. She worried that she'd gone over-the-top flamboyant too soon and maybe should have saved the outfit for Malmö. But it worked like a fan magnet. By the time she boarded the plane, she had already given out five autographs and nearly perfected her prepared speech about Bonnie and Eurovision:

"I watch the show every year," she recited again and again. "It's such a hoot. And to think that my dear friend and fellow Welsh gal Bonnie should have the honour of taking part this year! I simply had to come and experience the atmosphere for myself."

It went down a storm with the Welsh crowd. At the rate Bebe was being asked for her fan materials, she was afraid she'd run out of the generous stock she had brought with her. Nobody mentioned the possibility of Bebe performing at a future competition, but the reception was so overwhelmingly warm, she wondered why more stars didn't take advantage of this ego-boost. She did regret having booked a Business Class ticket, because it kept her apart from the fans. She didn't recognise any producers or musicians in her cabin and no one in Business Class nor the crew paid her any attention.

At Copenhagen airport, the buzz around Bebe didn't recur. The fans were clearly eager to get to their hotels and let the celebrations begin. They stormed past her to immigration and the baggage carousel, leaving her feeling abandoned and insecure. Had she been a mere diversion for them while they waited for the flight to depart? Was this a taste of what was to come in Malmö?

She took a cab to her Copenhagen hotel which, behind the traditional façade, sported a very funky interior, full of abstract modern art, with what she thought of as Andy-Warhol-coloured walls. Bebe took the elevator to her room and unpacked. It wasn't the largest room, but it had an impressive design: Dark green walls with glitter on them and shiny-silver edging. Bebe found it almost overwhelmingly busy, but the huge heart-shaped bath tub with built-in Jacuzzi was extremely appealing. Noting the fully stocked mini-bar, she knew she would be fine here.

The TV was set to a Swedish channel apparently dedicated solely to Eurovision: Interviews with the stars, music from past competitions, documentaries on the arena, talk shows with experts and re-runs of previous shows. It was prefect. A switch on the wall allowed her to transmit the sound of the TV to speakers in the bathroom. She poured herself a glass of champagne from the mini-bar and took a hot bath, listening to the Eurovision channel. Some of the broadcast was in Swedish, but thanks to the largely international crowd attending, most was in English.

She was surprised by how modern so many of the songs were. She was used to the days of up-tempo pop songs and classic ballads with the almost mandatory key-change for the final chorus. There was a lot of diversity. The TV played last year's winner, which was a pop anthem with techno beats, followed by an Eastern European ethno-folk song and then an operatic number sung in falsetto.

The participants sucked up to the audience in the many interviews aired – they were all 'grateful to be here' and 'just enjoying the experience', 'didn't need to win' and 'hoped to do their country proud'. Bebe realised she would have to be distinctive in her own interviews, if it came to that, in order to stand out.

"Tonight, is the Big Six party at the Euro Café," the female presenter reported in impeccable English. "Just a reminder to all those people who are new to Eurovision. Six nations automatically go through to the final, they do not have to qualify via the semi-finals. These nations are called the Big Six and are: France, Germany, Italy, Spain, the UK and the host country, which this year is Sweden. These nations will be hosting a party to introduce their songs. They should be well warmed up after rehearsing for the last two days, while the semi-finalists have taken a well-deserved breather."

"Are you going to be performing, Carola?" a male voice asked the woman.

"Robin, tonight is your night," came the reply, and then she sang the tagline of the show, "It's all about you-hoo-hoo…" The singer had a beautiful and powerful voice, but without musical accompaniment and at this volume, to Bebe, it had the impact of a fog horn.

At least now Bebe knew exactly where she had to be that night. She got out of the tub and rang Tom to find out the details for the Big Six party.

He was surprised but ecstatic that she was in Copenhagen. Beth apparently had not mentioned a word about Bebe's plans.

"Listen Tom, I'm not going to be dragged into any detective work when there is a party for me to attend. I need to do my own networking, do you understand?"

"Of course," Tom said, a little too quickly.

Within half an hour, he called her back to let her know that he had organised a VIP ticket to the event.

Inspired by the silver-shiny look of her room, Bebe chose a very similar dress, reminiscent of her Disco days and befitting the glamour she expected to find. A small voice in her head warned her that she hadn't sized up the competition or their couture, but by then it was time to leave. She wanted to be early so she could chat with Bonnie and the other participants, along with the press and the stars.

Chapter 9

A taxi took her across the bridge to Sweden. The centre of Malmö was decorated with European flags and posters, street stalls sold Eurovision memorabilia and there were signs to the important locations, such as the Euro town and the Euro Café. Bebe was impressed, and relieved that in the colourful crowd of people here, she no longer stood out.

Amongst the glitter-clad revellers, a group of dancers in traditional Swedish folk costumes moved rhythmically past her to the sound of Abba's 'Waterloo'. Oh, this was fun.

By the time Bebe arrived at the Euro town, the number of street stalls and diehard Eurovision fans increased exponentially. The range of gadgets and flags for sale with the Eurovision emblem was phenomenal. Bebe bought a small UK flag and a Eurovision badge to stick on her dress. The saleswoman also gave her a town map and directions to the Euro Café.

On the walk there, she realised not one person had recognised or approached her. Had she made a mistake by coming? What if people were only interested in this year's performers and were going to give her the cold shoulder?

The Euro Café was an actual café, adjacent to an expanse of meadow tucked between large modern industrial buildings. Once she came off the road, though, she couldn't see anything but the café grounds. A cluster of trees surrounded a courtyard, and next to the overcrowded café was a red-brick building she figured was where the concert would be held later. The sound system played Bonnie's 'Holding Out for a Hero'. It was reassuring that people here were open to music outside of this year's competition, and to British music. Many people in the UK ascribed the lack of British success at Eurovision to political reasons, but Bebe blamed bad songs and bad luck.

"Bebe Bollinger!" a voice screamed from the café area.

Bebe smiled and turned to the source of the call. It was only Tom, sitting with a group of men with Welsh and British flags.

"Over here," Tom shouted. "We've kept you a seat."

Relieved to have company but disappointed that there was no sign of the TV cameras and press, Bebe made her way through the crowds to sit down at Tom's table. She thought she recognised two of the men he was sitting with from the plane: Early twenties, ripped bodies, blond highlights, tight denims and T-shirts – one saying 'UK Twelve Points' the other 'Holding out for a Hero'. The third man had stunning Mediterranean looks, his eyes hidden behind pitch black sun glasses, the likes Bebe hadn't seen in years.

"We were waiting for you," Tom said. "It's time to go backstage and mingle."

"Is that where the press are?" she asked.

"Probably," Tom replied. "I want to introduce Hywel and Rhys from Cardiff. Both huge fans of yours." The two men nodded but kept their cool.

"And this is Giovanni, who recently joined my team on the blog."

Giovanni nodded coolly and gave her the thumbs up.

"Thank you," Bebe said and got up from her chair. "Sorry I kept you waiting. I could have sworn you said the doors wouldn't open for another hour or so."

"I did," Tom replied, "but you know the pattern of these events. There are so many interviews and publicity pictures for the stars to have taken with the VIP guests that the organisers schedule an additional hour-and-a-half before the show. Plus, with make-up and costume changes, they're always more or less late."

"Where is Beth?" Bebe asked. "I assumed she would be here with you."

"I set her up with two of Sweden's most notorious Eurovision fans. She's probably hanging out at their place, starting her own line of inquiries. There's no point in her following my every footstep. Wherever these guys take her, she'll be right in the thick of it."

"Then let's go." Bebe started walking.

The five of them pushed through the packed café, and Tom led them to the back, where two bouncers guarded a fire exit. He spoke with them in Swedish and showed them the tickets. Without taking their eyes off the crowd, the men opened the door and let the group into a narrow corridor. Tom grabbed Bebe's arm and led her through a series of doors until they reached a stylish lounge area with comfortable-looking white sofas. The room was packed with camera crews, journalists and important looking people.

Bebe had read a few articles about Eurovision but her knowledge of European geography, flags and languages was terrible. She hadn't remembered the names or song titles of any of the other singers;

however, she did know the flags on two of the tables: to her left was the German delegation and to her right was the Swedish. She also recognised the two presenters from the TV show that afternoon: A very young boy in denims and a woman in her forties with lots and lots of hair.

To her utter surprise and delight, she heard a very familiar voice calling her name and a TV camera moving towards her – a camera being one of her favourite things in the world. Because of the dark ambience of the room all cameras had tremendously bright lights, which blinded Bebe so much she couldn't even see the person who had greeted her.

"Darling," the voice said," so good to see you."

Now she knew who it was. "Peter Beatle," Bebe said and opened her arms wide. "What are you doing here?"

The cameraman switched the light off and let the camera sink to the floor. "I'm doing a documentary. What about you?"

"I came to support Bonnie," Bebe replied, "and to scout out the show and its potential. It's great fun."

Peter looked around the room before replying in a lower voice. "It is fun, but I'm starting to get nervous for Bonnie."

"What makes you say that?" Bebe was puzzled. Did Peter buy into the conspiracy theories as well?"

"The competition for Bonnie is much stiffer than I anticipated."

"Don't worry," Bebe assured him. "The bookmakers have her doing just fine. Where is she?"

"She's not here tonight. Must be her throat again. They've got Nicki French as a stand-in. You remember she topped the charts with a cover version of Bonnie's 'Total Eclipse of the Heart' and then represented the UK at Eurovision in 2000. Amongst the fans she's even more popular than Bonnie. Can you believe that?"

Bebe couldn't quite, but Eurovision seemed to be a world of its own.

"And here she is," Peter said, hugging a bouncy blonde woman at least ten years younger than Bebe.

"Bebe Bollinger." Nicki kissed her on the cheek. "I'm a big fan of yours, you know."

"Thank you," Bebe said, liking that woman already. "You must be so excited to fill such big shoes tonight."

"Absolutely," Nicki said.

"Do they have a piano around here?" Bebe asked.

"A piano? I should think so. Why do you ask?"

"Not to be presumptuous, but I want to show you what I think you could do with Bonnie's song to make it more appealing. My music is much closer to the Eurovision stuff than hers. If you're going to perform her song tonight, why not make it your own?"

"You have my attention," Nicki said. "Let's go upstairs on the stage and have a go." She led the way through two more sets of doors and a small staircase onto the stage. "I thought I'd seen a piano around here," she said and soon found a beautiful black concert piano in a quiet corner.

Bebe opened it, sat down and began to play Bonnie's entry 'Believe in Me' in the jazzy way she thought would make the song stand out more.

"That's quite nice," Nicki said. "But do you really think this will do better than the original version?" She sounded unconvinced.

"I don't know. I think it might, but none of us can predict what wins this competition. It's different every year. If you don't like it that way, then maybe nobody will mind if I use it on my next album," Bebe said, only half-jokingly. She could do with a fresh song and she doubted Bonnie would enter the charts with this, although stranger things had happened.

"I know," Nicki suddenly said and slapped her flat hand on the piano. "Why don't you come on stage with me tonight and you can play the song in your version? That way we can see how the audience responds. It will be all over social media in a cold minute."

"But I can't sing your song," Bebe insisted, although there was little she wanted to do more at that moment. "People came here to see and hear Bonnie and you're the closest thing."

"Bebe, we're all trying to outdo each other here," Nicki said. "But we do so in style. People sing each other's songs and perform duos and make sure they're seen to be nice. It feels like an election campaign or a popularity contest. I'll speak to Bonnie's manager, but I'm sure he'll be fine if you sing the song. I'll stick to 'Total Eclipse' and to the other songs we've rehearsed – that will do me nicely. Besides, it'll be fun to have you there. Big British names is what we need at this competition."

"Okay, but we've got to do something about her outfit," Bonnie's manager said when they were back in the lounge. "No offence, Bebe, but you look like that drag queen from the Ukraine."

"Don't be so rude," Nicki said but Tom, who had stayed behind here with Giovanni and the Welsh couple, nodded in agreement.

"I didn't want to say but it's true. A few years back the Ukraine came second with a great song and the artist was wearing a costume just like yours," he explained. "Only the man had a satellite dish as a hat, and he still roams the Eurovision sphere with the same costume. People will notice the resemblance and think it a rip-off."

"Oh dear, it's a bit late to go back to my hotel," Bebe said. "Maybe we can get away with it. I'll be sitting by the piano, so people won't see it right anyway."

"Nicki, have you got anything spare with you?" the manager asked.

"Let's have a look," she said and dragged Bebe by the arm towards her dressing room.

The make-up artist laughed out loud when Bebe entered and without having to be told what was to be done, she fetched a few dresses and, after holding each one against Bebe, Nicki picked a lovely classic black skirt and matching top, slightly reminiscent of Adele's style.

As soon as Bebe had put on the new attire, the make-up artist went to work with Bebe's face, adding touches to what Bebe had considered a particularly good job. Meanwhile, Tom and his entourage had joined them, bringing with them a bottle of champagne.

"Where's Nicki?" Bebe asked suddenly.

"On stage with the Swedish boy," the make-up artist said.

"He's a bit of a soft rocker and they're singing a few tunes together," Viktor explains. "Later he'll be singing with the German woman. Acapella versions of his song and of hers. They do that kind of thing here all the time."

"I'm glad," Bebe said. "I was wondering if me singing Bonnie's song would go down well or be seen as stealing her thunder."

The make-up artist laughed.

"Yeah right, steal Bonnie's thunder. Six million records sold and along comes Bebe Bollinger and steals the show. You've got a good sense of humour."

Bebe was furious.

"That's not what I meant," she said but Tom refilled her glass with champagne and toasted her, which was a welcome distraction.

When it was finally her time to go on the stage, Bebe was a bit tipsy. The audience seemed to be drunk, too, whether on alcohol or on Eurovision wasn't clear. They gave Bebe an enthusiastic welcome and held up lighters as her version of 'Believe in Me' electrified the room. Bebe got goose bumps herself. Only once in a blue moon did an audience connect with the singer and let music create such a magic atmosphere. Bebe was astonished.

Unfortunately, there was little time for her to revel in that feeling. Seconds after her song had finished the presenters announced the next singer. Bebe walked off the stage behind the thick curtain. The Italian contestant, a very handsome young man who looked a little tipsy, too, stumbled past her onto the stage to hysterical screams the likes Bebe hadn't heard since the Abba. In comparison to that, her warm reception earlier seemed tame and unimpressive.

"Well done," Nicki said and hugged Bebe. "Come on, let's go back to the dressing room for more bubbly. They don't need me until the end of the show when we're all saying goodbye..."

Suddenly they heard a metallic clunk overhead and then one of the spotlights came rushing past where Bebe and Nicki had been standing only a second before and smashed into the floor.

"Jesus!" Nicki hissed. "What on earth?"

Bebe was equally shocked and looked up to the ceiling and back down to the spotlight. Then back up and down again. Another spotlight 'accident'? It couldn't be. She examined the slivers of glass and metal. There were no strings attached to the spotlight and up there was no platform it could have been thrown from. It looked like an accident, albeit a very unlikely one. And that was just the point. It couldn't be. Who had heard of spotlights dropping just like that, twice in the same competition? She looked around her. The culprit couldn't be far. This part of the backstage area was very empty. Had nobody on stage heard the crash? The lack of stagehands was baffling. Bebe walked the entire length of the area, looking for clues as to how the spotlight could have come down. A few people came to investigate. They looked flabbergasted and in shock when they saw the monumental light in pieces.

In front of the curtain on stage the Italian song carried on as if nothing had happened.

"That was a close shave," Nicki said and began to laugh. "Phew."

"Phew?" Bebe mimicked her. "That spotlight could have killed us, and to be honest, I wonder if it wasn't actually meant to do just that."

"Kill us?" Nicki said, sounding more amused than shocked.

"Yes," Bebe said. "You know about Daniela, don't you?"

Nicki nodded.

"Must say that it reeked of a publicity stunt to me," she said. "I never took it seriously. I thought it was unfortunate for Bonnie that her insurance did take it seriously, but it got me here, so I'm not complaining. I don't think this was deliberate."

"No?" Bebe asked.

"No," Nicki said. "You know as well as I do that accidents happen all the time. However safe we think a place is, something can always go wrong. How would someone get a spotlight to fall at a specific time? And why would anyone try to kill us?"

The stage manager arrived with a few more of his staff. They examined the debris, cleared it up and promised to have the entire stage re-checked the following day, before any other show would be hosted in the venue.

"You need to call the police and have the scene examined," Bebe insisted.

"I'm not going to get the police involved," the man hissed. His face was flushed, the veins bulging dangerously close to bursting. Judging from his skin and belly size, he probably had issues with high blood pressure and anger management, so she let it drop, despite being deeply concerned. She considered telling the Malmö police anyway.

For now, she needed a drink to calm her nerves. She and Nicki returned to the dressing room and sipped more champagne which Tom and the boys had left. The two divas used the time to get to know each other, until Nicki was called back on stage for a final showdown.

"Come on," Nicki encouraged Bebe. "You should be up there, too."

"Sorry," said the stage manager, "we only need one stand-in for Bonnie. The stage is crowded as it is."

"Wait here then," Nicki said. "I won't be long."

Bebe shrugged and stayed put. When the noises indicated that the show had ended and thirty minutes later still nobody had come to the dressing room she got up and searched for the rest of the party. The lounge was almost empty and there was no sign of Nicki, nor her team. She found Tom and his three boys giggling with the German singer, a blonde bombshell Bebe was sure she had seen before Eurovision.

"Thank you for getting my ticket," Bebe said to Tom. He seemed too drunk and involved to take much notice of her. He waved her goodbye and then rolled onto his side, laughing at something the German woman had said.

Bebe headed home, disillusioned about her importance at Eurovision. She couldn't stop thinking about the accident backstage. How could nobody be bothered about this? Even if he didn't agree with the possibility of it being deliberate, the stage manager seemed unconcerned about the danger he was putting the stars in. It was outright shocking, especially since Bebe had always thought the Swedes had a strict adherence to standards. Had the same thing occurred somewhere else she wouldn't have been so surprised at the relaxed attitude. Bonnie and Daniela could play down accidents and death threats all they wanted, but something was rotten in the state of Sweden.

Chapter 10

Back in her hotel room, Bebe called Beth to tell her about the accident.

"I must confess I don't blame the stage manager and Nicki for being sceptical," Beth said after she heard the full story. "How could anyone have manipulated a spotlight to fall directly on you and Nicki, when right until then nobody would have known you and her would ever be standing there? Plus, how did they make it fall exactly at that time without being seen?"

"I know it sounds odd," Bebe said. "But the stage manager and his entourage were so quick in cleaning up the scene and suppressing any initiative to make a fuss about it, it's likely that any evidence of foul play has been destroyed before it could be found. And it doesn't surprise me that nobody saw anything. It's dark backstage."

"They called the police in Amsterdam and they found nothing suspicious."

"Maybe someone cleared up there quickly, too."

"That would explain a lot."

"Admittedly, Nicki and I are unlikely targets, which makes me wonder if someone is trying to sabotage the whole event by spreading panic. Maybe they're not just picking on individual contestants."

"I can see the logic in that," Beth replied. "But if you think about it, then it doesn't make sense. The incidents are too random and too low profile to have such an effect on the public."

"They wouldn't be low profile if either of those two events had hit their target."

"Then we're dealing with the possibility that a total amateur and idiot is behind this," Beth said. "There would be better and more efficient ways of spreading chaos than random acts backstage. Are you sure you didn't see anybody?"

"Yes," Bebe replied. "And I searched the place thoroughly. It's a mystery."

"I admit, the business with the spotlights sounds suspicious but it doesn't make sense," Beth said. "Why target two out of forty-odd participants randomly in such an amateurish attack? I've been talking to Eurovision fans and trying to find possible motives; to no avail. Bonnie is well liked in the industry and she's been married for decades with nothing indicating jealousy, separation or any other type of drama.

"Daniela is a bit of a dark horse, but if we agree to rule out regular professional jealousy or something very private, there is no reason to believe this is personal either. She gets on well with her exes and their new spouses. She's an ultra-modern and cool mother and lover, according to those who know her."

"Then I suggest we investigate the two events and see if we can narrow down the suspects," Bebe said. "Ask Tom if he can get the guest list from the Amsterdam event and the VIP list for the show tonight."

"I've tried that already," Beth said. "Unfortunately, because the Dutch police got involved, Tom had no joy in getting his hands on the list of attendants at Amsterdam. He has compiled an incomplete list from eye-witnesses, but that's of little use."

"Don't say that," Bebe said. "It gives us at least a starting point."

"You were marvellous last night," Tom said when Bebe called him the next morning. "I just wish you had stayed longer. The after-party was such a hoot."

"I'm so glad you enjoyed yourself. Thanks again for getting me those tickets. Now darling, I have another favour to ask of you," Bebe said and explained.

"What an excellent idea to get last night's guest list. Why didn't I think of that? I can't promise you anything but leave it with me," Tom said. "I'll see what I can do."

Bebe treated herself to another long soak in the enormous bath tub and listened to the Eurovision channel over the loudspeakers. To her delight they aired a report about last night's show at the Euro Café.

"Nicki French, the UK's 2000 contestant stole the show at the Big Six party in the Euro Café yesterday," Carola told her viewers. "She stood in for Bonnie Tyler, who due to personal reasons had to cancel her appearance at the last minute. Her stand-in, Nicki, sang versions of all the Big Six entrants and then, instead of singing this year's UK song, she let an old friend sing an altered version of 'Believe in Me' on stage. How cool is that?"

Bebe sneered at the 'old friend' but continued to listen with intense interest.

"Very cool," Robin replied. "I'm so glad Nicki is coming back into the limelight. She's so talented and super nice."

"How did you feel about Nicki singing your song, Robin?"

"A little uncomfortable," Robin joked. "She's too damn good."

"She's very good, indeed," Carola agreed. "And a lovely woman. I met her in Stockholm in 2000. I'd love to sing with her one day."

"I'm sure she'd be up for that," Robin said.

"Now which one of the songs from yesterday's Big Six party was your favourite?" Carola asked.

"Nicki's version of the Spanish song. I think it's the weakest of the Big Six and she really spiced it up."

"Well, my favourite was Bonnie's song as sung by Bebe Bollinger. You're too young to know much about this but she was a well-respected star in the Seventies and Eighties."

"Like Engelbert?"

"Well, she didn't sell as many albums as he did, but she had some great songs."

"Let's play a clip from the show," Robin said.

Bebe jumped out of the bath tub to get a look at the screen in the other room, but slipped on the tile floor and twisted her ankle. She was in agony, yet her vanity and curiosity were strong enough to help her limp into the other room, wrap herself in a towel and watch a clip of Nicki singing with Robin. She rested her foot in the ice bucket still there from yesterday's celebratory bottle of champagne. The water was still cold enough to have a mildly soothing effect. She stared at the screen. At last they showed the long-awaited clip of Bebe performing 'Believe in Me'.

"Beautiful," Carola said. "What a great voice."

"She has indeed," Robin said and grinned mischievously. "And she has the weirdest dress sense imaginable. Look at these pictures from yesterday afternoon. Bebe must have a wicked sense of humour to have come to the Café in this frock.

Carola frowned.

"And Bebe must be brave," she said. "She almost copied the dress from Verka, the Ukrainian drag queen. I wouldn't dare mess with him!"

The screen showed the image of an unnervingly masculine man in make-up, a very similar glitter outfit, with huge glasses and a satellite dish on his head. He looked hilarious and frightening at the same time. Bebe could see the unflattering resemblance and cringed.

Unfortunately, that was the end of the report on yesterday's show. Robin and Carola now welcomed Krista, the woman representing Finland. A very pretty girl, Bebe thought, as she got up to see how badly damaged her ankle was. It seemed okay, so she returned to the bath tub.

"I wrote 'Marry Me' to propose to my boyfriend," the Finnish girl bubbled excitably over the loudspeaker. "But I won't enjoy my wedding knowing that so many of my gay friends aren't able to celebrate theirs yet. So, I'll dedicate the song to the gay community and their fight for equality."

"Cynical voices say that this is a calculated move to mobilise the gay vote for your song," Carola said. "How do you respond to such accusations?"

Kristina laughed.

"Let them be cynical," she said. "I hope they dig into my background and find that a lot of my friends are gay. Eurovision is a very gay-friendly environment and I don't think anyone here has to suck up to that community. Being here is a statement in itself: My point for marriage equality is to the viewers who aren't gay, and I'd imagine that will lose rather than gain me votes."

"That's sweet of you," Carola said.

"How do you rate your chances?" Robin asked.

"That's difficult to say," Kristina said. "It depends on many factors, mostly on luck and timing. When I first kissed my backing singer on stage in Amsterdam my betting odds shot through the roof, especially as Daniela had the accident and didn't perform since that night. People weren't betting on her and put their money on me instead. Then Bonnie cancelled a show and I climbed higher in the rankings. Whether or not that means anything, I don't know. I'm just happy being here."

Bebe grinned at the over-used phrase. She had noticed that everyone here was doing this, so she couldn't blame the Finn. It was just so different from Bebe's days on 'Top of the Pops', where the unwritten rule had been to be as cool and unexcited about being somewhere as possible.

Her bath got interrupted by Tom who knocked on her door to deliver the list of backstage ticket holders and potential suspects.

Bebe put on a comfortable soft dressing gown and got him to sit on her large bed with her.

She looked at the computer printout. It had more than 100 names on it.

"Oh dear," she said. "That's far too many suspects."

"I agree," Tom said and pulled out another sheet.

"These are the names that I would flag," he said.

Bebe took the paper and had a look: only twenty names, all of them with a short paragraph about what made them a suspect. Fans who didn't like the UK or Bonnie representing the country, people with professional grudges against the competition, people who didn't seem to be actual Eurovision fans and some who just appeared angry and hate-filled.

"You can't possibly know all of the 100 guests," Bebe said.

"Of course not," Tom admitted. "But I had long gossip sessions last night with the other entrants and with one of the bouncers after hours and that should cover anyone who went backstage."

"Marvellous," Bebe said. "Can you cross reference them with the list you compiled of people at the Amsterdam Eurovision party?"

He took the short list from Bebe, crossed out a few names and made a few amendments to some of the paragraphs he had written about each suspect.

"That takes it down to seven, although I would probably discount these two," he crossed out two more names, "since they only hate the UK but speak highly of the Czech Republic and Daniela."

Bebe took the amended list back. The highlighted suspects were:

Peter Beatle, DJ and hardcore Eurovision fan for years. Declared that the UK and the Czech Republic were two of the worst songs in the competition this year and advocates that the show should be for new talent only.

Jan Ola Nielssen, miserable drug head who does nothing but moan about the contest, gets awfully drunk and was once banned from a Eurovision party in Riga because he started a fight with other fans.

Marcha De Poel, an X-Factor runner-up who expressed interest in performing for the Netherlands this year but missed out when the national broadcaster announced there wouldn't be an official heat and instead commissioned Anouk to write a song. Marcha stated on TV that the UK should not get automatic entry to the final and should have to qualify via the semi-finals like everyone else.

Mark Evans, a notoriously annoying online troll who has been barred from several internet Eurovision forums for his nasty comments and divisive behaviour. He's from Wales but advocated quite graphically that he doesn't think Bonnie should be representing the UK, even though she is from Wales, too.

Claudia De Poel, cousin to Marcha. She sang backing vocals to Anouk in Amsterdam but was replaced by Shirma Rouse. Claudia was furious about it. Her presence in Malmö without having a musical gig doesn't make sense. And what did she do as VIP at the Big Six party?

Bebe whistled through her teeth.

"Those are some hilarious motives for murder," she said. "Can we meet with these people and question them?"

"Of course," Viktor said. "The ticket sales printout has all of their contact details."

He turned over the sheet with the full 100 names and pointed at the list of phone numbers and email addresses.

"How did you get these?" Bebe asked.

"I made some useful friends last night," he said and winked at her.

"Well, thank you my dear."

Chapter 11

Two hours later, Bebe sat in a fish restaurant in Malmö, impatiently waiting for Beth to discuss the list of suspects and figure out how to get them to talk to two amateur detectives.

At the table to her left sat a Swedish family, the children glued to their mobile phones and the parents looking miserable as they ate their salmon. To her right sat a group of Spanish people who were involved in a lively and noisy discussion.

Bebe's foot was still hurting, as was her ego after seeing the Ukrainian drag queen on TV. She had packed deliberately for this occasion and, as it turned out, exactly opposite to how she should have. This afternoon she had settled for a dark blue dress which was simple enough, had it not been for the puffed up short sleeves. She felt ever so self-conscious and disappointed that the glamour seemed to be limited to performers on stage only. That wasn't how she had envisaged the scene here at all.

Eventually Beth turned up, plonked herself down and ordered a stiff drink from the waiter.

"Sorry," Bebe said. "I never got to ask you about your evening last night. Where did you end up?"

"Oh God yes," Beth said. "My landlords Lars and Ola kept me company for most of the evening. We were meant to go to the Big Six party, too, but we stopped at the Greek reception on the way and never got out of there in time. The Greek song is called 'Alcohol is Free' and that wasn't a lie yesterday. Ola and Lars have this remarkable talent for remembering song lyrics and mimicking dance moves from each song. The hosts never saw it coming but my boys stole their thunder. I had a great time. This music does my head in, but the fun of it all makes it bearable."

"Did you find out anything?"

"Not much, but to be honest, we're stabbing in the dark. Daniela is deemed as arrogant by some and was slammed for not being willing to perform in a national selection show. She was selected internally, saving herself a possible defeat by the hands of the telly voters. A lot of people took offence at that since Eurovision is all about the voting, and she had by-passed this. As for Bonnie, the same should be true but everyone likes her and her friendly attitude. Resentment against the UK is felt mostly towards the commentators."

"I find that hard to believe"

"If I'm being honest, me, too. Yet, on the online forums and in discussions it is brought up time and time again by all nationalities. Which is a shame, because I do enjoy the odd sarcastic comment about the more outlandish entries," Beth admitted. "Is that really so bad? Does the UK have to be punished for this by being passed over when it comes to the voting?"

"I can hardly recognise it as a reason for murder," Bebe said. She opened her handbag and handed Beth a sheet of paper. "Well, here's the list of suspects," she said.

Beth took it and studied it hard.

"Are you sure we're not wasting our time here?" she asked.

"You'll get paid, don't you worry."

"It's not that," Beth said. "I wonder if any of these people would go to such lengths over a musical competition."

"There's only one way of finding out," Bebe said and handed Beth the telephone. "Let's call them and arrange some meetings."

Their first suspect was easy prey. Bebe had spoken to Peter Beatle only yesterday and he had been so much nicer to her than he was on his show. The question was, where had he been at that precise moment when the spotlight came down? When Beth said she wanted to do an interview with him for Tom's blog he was instantly available and offered to meet them at a bar not far from the fish restaurant only twenty minutes later.

Peter had shaved his head, he wore denims and a tight white shirt that accentuated his flabby physique. How that man could be fashion guru was beyond her.

He eyed her costume.

"I wish you'd worn that when you came to my show," he said and grinned. "I would have had a field day with that."

Bebe laughed.

"Always the charmer," she said.

"Now Peter, tell me: who are your favourites at this competition?" Beth interrupted the two. "You must have some insight as to who will do particularly well. And which songs would you play in a nightclub?"

"Obviously, when I do a Eurovision gig I need to play requests and then I'll play anything," Peter said and patted his head. "But professionally, I'm most interested in Malta: it's an innovative happy tune that will do very well. Bulgaria is having a good shot at ethno pop but I doubt they'll qualify."

"What did you think of my version of Bonnie's song?" Bebe asked, only in part hoping to find out more about Peter's exact whereabouts during the moment the spotlight had fallen.

"May I be honest?" Peter asked with a serious face.

"Of course," Bebe said automatically, although she had her doubts she wanted to hear this.

"It's miles better than Bonnie's version. You understand your audience, you know the people who come to Eurovision and what they need to hear. Absolutely love it. And may I also please say that I'm glad you changed your costume. The frock you wore in the lounge before the event made me cringe."

"How about my vocals," she asked. "Were they okay? I mean, did you listen to the song in the audience or backstage?"

"I was backstage of course, in the lounge and watched you on the TV screen. Very nice vocals."

"What about the song from Italy?" Beth asked. It had been the act performing during the incident.

"He's okay, I guess," Peter said. "I didn't pay much attention to him."

"He was on stage right after me," Bebe said. "How could you have missed him?"

"I must have gone to the gents, or something."

Beth and Bebe exchanged a quick look.

Peter digressed into a monologue on what he called the ill-advised costume fetish. They let him finish to make this a more believable press interview.

"I heard that you said that the UK and the Czech Republic were two of the worst songs in the competition this year," Beth asked him when he was done. "Why's that?"

"Well the Czech song is dreadfully miserable and slow. It's nothing special at all, yet it's sold to us as a super offering from a country sending one of their best. It's boring and Daniela clearly isn't the star she's made out to be. The show really should be for new talent only. It's appalling."

"I don't know," Bebe intervened. "In the Seventies and Eighties all the biggest names participated. Why shouldn't they do so now?"

"Eurovision is a niche market. The big stars don't come here anymore, only people who see it as a change at a breakthrough. Oldies who hope for second chance or one more comeback spoil it in my opinion. Sorry!"

"Why's this so important to you?" Bebe asked. "Why not lean back and watch what happens with amusement and get on with it?"

Peter's face grew red with anger.

"Eurovision is not just any minor show for me," he said. "I love it and I take a great interest in the direction its format is going. As a DJ, people ask me to play songs from Eurovision artists. I don't want to play old stuff from Bonnie Tyler, thank you very much. She walks in here with her Grammy nominations and takes over the space that should be for people who sing chansons, Eurovision fare, made for a very specific audience. She's hijacking the show for her own needs. I find that type of thing very offensive."

"Are there any other performers you hate this much?" Beth asked.

"The German singer, Cascada," Peter said. "She's got a career already and her song sounds just like last year's winning song. I don't care that the courts ruled in her favour. I believe that she copied that song and she should have been disqualified from performing. I was invited to the German final and they had a lot better songs than hers. They should get a chance instead."

"Do you think anybody might feel as strongly about this as you and try to sabotage any of the performances?" Beth asked.

"They should," Peter said.

"Would you consider taking such action?" Beth asked.

"Absolutely," came the instant reply. "If I could I would pull them off the stage myself. I've started an online petition and have written to the producers."

"What if I told you that those very two singers have been victims of attacks?" Beth probed.

"I'd say thank God for that," Peter said. "I hope they pull out of the competition. I've been a Eurovision DJ for years and I know I'll never play their songs voluntarily. I've got standards. In this business you need to watch your reputation. You can tell Tom's blog readers that Peter Beatle is a man of passion and integrity."

Beth couldn't help but giggle.

Peter looked at her with contempt but then his face cracked and he burst into a laughing fit himself.

"You're right, darlings," he said. "I sound so pathetic. At the end of the day it's just a show and please don't think that I'm not having a good time here, because I am, despite all my moaning. That's part of my job."

He emptied his champagne flute and got up.

"You're actually dressed mighty fine for the occasion," he said to Bebe. "However, saying that won't get me the viewer figures I need."

He sent them both air kisses.

"See you around."

"What do you make of Peter?" Bebe asked once he was out of ear shot.

"That man's a weirdo," Bebe said, "that much is clear. At the same time, he's got a radio gig and a career to lose. I don't think he did it, but we can't rule him out."

"I agree," Beth said. "He was backstage both times. And you know what? Something in the way he owned up to it made it sound as if he was trying to provoke us. It was like a 'look, I don't have an alibi and I'm not hiding my motive. Accuse me if you dare – you've got nothing on me.' It didn't sound as if he said all of this so we wouldn't suspect him."

"Well, he doesn't know we're investigating the spotlight crash, so I'm not sure he thought about giving himself an alibi while talking to us."

Bebe got her phone from her purse and handed it to Beth.

"Now let's call the next one on the list and get an appointment."

Jan Ola Nielssen, the borderline violent 'psycho' as he had been described by Tom on the list, loved the prospect of doing an interview with Tom's blog, too, and also agreed to meet them at the Euro Café within an hour. This left the ladies enough time to make their way to the café in a leisurely way and have their first glass of champagne together.

"I missed this," Beth said and patted Bebe's hand.

"Me, too," Bebe admitted. "Having a career can be incredibly lonely."

"Well, I wouldn't know about career," Beth grinned. "I know about lonely, though."

"You must get out of that place and make a fresh start, away from that woman."

"Fred and I are still good friends and very fond of each other," Beth said. "I can't cut her out of my life."

"You must learn how to do that," Bebe insisted. "Every time she starts a new fling you're getting hurt and when she ends it you hope that it's your turn again and that she will finally see that you're the perfect woman for her. Don't kid yourself. I love her to bits but for you Fred is bad news."

They were interrupted by Jan Ola Nielssen, whom a waiter accompanied to the table. Nielssen was petit and slim, in his forties and was wearing a tight T-shirt with the Eurovision emblem, and blindingly pink trousers.

"Hi", he said and sat down with his legs crossed.

He grabbed one of the empty water glasses and poured himself a glass from the champagne bottle.

"Nice," he said after he had one sip, then he emptied the glass in one go.

"So, what do you want to know about me? "

"You're a big Eurovision fan, we take it," Beth asked him. "You went to the party in Amsterdam and now you're here. Who are your favourite acts this year? Who do you like and who don't you like?"

"Oh, I do like the man from Azerbaijan," Jan Ola said. "He's gorgeous. And the Irish song isn't half bad."

"That's it?" Bebe asked. "Only those two and nobody else?"

Nielssen stared at her and then suddenly snapped with his fingers.

"Oh, it's you," he said and pointed at her.

Bebe smiled, always happy to be recognised and praised.

"How did you get Bonnie to agree to let you sing her song?" he asked. "We didn't pay all that good money to hear her older sister perform. That was outrageous."

"I take it that you didn't like it then?" Bebe asked, her hands crossing over her chest.

"You catch on fast," Nielssen said and poured himself another glass.

"Never mind about Bebe," Beth said. "What do you think of Bonnie's original version?"

"Bonnie's okay, I suppose," he said. "She's got a great voice, but she doesn't use it for this song, which is a big shame."

"How about the Italian guy and his song?"

"Yeah, he's cute. We were chatting in the smoking area when your song was playing," he said to Bebe.

"What about his song?"

"The song is boring, but who cares if the package is so nice."

"What do you think of his performance at the Big Six party?"

"To be honest I can't remember much. I was drunk and most of the night is a blur."

"Yet you remembered me?" Bebe asked.

He rolled his eyes.

"Yes, I remember you."

There was an awkward silence as Nielssen lit a cigarette.

"This is a non-smoking café," Beth pointed out.

"Let them kick me out," he said and blew the smoke at her. "Listen darlings, you said you wanted an interview with a hardcore fan, so far you've been asking nothing but the most unoriginal questions. Let me help you out. I watched my first Eurovision when I was twelve. The bloody Germans won, but the song was okay I guess. We Danes didn't do great, but then we dominated the contest for a decade. I've started watching the competition live since 1998 and have never missed a year since."

"What happened to you in Riga?" Beth asked, obviously hoping she had caught him off guard enough to get him uncomfortable, ready to reveal something he would otherwise have hidden.

Nielssen rolled his eyes and took a deep drag from his cigarette. How he had got away with smoking in here was beyond Bebe. Nobody seemed prepared to take the man on, not even the waiters.

"So, you heard about that? Well, to be blatantly honest, I have no idea," Jan Ola said. "I was very drunk, and I guess some idiot must have said something that annoyed me, so I – how do you British say – lamped him one. People can be so rude."

"Thank you," Beth said. "I think I have enough information for today."

"You haven't asked me anything that matters," Nielssen protested. "It was hardly worth my while coming here."

He stood up, extinguished his cigarette in Bebe's almost empty champagne glass and stormed off.

Bebe and Beth burst into laughter.

"What a nutter," Bebe said.

"Yeah," Beth agreed. "If he could stay sober long enough he could well be the man we're looking for, but I seriously doubt he could get through an involved scheme without passing out from drink beforehand."

"He must be sober enough to make money from his business," Bebe pointed out. "It says here in the notes that he's got his own IT company and sponsors the London Eurovision party every year, so he must be brighter than we can assume from his appearance. Could that be a plan to throw us off course?"

"Absolutely," Beth said. "You've got to trust your gut instinct when you speak to these people, but don't trust anything they say. Some suspects are fantastic actors."

"Mind you," Bebe said. "My gut doesn't say much about him other than that I don't like him."

"Then your gut is at least right about one thing," Beth said. "Next!"

Chapter 12

It proved difficult to get close to the other suspects. Marcha, the jealous X-Factor runner-up, was working on a documentary about Eurovision with a Dutch TV crew and was busy all that day. She was keen to promote herself outside her home country and promised to make herself available the following morning

Her cousin, the backing vocalist Claudia, didn't event answer her phone and returned neither Bebe's calls nor Beth's.

Mark, the online troll, also didn't respond to their messages, which left the two women time to catch up on their gossip. They walked back into town and found a pizzeria near the station.

"Helena has run out of cash again," Bebe said after they were digging into their dishes. "I bailed her out the once a few months ago; I know her father did the same at least one other time and she's already leaving me messages with obscure reasons why she can't get the money herself. I've stopped taking her calls, as much as my heart bleeds."

"I'm glad I don't have kids," Beth said. "I'm too selfish and would make a dreadful mother."

"What's worse than selfishness is helplessness," Bebe said. "I know I'm egocentric, but I gave it all up for Helena, ready to put my life on hold. The problem is that she and I are such different people and don't understand each other. I thought I'd get a mini version of myself, but ended up with this person who hates me and everything that I do. We simply never got on."

"That's bad, especially since she won't leave you alone."

"Tell me about it," Bebe said. "I enjoyed my time on the cruise ship, not least because I knew Helena couldn't just show up and make a scene."

"Is she seeing anyone?" Beth asked.

"I'm sure she is," Bebe said. "I doubt it will last, though. She's so flighty."

"I remember," Beth said and grinned.

"Where's Tom by the way?" Bebe asked. "I thought you were meant to work together?"

Beth's head sank.

"At the Big Six dress rehearsal I believe," she said. "He never tells me details. I think he's started seeing that Italian guy who's working for him, Giovanni. He spends all his time with. He's given him a job at his blog and arranged press accreditation for him."

Bebe got up and gave Beth a hug.

"Oh dear," she said and after a few seconds she broke free and sat back down.

"Tom is a bit of a fickle man. I wouldn't take it to heart. I know he trusts you more than his own investigative talents, so keep doing what you're doing."

Beth nodded.

"I know. It's just that I thought we were becoming friends and now I feel dumped like a hot potato. I'm not used to that coming from men."

Bebe took her friend's hand and stroked it.

"Tonight's the Dutch party," Beth said. "Anouk has invited the press and fans to a marquee in the town centre. It has everything, from drinks, music and celebrities – the works. Fancy coming as my guest?"

"What about Tom? Why didn't he want to cover that event himself? Him speaking Dutch would make him the obvious choice, if he insists you two work separately."

"He thought he's too well known in those circles to be an effective spy."

"Well never mind," Bebe said and devoured the last piece of her pizza.

"I'll come along."

"Thank you."

Bebe emptied her glass and pushed her plate away.

"That was lovely," she said. "Promise me never to take me to a pizzeria again. It's so bad for my figure."

Beth promised and asked the waiter for the bill. As she looked through her handbag to find her purse, she briefly checked her phone and saw that she had missed two calls from Tom.

"His ears must have been burning."

"Call him back," Bebe said.

"Oh, my God," Tom said without any introductory pleasantries when he answered his phone on the second ring. "There's been another accident."

"With Bonnie?" Beth asked.

Bebe almost forgot to breathe. So, their fears had been justified?

"No," Tom said. "With Cascada from Germany. She uses giant steps for her act and they hadn't been locked in place. Cascada walks down from the top of the stairs during her act. When they started moving she lost balance and tumbled onto the floor."

"Is she okay?" Beth asked.

"She sprained her ankle, broke a few nails and the heel of her left shoe has come off. She was shocked at first but immediately tried to get up and continue with her performance. She was limping through the song like a brave trouper."

"Oh my,'" Bebe shook her head. "Another 'accident'?"

"This is the first time she rehearsed with this particular set of steps. They didn't get here in time for yesterday's rehearsals, so everyone thinks it's damaged from the express transport."

"Are any of our suspects at the event?" Beth asked.

"I don't know. They wouldn't necessarily have to be here," Tom said. "The steps could have been tempered with ahead of the rehearsals."

"Can you use your friendship with Cascada to track the exact movements of the steps between Germany and Malmö?"

"Of course, I'll try my best."

"Excellent," Beth said.

"Giovanni's sure there's a story in all these 'accidents'," Tom said. "He wants to meet you both to have a chat about it."

Bebe grabbed the phone out of Beth's hands.

"I don't think so," she said. "It's not something we should seek publicity for. Publicity makes criminals hide more carefully. Tell him thanks but explain to him that we need to operate undercover. It's the only advantage we have, since the police aren't doing a good job as far as we can see."

"You got it all wrong," Tom insisted. "He wants to do a documentary about it next month, not a scoop while Eurovision is going on."

"I don't care what the man tells you," Bebe said. "You've only known him for five minutes. Journalists cannot be trusted with this, even if they suddenly work for you. There are lives at stake."

"Suit yourself," Tom said and hung up.

"Someone's overly sensitive," she said and handed the phone back to Beth.

"It's already time to go to the Dutch party," Beth said. "Do you need to go back to the hotel and change?"

Bebe looked down at herself.

"What do you think?" she asked. "Ever since they compared me to a drag queen I'm too self-conscious to make up my mind what to wear."

"You look mighty fine in my eyes," Beth replied. "Don't let people get to you. You really should grow a thicker skin if you want to continue in show business. There will always be people who criticise you, especially here at Eurovision. It's really funny if you think that the UK has got a bad reputation for poking fun at the competition, and then you get so much badmouthing and bitching about bad costume choices from everyone else. It's a bit rich, isn't it?"

"I know," Bebe said. "Tom told me that there is an award for the worst costume each year."

The marquee for the Dutch party was only a few blocks away. The May sun had been surprisingly strong during the day but now that it was evening the temperature had dropped. Bebe was glad she had brought a large square throw that worked as a scarf as well as an improvised jacket to keep her warm.

"I hope they won't play cheesy pop all night," Beth said.

"What do you expect them to play?" Bebe asked. "Heavy Metal? The Dutch song is a nice enough ballad but it's only three minutes long. Cheesy pop is part of the deal here. If you're lucky they have Loreen and her techno song."

At the entrance to the marquee the bouncers checked Beth's press pass. When Bebe couldn't find hers they asked her to queue for a ticket.

"You don't understand," Beth told them. "This is Bebe Bollinger, the singer from Britain."

The bouncer shook his head.

"Nice try. The singer from Britain is already inside."

"Bebe was on the Big Six stage yesterday. Did you not see it?" Beth asked.

"I know she wasn't singing here yesterday," the bouncer replied.

He pointed at the ticket queue and turned away, scanning the surrounding area with his eyes like a sniper searching for his target.

"I could go back to my hotel in Copenhagen to get the press pass but that will take hours."

"I appreciate that," Beth said. "I'll see if I can find someone who can get you in. If I'm not back in a few minutes, start checking, just in case.

Bebe's heart sank. She had come a long way down from being the entertainer on the Eurovision stage only last night to being the entertained and having to queue for the privilege tonight. It was at moments like this that she wondered if the results were worth the effort she had to make. There were these short glorious moments of being recognised for her talent and adored by fans, and then all was gone and she felt like nobody. Her career was a constant struggle and she just about had enough trying, scheming, begging and hoping. As she had feared all along, there was no magic opening of the marquee door for Bebe.

Reluctantly she joined the queue, which was not only rather long, but also hadn't moved for some time. Maybe a taxi to Copenhagen would be quicker after all. She overheard a group of youngsters whisper something about Miss Marple and giggle. She could feel her cheeks warm with a rush of blood. How many more insults should she expect tonight, she wondered? She opened her purse to see if she had any messages on her phone. At least that way she would blend in with the millennials while waiting.

"Isn't that the woman who sang Bonnie's song last night?" she suddenly heard from further ahead in the queue. She pretended that she hadn't heard this and stared focused on her phone. She prayed that this was not going to be followed by something rude.

"I'm not sure," came the reply from within the queue. "I'll find out."

Before she knew it, a young man tapped her on the shoulder.

"Excuse me," he said with an Eastern European accent. "Did you sing a version of 'Believe in Me' on stage yesterday?"

Nervously she turned around and put her phone away.

"I did indeed," she said. "I'm Bebe."

"Oh wow," the young man said. "Just wow."

"Thank you," Bebe said, "what's your name?"

"Atis," he said, "me and my friends are from Latvia."

She looked at him: he was only about twenty, very smiley and handsome.

"Nice to meet you," she said. "How are you enjoying the spectacle, so far?"

"Fantastic," he said. "You were very good. My friend Elisa, she downloaded your album yesterday. She was wondering if you would mind signing her i-Pod?"

"Signing her i-Pod? I've never heard of that." When she saw his smile drop she added: "But of course I will."

"Why don't you join us in the queue?" Atis asked and to her surprise the people standing in between Bebe and the Latvian group gestured for her to go ahead.

"Why thank you," Bebe said and followed Atis to where his friends were standing.

Elisa, an equally young and beautiful girl, got out her i-Pod and handed Bebe a pen.

Bebe signed it with love and then pulled out a few autographs from her hand bag. She always carried some with her. 'Never disappoint a fan' had been her motto throughout her career.

"Have these, too," she said, happy that a group so young were complimentary about her music.

"May I have one as well, please?" someone else asked. Bebe turned around and handed an autographed picture of her to a big lady with dark, Mediterranean looks.

"Thank you."

"Can I have one?"

"Me, too, please!"

"And me!"

Suddenly half of the queue had turned around and demanded her autograph. People pushed her towards the front of the queue.

"That's the UK entry," she heard someone say.

"No. That's not Bonnie Tyler." Someone else disagreed.

"It sure is," the first voice insisted. "I saw her yesterday singing 'Believe in Me'. I recognise it from the CD.

"It says Bebe Bollinger on the autograph," a third voice chipped in. "I never heard that name mentioned anywhere."

"She sang Bonnie's song yesterday," a fourth person now got involved. "They are good pals those two."

Bebe was too busy handing out autographs to follow all conversations around her. The unexpected attention, right after she had settled into the humbleness of waiting outside to be let into the

84

Dutch party, was extremely welcome. It didn't matter if some of this was overexcitement by Eurovision fans who didn't necessarily know who she was.

"Come with me," she suddenly heard the bouncer say, the very man who ten minutes ago had been so incredibly rude to her.

She followed him as he led her towards the marquee. Bebe half expected to see Beth or Bonnie standing there but it seemed as if the man had taken her previous statement more serious once he had seen the fuss that had been made about her. So, she had got in on her own merit.

The grim-looking man held the door open for her and almost gallantly swung his hand forward to invite her in.

The inside was larger than she had expected. A few high tables for people to gather around had been planted on the side of the marquee, leaving a large area in front of a stage which formed the centre of the room. People were busy mingling. Bebe could find neither Bonnie nor Beth. Maybe there was a VIP area elsewhere?

The DJ was playing dance tunes, which Bebe had to assume had been part of Eurovision at some stage. She had never heard of them but she enjoyed the music all the same. They were quite catchy.

"I believe you're looking for me," a beautiful young woman addressed Bebe.

She had long dark hair, dark sparkly eyes, a big mouth with a flawless white set of teeth and an enviable curvy figure.

"I'm sorry my dear, but who are you?" Bebe asked. She knew it was one of the De Poels but not which one.

"I'm Marcha," came the reply. So this was the jealous X-Factor runner-up.

"Oh yes, of course," Bebe said. "My friend was going to interview you. I'm afraid we've been separated; I'm not sure where she is; probably in a press room somewhere."

"Never mind," Marcha said. "I just wanted to apologise for not getting in touch with you sooner. I've been so busy with the documentary about 'what I missed out on'."

"You must be gutted," Bebe said.

"Not really," Marcha replied. "In fact, I get to see everything that there is to see, I get to party and I can drink because I don't have to perform the next day. I meet producers and people from all over Europe and at the end I won't be judged by my country for how many points I bring home. The Netherlands have done badly for the last ten years. I won't hold my breath for Anouk even qualifying. If she does, millions of people will watch her sink to the bottom of the scoreboard and her career will be finished. She'll have some more kids, I guess, and spend her spare time kick-boxing after this."

"Those are harsh words," Bebe said. "Maybe you could have done better with the right song and be known for restoring your country's standing?"

"Could have, would have, should have… " Marcha laughed. "I'm having a great time and wish Anouk luck. She needs it."

Bebe registered the thinly disguised spite and she remembered how Marcha had stated on TV that the UK should not get automatic entry to the competition as it currently did. She had held a passionate speech how the Big Six countries should have to qualify via the semi-finals like everyone else. Bonnie and Cascada were both part of the Big Six group.

"What do you think of the songs on offer?" Bebe asked. "Which ones are your favourites?"

"Oh, they're all cool," Marcha said. "I doubt any one of them will get into the charts, though."

"Yet, you planned on participating yourself?" Bebe asked. "That's strange."

"Yes," Marcha admitted. "That was when I thought I'd be voted off the X-Factor. I recovered and nearly won the show. You know as much as I do that you need to fill newspaper columns and Eurovision was simply one of those. Anouk had already been picked, so it was safe to say I should be doing it instead of her. Once in a blue moon a Eurovision winner makes a career or a half decent living out of the show; everyone else goes home as a failure, never to be heard from again. I never wanted to take that risk."

"How do you feel about Anouk, then?"

"She's okay, I guess," Marcha said. "Her song is weak and so is her staging. I don't envy her place. Doing this documentary is much more fun."

"Come on," Bebe said. "Don't tell me a stage this huge, a combined TV audience of almost a billion, can't tempt you, regardless of the outcome. You're lying."

"Of course, I'm tempted," Marcha admitted. "Who wouldn't be? But somehow my gut is telling me that this isn't going to end well.

Songwriters in my country don't give their good songs to this competition anymore."

"I know you're doing this documentary now. And I heard also that it only started once you were here. Why did you come to Malmö, if the filming hadn't been the primary reason?"

"To make up my own mind," Marcha said. "And to stay in people's minds. After all, fame can be fickle, as I'm sure you know yourself. X-Factor fame is particularly short-lived. I started the Eurovision envy game, so I had to continue."

Bebe wanted to ask more questions but she was interrupted by the sudden arrival of the friends she had made earlier in the queue. As the group came up to her one held out his phone, which was playing the YouTube clip of Peter's radio show with Bebe giggling over that terrible word.

Marcha looked shocked.

"That is so rude!" she said.

"It surely is," Bebe admitted. "I didn't think your generation minded that kind of language."

Marcha was about to answer but the group of fans surrounded Bebe chanting the outrageous word and then dragged her to the bar where they treated their 'new best friend' to champagne and kept her busy with chit chat. By the time they let go of her, Marcha had long disappeared.

Bebe was disappointed. On reflection, it struck her as odd that the Dutch girl would volunteer so much information about her career tactics to the friend of a journalist. That seemed very naïve and unguarded, unless it was meant to mislead her.

The place had filled up quite a bit within the last 20 minutes or so and technicians were setting up sound equipment on the small stage within the tent. The DJ was still spinning catchy tunes – surely those couldn't be the recent Dutch songs that had so famously bombed at the contest. Bebe remembered that she was here for a reason and looked for the entrance to the VIP lounge.

"There you are," she heard a familiar male voice behind her.

"Peter Beatle!" Bebe called out and hugged him.

"Bebe, you dirty minx," he said and took a sip from her champagne. "Let's get more booze."

He grabbed her hand and pulled her towards the bar, where he ordered a bottle of champagne.

"It's so exciting you are here. You're so wicked!"

Bebe laughed, slightly helpless against his forceful behaviour.

"There are plenty of people I've got to introduce you to," Peter said as he poured them both a glass. "Don't go anywhere."

He went to the DJ booth and handed the man a memory stick, then he spoke with one of the technicians on stage before waving at a few people and dragging one of them to the small table near the bar where Bebe had positioned herself. The sound system was blasting an Abba track and the crowd was loving it.

"This is Edsilia," Peter said on returning to the table, pointing at a dark-skinned woman with a fabulous smile, "a former Dutch contestant and great fun."

"How do you do," Bebe said and shook her hands.

"Edsilia will be singing in a minute," Peter said. "She's such a darling to look after us tonight."

"Thank you," Bebe said. The music was loud and she found it hard to understand. The DJ must have turned up the volume. The new track sounded familiar, too.

"You should really do Eurovision," Peter said. "Ask Nicki, she came 16th but she's almost made a living out of it."

"Nicki's here?" Bebe asked.

"Yes, over there," Peter said and pointed across the room. He waved and Nicki picked up her glass and came to join them.

"Is it true?" Bebe asked Nicki after they had exchanged pleasantries. "Peter said you made a career out of Eurovision?"

"Absolutely," Nicki said. "And it's so much fun."

Now Bebe recognised the track. It was the remix of her giggle at the Peter Beatle Show, only someone had blended a clip from 'He's the One Who'll be Sorry' in. To her amazement the people in the marquee danced to it and seemed to have a good time.

Edsilia went to the stage and grabbed a microphone.

"Welcome to the Dutch party everyone," she said. "Thank you all for coming. We're still warming up as you might have gathered, but boy, are we hot already."

She paused and right there the rude word came up again, and Bebe's giggle.

Edsilia laughed.

"You're probably wondering why we're playing this song," she said. "Yes, it's not a Dutch song and neither is it strictly Eurovision, but there won't be many stars from the competition that haven't eyed up songs from this singer's repertoire at one stage in their career or another. I certainly covered a few of her songs in my shows and would cover more if my manager allowed me to. Please give it up to the one and only Bebe Bollinger."

Bebe smiled and waved at the people around her. There weren't many who seemed to reconcile the words they heard with the waving woman.

"This is bullshit," Peter said and pulled Bebe through the crowd towards the stage. "Up you go," he added and pushed her up the two steps.

Edsilia was as unprepared for this as Bebe and looked confused.

"Can we have a second microphone?" she asked and then whispered to Bebe: "I didn't bring the backing tracks for my remakes of your songs. We could sing 'Holding Out for a Hero' or what Eurovision songs do you know? 'Euphoria'?"

"What about my version of 'Believe in Me'?" Bebe asked.

"Too slow," Edsilia replied. "Any other ideas?"

"No," Bebe said. "It'll have to be 'Holding Out for a Hero' then."

Edsilia signalled the DJ a flexed biceps and on cue he started to fade out the track with Bebe's giggle.

"So Bebe and I are going to try a little duet," Edsilia said. "We're both big fans of Bonnie Tyler, who couldn't be with us tonight, so we're going to pay tribute to her with this lovely track."

The fans went barking mad when the legendary drum intro to the song roared over the speaker system.

"Who sings which line?" Bebe asked. Edsilia pointed at herself and began to sing. She wasn't one for moving madly around the stage. Her forte was her smile and her ability to hold the gaze of anyone and make them smile. When it was Bebe's turn Edsilia pointed at her and then did the rock star thing where she shook hands with as many fans in the front row as she could.

Both singers had husky voices which worked very well for this song. When it was over Edsilia thanked Bebe for being on stage and signalled the DJ by giving him a repeated thumbs-up.

When a few piano cords started playing the crowd went mad again. Edsilia started to sing a ballad over the cheering while Bebe returned to where she had left Peter and Nicki. Unfortunately, they had disappeared and had seemingly taken the champagne with them.

Chapter 13

The loneliness didn't last long because Beth appeared out of nowhere.

"Where on Earth have you been?" Bebe asked.

"Back in the VIP lounge, waiting for you. Then I heard your voice. Luckily, I had the most amazing chat with Claudia de Poel, the rejected backing vocalist."

Bebe couldn't decide whether to be more curious or outraged.

"Well, you could have checked in with me, couldn't you? It was unlikely for me to be let into the VIP lounge if they wouldn't let me into the marquee to start with," she pointed out.

Beth ignored the outburst: "Turns out, Claudia is completely cool with not being backing vocalist this year."

"How so?"

"When her cousin Marcha made all these remarks about Anouk cheating her way out of a qualifying round, they couldn't go ahead and hire the cousin of Anouk's hardest critic. Claudia appreciates this situation and she has signed a deal with Anouk's record label to go on tour with several other Dutch artists. The contract is for two years, so I don't think we have a suspect there."

"How do you know she's telling the truth?"

"I spoke to Anouk as well, who confirmed all the details."

"I get that we're able to eliminate one more suspect, but why did you say that you had the most amazing conversation with her?" Bebe asked.

"She's very witty."

"If she's anything like her cousin Marcha, then Claudia must be," Bebe said.

"How would you know that?" Beth asked. "Have you met her?"

"Yes, just a few minutes ago. She approached me and apologised for not getting in touch with us. We got interrupted, though, and I never got to ask her all the questions I had wanted to."

"Now that's funny, because Claudia said that Marcha had already left the country."

"Then Claudia's clearly mistaken. Did it sound like the two cousins were particularly close to each other?" Bebe asked.

"Quite the opposite," Beth replied. "It sounded to me as if there's a deep rivalry going on. Claudia even said that she thought

Marcha capable of almost anything, that Marcha is career obsessed and would walk over dead bodies to get where she wants to be. They didn't speak for months when Claudia was hired by a recording studio and Marcha missed out. Then Marcha got into the X-Factor and they made up. Since the show is over and Marcha hasn't landed many jobs there's more animosity again."

"Where's Claudia now?" Bebe asked.

"Having her make-up done backstage. She'll be on stage shortly with one of the next few acts."

"And that explains why she's in town," Bebe said. "That all makes sense now."

"Did you hear about Bonnie's accident?" Beth asked.

"No," Bebe said. "But I remember Edsilia saying that Bonnie couldn't be here tonight. I completely forgot about it. What happened?"

"The steps for Cascada happened. Bonnie stood backstage waiting for her cue when Cascada's steps suddenly started moving towards her. Luckily Bonnie saw it and got away. While doing so she fell over and has a slightly sprained ankle, though. Nothing to worry about, the doctors say, but she needs to rest it tonight or the ankle will be swollen to twice its size."

"That's shocking," Bebe said. "Especially since Cascada's stairs weren't locked solid in the earlier rehearsal. How could that same mistake happen twice? Were there any witnesses who saw what happened?"

"The wheels of the steps aren't locked before they go on stage to save time. They shouldn't move unless pushed anyway. Nobody saw anything, as usual. At an event this big with so many helpers, it's shocking indeed. I wonder how all these accidents don't ring more alarm bells."

"Didn't you say yourself at some stage these were all unfortunate coincidences and that there was no case?" Bebe asked.

"Absolutely," Beth said. "As an outsider I think there's a pretty good chance that these are coincidences. The organisers and the local police, however, shouldn't afford such a relaxed attitude. Tom said they sent one policeman who spoke to the security staff and then wrote his report without checking out the scene personally."

"I agree, that's outrageous," Bebe said. Then she stopped for a moment.

"Did you say Tom?" she asked.

"Yes, he was there with his Italian journalist and immediately called me with all the details," Beth said. "He's such a sweetheart, after all."

"What time did the accident occur?"

"Half past three."

"That would have left enough time for Marcha or Claudia to leave the arena, take a train and be here as if nothing ever happened."

"True. And Peter was at the rehearsals as well."

"But how?" Bebe asked.

"As radio DJ, he has a press pass and is allowed access during this round of rehearsals," Beth replied. "From tomorrow on, members of the public are admitted to the rehearsals, too. The organisers even sell tickets for these shows. Keeping track of suspects will be tougher."

"Nonsense. There's tight security in the hall. The real question is motive," Bebe said. "Why are those singers or countries being targeted? And why are the authorities so slow?"

"I wish I knew," Beth said. "Maybe the police know more than we do and these are all perfectly legitimate accidents after all."

Edsilia had finished her set a while ago and the DJ had entertained the crowd with contemporary Eurovision music and some classics. Now the music had stopped and the DJ introduced the star of this evening: Anouk.

The Dutch singer limped on stage with a pained face. Her foot was in a massive plaster cast, which looked so much bigger and more dramatic than in the pictures of her online.

"She's putting this on for show," Beth said. "When I saw her last the cast was half the size."

"This is probably an extra-strong model," Bebe disagreed. "So, she can move. You stand an awfully long time during rehearsals."

"Goedeavond," Anouk said. "Welcome everyone to the Dutch party and thanks for coming. For some reason my foot hurts more today than usual, so I'll go straight to the point where I sing my song and you scream with excitement. How about that?"

She laughed and the audience laughed with her. Then she launched into her number.

"How depressing," Beth whispered. "Maybe the spotlight tried to kill itself over this dreadful song."

"Sshh," Bebe said, but she grinned. "Have a look at the crowd to see if you spot anything suspicious. That's what we're here for, not for the music."

Bebe also let her eyes wander around the room for familiar faces or odd reactions. Not all in the name of protecting Anouk but, if she was honest, more so to see how people responded to this song. Musically, Bebe had a lot in common with Anouk, even though she fancied herself as slightly more accessible and her songs of higher quality. Currently, it seemed the record-buying audience favoured Anouk, and Bebe wanted to know why that was.

Anouk sang another song but then excused herself and retreated to a seat in the corner, where eager fans asked for autographs and chatted with the star. Beth managed to stand right beside.

Meanwhile, Edsilia went back on the stage. In the middle of her set she asked Bebe to join her once for more a duet. The two sang 'Waterloo' by Abba and then Edsilia did an impressive version of Bebe's 'Losing My Mind'.

"Get out of town," Bebe hissed jokingly and applauded her.

The evening started to frizzle out and had it not been for Beth's dedication to watch over Anouk, Bebe might have left a long time ago. She was still sipping champagne and had the odd chat with the other party guests when Tom arrived, without his Italian journalist.

"Were there more accidents tonight?" he asked.

"Fortunately not," Bebe replied. Beth had cautioned her not to mention too much of the investigation to Tom since he was now effectively a paparazzi in her eyes. Now tipsy, Bebe didn't agree and since she was desperate to talk about her findings and reflect upon them, she relayed the conversations with the two De Poel cousins.

"Oh, no," Tom said and laughed. "The two are best friends, and always have been. They're putting on a show for the media with their constant arguments."

"How would you know?"

"They say all these nasty things about each other on TV and in the interviews but then, again and again, they're seen together in private. Not many people buy into their feud, but nobody cares because it's entertainment for some and irrelevant to others."

"What do you think this is all about?" Bebe asked him.

He shrugged his shoulders, a tad too quickly in her opinion.

"What we need is a new lead or a new attack," he said. "With the latest events we can already eliminate Mark, the online troll, but we still have too many suspects for my liking."

"How can you eliminate Mark?" Bebe asked.

"He was at the Scandi party today and we have reliable witnesses for this. He couldn't have been involved in the accident today."

"What was his background again?" Bebe asked.

"Mark Evans, the notoriously annoying online troll."

"I start to wonder if it isn't someone backstage," Bebe said. "Didn't you promise me to find out if anyone worked in Amsterdam as well as at the Big Six party?"

"I did but unless you count people who are personal assistants to the participants then we've got zero."

"Why shouldn't we count personal assistants?" Bebe asked. "They're often the most intense people and hard core supporters of the stars they work for. I'd say they're one of our top suspect groups."

"Fine," Tom said. "I'll get the list to you tomorrow morning. How about you and I meet at nine for breakfast and then go to the arena and watch the rehearsals? Tomorrow is the final stretch for the first semi-final. They'll do two rehearsals tomorrow and then it's the actual semi-final on Tuesday. Anouk is in this semi-final, so we should be watching this closely."

"I haven't got any tickets," Bebe said. "Looks like you'll have to go alone with your journalist."

"I've got a spare ticket," Tom said. "Giovanni can't make it."

Bebe smiled. "Always happy to be your second choice," she said.

Chapter 14

Tom accompanied Bebe to her hotel. He insisted on having a nightcap with her in the foyer. He had the kitchen send them canapes and got her a glass of champagne.

Bebe was glad to be sobering up and only accepted the drink so as not to be rude.

"I hope you don't mind," he said, "but I've seen that you don't have a Facebook page or Twitter account, so I've taken the liberty to set them up for you. I can make you and your manager administrators so you can take it over whenever you're ready. You should see how many Likes and followers you already have."

He pulled out his smartphone and showed her. She didn't understand the significance of those numbers: 1200 Likes on Facebook and 1800 followers on Twitter.

"That's only within the last few hours," Tom said. "That's huge."

"Well, thank you," she said. "I hope Fred will be fine with this. She's my manager and she did a decent job since she took over. I don't want to upset her."

"If she knows what's good for you then she'll thank me on her knees for doing this," he said. "It's a major oversight on her behalf not to have done this. Seriously, on what planet did you find her?"

Bebe was taken aback.

"Fred knows about Twitter," Bebe said. "She told me I was trending on it. I've asked her to leave me alone with social media: it frightens me."

"Darling, social media can be great fun and it's possibly the best way for you to rise back to the top," he said. "You can bypass all media and journalists and make your own stories and talk to your fans directly. It's so useful. Look!"

He tapped frantically on his phone and then showed her the Facebook page. It had plenty of lovely posts from fans and adorable comments about her comeback.

```
We missed you
Once our Diva, always our Diva
Love your sense of humour...
```

She was moved to tears. She should check this out the next time she had doubts about herself. Usually she went to one of the piano bars to get that type of fix. Now she had it at her disposal at the click of a mouse.

"Why did that never happen on the website?" she asked.

"People have to go to your website to find it, but on social media everything somehow comes together and fans get shown posts and tweets from all different sources and you can reach people who didn't even know about you – it's very sophisticated," he replied.

"So, what do I do with it?" she asked.

"Well you just post like this," he said and typed:

```
Having  a  fantastic  time  at  #ESC2013  with  my
friends   @EdsiliaRombley   @BonnieTOfficial   and
@PeterBeatle
     Love Bebe
```

"That's all?" she asked. "I don't get it."

"Watch," Tom said and within seconds she saw people reply to the post.

```
Shame  we  missed  you  at  #ESC2013  –  where  are
you going to be next? Be great to meet you!
```

```
Don't tell Bonnie but your version of 'Believe
in Me' is awesome
```

She was in heaven.

"Thank you so much for this," she said.

But then she saw another string of comments:

```
Go  home,  you  old  crooner.  Enough  of  UK  has-
beens already!
```

```
Shut up Mark and leave Bebe alone
```

```
You shut up and tell her to shut up, too'
```

Tom pulled the phone away from her.

"Aw well," he said. "A bit of bad pops up amongst the good. Don't get stressed about it: it comes with the territory."

She took a sip from her champagne and forced a smile.

"Of course," she said. "Not the first time I got bad reviews."

"Well, you get trolls on the internet," he explained. "They shout abuse at everyone and stalk you without any real reference to what or who you are. I guess it's jealousy and boredom and anger, all coming out and targeting the first person they can find or think of. Don't take it personally, because it isn't."

"I know," she said. "I wonder if that Mark is the Mark Evans we had clocked as suspect."

Tom checked.

"Yes, it is," he said. "Well spotted. He's one of the few trolls who publicly admits to his identity. Strictly speaking that doesn't make him a troll, I think."

"Might be an idea if you keep an eye on this social media thing for now," she said. "I better go to bed, if you don't mind. I'm shattered."

He helped her up from her chair and then walked her to the elevator.

She kissed him on the cheeks as well and stepped inside.

"Goodnight."

Back at her room, Bebe realised that her phone had been out of battery. She plugged it in near the desk and went to the bathroom to take off her make-up. By the time she returned there was already some sufficient charge on the phone and she saw that it had sprang into action with frequent beeps and vibrations. She picked it up and found heaps of messages for her.

Apparently, Fred had tried to call her numerous times. There were text messages and a voice mail:

Call me back immediately. Big news!

It was past one in the morning but the urgency made her forget about that. This was so exciting.

"Fred, what's so important?" Bebe asked when Fred had picked up on the second ring.

"The people love your version of 'Believe in Me' and the team spirit you're showing being here," Fred said. "One of the producers was so excited that there's some star power behind Bonnie and their whole campaign this year that he's commissioned a documentary with you."

"That's wonderful," she said.

"They're sending a small team over tomorrow and they'll come with you to all the rehearsals and parties. You're going to be very busy over the next week."

"How marvellous," Bebe said.

She texted Tom to tell him that she probably wouldn't be able to come to all the rehearsals with him now due to the filming, but he immediately texted her back to say he was more than happy to help her with the documentary, especially since the rehearsals were where they were meant to do their investigating, anyway.

Then she texted Beth that her commitment to the investigation now was compromised.

Beth texted back.

```
Don't be silly. You'll be more useful to the
investigation than ever. Speak tomorrow.
```

Bebe was too excited to fall asleep. She tossed and turned for half an hour, but she wouldn't drop off. She kept picturing herself on TV. It seemed so long since she had been the object of a TV programme rather than one participant of many in talk shows.

When sleep wouldn't come she got up and checked her phone again. In times of waiting for good news this was the worst kind of addiction. And, indeed, there were more messages for her: Helena, asking for money, Helena threatening to come to Sweden to 'earn her keep', Helena offering to support her mother's comeback.

Now that was a scary prospect for Bebe, but Helena was unlikely to have enough money for the air fare over here, let alone find Bebe's hotel and whereabouts.

The last message stopped her in her tracks, though.

```
Dear Bebe, due to an illness one of the UK jurors
had to pull out. Could you be persuaded to join
the team? Best Tonia
```

Could she be persuaded?

Dear Tonia, I'd be delighted to, but unfortunately
I'm at the contest in Sweden and unable to fly
back to the UK for this due to work commitments
Thank you so much for thinking of me

Dear Bebe, that's why we need you. The UK jury
will vote in Sweden this year as part of a special
trial. Welcome to the team!

Bebe was so glad she had come to Malmö.

The next morning, she felt surprisingly refreshed, despite the very early hour of her alarm and all the alcohol she had consumed the night before. She had a shower, put on a dark purple dress that she considered the least outrageous of her limited choices and did her make-up, all the while singing 'Believe in Me' by Bonnie. The song truly had a great feel to it, it had grown on her so much, she would have to make it part of her repertoire in the future.

Downstairs in the breakfast hall she wanted to hug every person in the room. Wasn't life wonderful and weren't people lovely?

A documentary about Bebe in Sweden, attending Eurovision and releasing a better version of 'Believe in Me' than Bonnie Tyler – she couldn't help dreaming about the possibilities that would open for her. She always remembered how a fly-on-the-wall documentary about cruise ships had catapulted singer Jane McDonald to stardom and chart success. Such hopeful visions hadn't always worked out for Bebe in the past, so a part of her remained naturally cautious. The other part of her wanted to enjoy this feeling and tried not to think of all the things that could go wrong.

It was just as well she had eaten at least something at her hotel in Denmark. When she met Tom at the café in Malmö he got up from his seat and immediately steered her towards the arena.

"Rehearsals start at 10," he said, "and we have to queue to get in."

"I thought we were press," she said.

"Press also have to queue and go through security."

She suddenly froze. How could she have forgotten?

"My press pass is missing."

"No it's not," he said and produced it. "Giovanni and I found it on the floor in the Euro Café the night of the Big Six party."

"And you didn't tell me?" she asked.

100

"Sorry," he said. "I was busy with a thousand things."

The queue wasn't long, though, and the security procedures were painless. Tom and Bebe found themselves seated in a fairly empty arena a mere twenty minutes later.

"It will fill up," Tom reassured her. "The downstairs section here is reserved for press, the upper tiers are for the regular punters. It won't be packed, but it will be a lot fuller than it is right now."

Bebe saw everything around her no longer only as a possible crime scene but as the backdrop for her marvellous documentary and the many questions she might be asked:

'What does Bebe think of Austria's entry?' – 'Will Bebe award points to Belarus?' – 'How an industry expert of twenty years judges the offerings from Moldova'.

She had done her research yesterday: there were 16 countries competing for 10 spaces in the Grand Final on Saturday. Today would be the first rehearsal of all 16 songs in one go, including their props and full stage show. Media coverage of this performance was crucial and heavily influenced the bookmakers. The press was awarding its own prize and was rating each song, which fuelled the hype around who would be the eventual winner.

Bebe sat through the first few songs and felt utterly bored. As far as she was concerned, none of them were any good. The Danish song was next, one of the show's hot contenders. The flute intro was catchy but also an obvious appeal to the folk music fans all over Europe.

Russia and Ukraine followed, both great ballads, but Russia got booed, due to its current unpopular politics and Ukraine got laughed at because they had hired a really tall man to carry the really small singer on stage. You couldn't make it up.

"The Netherlands are next," Tom said. "Watch out."

Anouk was brought onto the stage in a wheelchair. She stood up at the last minute and stood motionless, singing to a backdrop of visuals on the screen behind her.

"Clever," said Bebe. "There are no props that could fall onto her, are there?"

Tom pointed at the many ceiling lights and Bebe flushed. How stupid she could be.

"Not a vintage year," he whispered in Bebe's ears. "This isn't a great start to the show."

"I'm glad you said that," she said. "I had higher expectations for the quality of songs, although I hope this will help Bonnie make a good placing."

All around them journalists were busy taking photographs or making notes on their i-Pads or phones. Bebe wondered what they made of the show. Were they fans or forced to be here? There was so little coverage of the show in the UK until the final night, it seemed rather surprising to see so much news presence here so early in the game.

Just then there was a huge scream on stage. The performer from Moldova, an incredibly pretty girl with a slow ballad, had been singing her song propped up by a raised platform hidden beneath her excessively long frock. It had looked borderline silly to Bebe but if the objective was to get noticed, it certainly had done the trick.

Something must have happened to the platform. The singer was doubled over, half dangling down but held in place by whatever prop had supported the extension of the dress. It made for a bizarre image and Bebe was sure it had to have frightened the living daylights out of the poor girl, suspended in mid-air.

The audience murmured; the photographers were not taking their lenses off the stage where a group of technicians with ladders came to the singer's rescue. The music stopped and the woman was freed. The costume had been ripped and Bebe could now see that the prop holding the woman up had been a set of rolling steps. The front wheels had collapse which had led to the forward bend.

"Another sabotage," Tom said and added almost triumphantly: "She's not a favourite in the betting, not an established singer and not pre-qualified. It's as I suspected: we're having a full attack on the show itself. You can't call these dramas 'accidents' any longer. It's impossible... not after Cascada's steps were tampered with, too."

"You have a point, but there's no way we can be sure that this latest incident is necessarily connected with the others."

The show stopped for a few minutes. The Moldovan singer came on stage to finish her song without the prop.

"Twitter is going bonkers over this," Tom said.

"And are they also calling it sabotage?"

"Not yet. It's mainly videos of it."

There wasn't much time to think about the event in any case. The next act, which was from Ireland, rolled on and it was one that easily distracted the audience from what had gone on before.

Extremely handsome and topless drummers banged on large drums with a front man in a macho leather costume. Ireland had gone all sexy and it looked as if the people in the arena were appreciating it. Screams of enthusiasm and entranced faces staring on the stage were proof of it. The show was mesmerizing. Tom was looking at the stage with his mouth agape. Surely, he had forgotten Bebe even existed; or his Italian friend for that matter. Where was Giovanni? She wondered. Why had he not been able to make the dress rehearsal? Wasn't he a big fan?

A huge crash on the stage pulled her out of her thoughts. One of the drums had collapsed onto the hot-looking man beating it in the manic rhythm of the song. The singer briefly turned back to see what was going on but carried on regardless. Technicians ran onto the stage and freed the poor drummer, who seemed shell shocked but unharmed.

"Now do you believe me?" Tom whispered.

She nodded.

The rehearsal continued with the last few songs. The journalists were typing frantically into their phones or sat together in clusters to discuss what they had witnessed. Tom showed Bebe on his phone that the organisers had posted a press release on the official website playing down the incidents as stage management issues but promised an investigation.

Although she remained sceptical that every incident was the work of a madman on the loose threatening and sabotaging Eurovision entrants, Bebe couldn't deny that something sinister was going on.

Since Tom was glued to his phone and ignoring her, she got her own phone out and saw she had messages: She was due to meet the other members of the UK jury in half an hour, in the arena. It was lucky she had checked her phone.

Chapter 15

The directions to get to the UK jury room on the top floor of the arena were simple enough. At yet another set of security checks she was pleasantly surprised that her name was on the list of people allowed to enter.

"Down the corridor, second room on the right," the doorman said as if he didn't even see her. The jury room was small and furnished with nothing more than a tiny leather sofa, two tables, chairs and a TV. A lanky Swede with dreadful blond highlights and a sweater vest from the Eighties greeted her.

"Fabulous to see you Bebe," he said. "My name's Magnus and I'm your European Broadcasting Union, EBU, jury supervisor. I wish everyone was so prompt."

He handed her a leaflet.

"Here's all you need to know about the voting system."

"So, what happened to the other juror?" Bebe asked, fiercely suspicious of anything irregular regarding this contest.

"To be honest, I haven't got a clue," Magnus said. He pulled out a handkerchief and blew his nose, but instead of putting it away he also used it to clean his horn-rimmed glasses.

"It's not rocket science," he carried on. "You'll be voting tomorrow in the dress rehearsal for the first semi-final and then again on the grand final on Saturday. The rules are in the book over there."

He pointed at a small coffee table in the corner with one hand while the other combed through his hair.

"You'll be watching the performance here in the room with your fellow jury members, so you're away from any influence. Be fair and judge the songs on the criteria outlined in the paper."

"Of course," she said and began reading.

She let the live performances she had just witnessed in the arena go through her head once more and tried to assess them in her mind:

'Vocal capacity of the singer, performance on-stage, composition and originality of the song, overall impression of the act...'

That was going to be tough. The accidents she witnessed had made the biggest impressions on her. She surely wasn't meant to award points for those.

One by one her fellow jurors joined her. She was delighted that the charming Tonia Carmichael turned out to be chairperson. Tonia said a brief hello to Bebe but then she got an earful from Magnus, who instructed her on her duties and gave her a pile of paperwork to go through. Tonia sat in the corner, her head resting on her arm and her eyes fixed on the papers.

Next in was an opera singer, a big lump of a fellow with the obligatory long scarf, dramatic movements and a box of chocolates in his hands, which he put on one of the tables and silently indicated for Bebe and Tonia to help themselves.

Bebe had no idea who the other two members of the jury were: A young man whom she had never seen and whose attire didn't give anything away. He wore track bottoms, a wide fluffy shirt and several chains around his neck. A white rap singer, she wondered?

And another woman, the ageing business executive-type with looks that implied an official capacity, a perfect figure, make-up and a flaming red dress that few people would get away with.

"Let's get down to business," Tonia suddenly said and jumped up.

She handed everyone a few pieces of paper.

"Please read these carefully and sign them. You need to declare any interest as part of the jury code of conduct, so we know if you have connections to any of the participants, their relatives, record companies, et cetera et cetera. It's all common sense, so don't sweat it. You'd know if you shouldn't be here. We'll do a dry run today, so we'll be watching the songs from the first semi-final on this TV screen live as they are being rehearsed again. I'll ask you to make notes during every song and judge the music in all categories outlined. Then I want you to rank the songs and then we combine all of our votes to make the UK Jury Top Ten."

She looked around the quiet room.

"Any questions?"

Everyone shook their heads. Bebe tried to establish familiarity with Tonia by smiling at her, but today the woman was nothing but cold professional.

Bebe sat down next to the opera singer, resisting the siren call coming from the chocolate box. No, she had fought too hard for her figure to let herself go now.

"So nice to see you," she said, only now realising that she couldn't remember his name. It had been a very long time since she had last spoken to him and the man was past the height of his career, with the few TV appearances he had landed now being in the distant past. The honour to be here seemed suddenly much smaller.

The man nodded, and kissed her on the cheek,

"You, too, Bebe," he said and grabbed another chocolate. "You, too."

While they waited for the show to begin, Bebe saw that she had more begging texts from Helena and a message from Fred: a magazine wanted to do an interview on Bebe's time at Eurovision and when the jury duty that afternoon was over, the TV team would be waiting for her in the press hall.

Without warning, the TV in the room came on and Bebe could see the first contestant standing on stage, waiting for her cue to sing. The music sounded odd in the slightly empty arena. Between her duty of judging the songs and the associated writing on forms it seemed time passed very quickly. Daniela's turn to sing soon came. Bebe's eyes were glued at the TV screen, waiting for something dramatic to happen, but nothing did.

The song from Moldova had to be presented without the rolling steps and the Irish drummer was back on stage as if nothing had happened a mere few hours earlier.

Calculating the scores was a drawn-out process.

"Can we go now?" the young rapper asked.

"Of course," the Swede said, "same time tomorrow, but then with the real vote."

Everyone but Tonia disappeared.

"So sorry it took me so long to get my votes together," Bebe apologised.

"That's alright," Tonia said calmly.

"How did you end up with this job anyway?" Bebe asked.

"As I said on Peter's show, I did Eurovision a long time ago and I never managed to wipe that off my slate," Tonia said. "I thought I might as well join them if I can't beat them, so I embraced the shame and took it on."

"Shame?" Bebe asked. "Is it that bad?"

"For the career that I had in mind it was like dog poo on my shoes. I couldn't get rid of the stink. Wherever I went, someone dug out the archive footage and had a laugh at the choreography and our cheesy lines."

When she saw that Bebe was seriously shocked, she hit her gently on the shoulder.

"I'm only kidding," she said. "It isn't all that bad. It got me a few regular annual gigs, I'm not complaining. And at least we did reasonably well that year."

"What do you make of Bonnie's song?" Bebe asked. "How do you fancy her chances?"

"I'm delighted for her and the UK and think she'll do marvellously," Tonia said with a smile hammered in her face. Then the smile faltered and Tonia added: "That's the official story. Between us, I think it will sink."

"Even with this lousy competition?" Bebe asked. "I could hardly find a handful of songs to award points to, let alone the required ten."

"Darling, Europeans have weird tastes," Tonia said. "My only worry is that the UK might decide to pull out of the competition someday. People are less and less interested, they complain about the money we have to pay for it and then what can I do?" Tonia said. "I've done the circuit of reality shows and I'm running out of options. There's always newer and younger talent around, so work is getting scarce. This is a safe job, out of the limelight but worth a few interviews; plus, the networking with European musicians. They all want you to like their songs and try to woo you. It's rather handy… you'll see."

Bebe kissed Tonia goodbye and made her way down the stairs to the press hall, to meet the documentary team.

She was over the moon to find that the delightful Peter Beatle was part of the show. The documentary director's name was Morgan. He was a camp hippy-type with greying unwashed hair, worn black Levis, which he seemed not to have taken off since he was a teenager.

"I cannot believe nobody has given her the script," he yelled and threw his hands in the air.

"Relax, Morgan," Peter cut him short for her. She loved his confidence.

"Bebe's a professional, and who needs a script for a documentary anyway? Just tell her what you want her to say and where you want her to go and she'll do it."

He added a quiet: "For crying out loud!" and rolled his eyes.

"Don't let this moron annoy you," he warned her.

Morgan ignored the remark and instructed his assistant to brief Bebe, while he himself conferred with the cameramen.

Bebe was to walk down the empty seat rows of the arena and welcome the audience to Malmö. The lines she had to read had been written in the most unimaginative style, just what she had expected from a documentary that had been quickly pulled together overnight. Anyone could have done better than this. She was so pleased that Peter was here. He was the king of improvising and would support her if she tweaked the odd sentence to make it a little more interesting. Who wanted to know all the boring details and not have spilled some of the gossip and the glamour of this show? She was sure she could spice it up.

She read through the lines a few times and got into position on top of the arena. The steps up here were steep and Bebe had to take off her heels to feel remotely safe.

"Welcome to the Arena in Malmö," Bebe said, slowly taking one step down. "This is the fifth Swedish win to date, giving us Brits a run for our money as the country with the second-highest number of wins so far. The UK had to dig deep into its pockets to send real star power to Malmö to bring the accolade home and regain our status as…"

Bebe almost fell over. The height was dizzying and the text so uninspiring.

"Sorry," she said. "Can we do this again?"

Morgan briefly nodded and shouted: "From the top, and put your heart in it this time. You're a star. Prove it to me!"

Bebe slowly ascended to the top of the arena and started again.

"I'm here in Malmö with my dear friend Bonnie Tyler," she said, off script, "and we're going to do our best to win and bring the trophy back to the UK. The Swedes have won far too often for our liking. The UK has been holding out for a hero to do this and Bonnie has heard their calling."

"Stop," Morgan interrupted. "Please stick to the text we gave you."

"I can't," Bebe said. "It's rubbish."

"I know, darling," Morgan said. "I do know."

"Who wrote this piece of crap, anyway?" Peter muscled in. "Why can't Bebe and I do this our way?"

"I've got strict orders," Morgan explained. "We need to demonstrate to the rest of Europe that we respect the show and that we take it seriously. If we make fun of it one more time we'll never get anywhere, regardless of who enters the competition for us. So, please let's get on with the job as per script and hope that the executives know what they are doing with this rubbish."

Bebe gingerly climbed back to the top of the stairs and reeled off the text exactly as instructed. It was hard to put any feeling into it. Given the recent image change from workaholic to fun and naughty Bebe she could only see this documentary flop. She caught Peter's eye, who seemed to feel her pain. Wasn't he simply too good to be true? She had to remind herself that he was a suspect. What was it that Tonia had said? The UK might pull out of the show. Tonia's livelihood seemed to depend on it and come to think of it, Peter got a lot of mileage for his career out of it. She couldn't put it past him to create some mayhem to keep the show going.

When the filming of this segment was over, two hours later, she had heard enough of statistics and boring details about the singers and countries. Peter had been given very similar lines, although he managed to sound far more interested in those details than his off-screen comments had suggested.

"Let's go for a beverage," he said. "I want the dirt on the jury you're working with."

"I've signed papers not to tell," she said cautiously, "but I'll join you for a drink."

"Follow me," Peter said. He led her out of the arena and hailed a taxi that drove them to the Euro Café. There was another party going on and Peter managed to get the two of them in to the VIP section. Half of the Eurovision participants were here, chatting and drinking.

Peter bought her a Bloody Mary and then started to grill her about the other jury members and who the UK would be giving their votes to.

Bebe resisted spilling the beans and it wasn't long before Peter lost interest and disappeared with his drink. She made her way to the bar to get another drink for the road. Tomorrow would be a busy day with more of the same: tough documentary work and listening to the songs from semi-final one yet again. She noticed that behind her in the queue for the bar stood the Irish singer. He looked much younger than she had imagined.

"What on Earth happened on that stage this morning?" she asked him.

"Oh, you mean that drum?" he asked. "Stupid mistake that."

"It could have killed the guy," Bebe said. "I was so frightened."

"Bill's a tough cookie. He's as good as new and there wasn't any damage to the drum either. Just one of them things."

"Doesn't it strike you as odd that there could be so many accidents on stage? Do you feel safe?"

The guy shrugged his shoulders. "When you do Eurovision you can get paranoid," he said. "Suddenly you get trolls on the social media and hate mail. It's part of the package, I guess."

"I worked in the show business for decades and nothing of that sort ever happened to me," Bebe said. "What kind of hate mail did you get? Anything credible?"

"Na," the young man said. "I shouldn't think so. I'm not paying any attention. I'm here to sing and to enjoy myself."

"Some people say that all these little accidents are linked," Bebe said suggestively.

"You mean, like sabotage so we have to pull out of the competition?" he laughed.

"Stranger things have happened for less," Bebe said. "Have you found anyone particularly competitive?"

"Sorry," he replied. "Everyone's just really lovely and the things that happened weren't that dramatic, don't you think?"

"I suppose," she said, unconvinced.

She decided against another drink and dropped out of the queue. She better be rested for tomorrow. On the way home Bebe called Beth, but the phone went directly to answer. Tom didn't pick up either. When she got to the hotel, the receptionist sitting by the desk was so engrossed in her papers that she didn't even move her head when Bebe walked past.

"Mother," Bebe heard the all-too-familiar voice of her daughter. She turned on her heel.

"What do you think you're doing here?" Bebe hissed. How had that minx managed to find her? This was unbelievable.

"Don't be like that," Helena said and got up from her seat in the lobby. "I thought we could spend some time together here on your holiday."

"Holiday?" Bebe snapped. "Are you out of your mind? I'm working, darling, and the last thing I want to do when I get to my hotel is having a selfish little princess trying to take me for a ride. Only a few days ago you told me you had no money and I needed to help you out, and now you're here, so you obviously had enough for the air fare. You tell nothing but lies."

"Dad helped me out in the end, but he didn't give me any spending money. He said that was your responsibility."

"Oh, darling daughter," Bebe said. "If you want spending money then you'd better earn it. You were not invited, so don't make me pay for your own silly decisions. It doesn't work like that. You really must grow up, Helena. I can't continue to prop you up. You need to start doing that for yourself."

"I've got a job," Helena said, triumphant.

"Doing what?" Bebe asked.

"I'll be a waitress in the Euro Café," she said.

Bebe laughed.

"Sweetheart, they're only open for another week, then what are you going to do?"

"I'll figure something out," Helena said. "All I need is a little spending money until I get paid."

Bebe sighed and opened her purse.

"Here are some Krona" she said and handed her a few notes.

"That's next to nothing," Helena complained.

"I tell you what. I'll show up at the Euro Café tomorrow and see whether this is true or not," Bebe said. "Then I'll consider a loan. It's a sad state that I always have to verify everything you tell me."

"Thanks mother," Helena said. "Now can we have some quality time at the bar?"

She tried to grab Bebe's elbow and pull her towards the restaurant but to no avail.

"I'm sorry," her mother said. "Not after the day I've had. I'll have to see you tomorrow."

She kissed Helena on one cheek, smelling a fair bit of alcohol on her daughter's breath. Then she headed for the elevators and made her way up to her room. It was time for a hot bath and relaxation. It had been a taxing day and she enjoyed a few moments of tranquillity and peace.

She couldn't help notice that she had met some strange characters over the last few days.

The five suspects, for instance, all seemed dodgy in their own ways. The provocative DJ Peter with his almost ideological or political views on the song contest – could his obsession make him a killer? Although he had almost become a friend and ally, she couldn't shake off the feeling that she had to watch him, however normal obsessive behaviour seemed to be in the Eurovision fan circles

Then there had been Jan Ola Nielssen who had been so blatantly rude and tactless and who had a record of somewhat violent behaviour. But 'lamping' someone when drunk was not the same as plotting attacks.

Mark Evans, the online troll had an alibi but he, too, had a certain psycho look that stated alarm bells in Bebe's mind. She hadn't even met him; just seen his avatar and the comments he had left on the internet. If Nielssen was an obnoxious man, Evans seemed to be even worse.

Once people were this obsessed with something, anything was possible. Bebe had no doubt they were all capable of doing something stupid. Just how stupid, she wasn't sure.

The De Poel cousins were playing a game with the media, Tom was probably right about them. The entire pretence about liking and not liking each other was a thinly disguised ploy. Also, Bebe felt instinctively that the two would not be gambling with potential murder purely for the sake of publicity. At this moment in time neither of them was short of that.

There was of course Tom himself, the man who had been at all events. As a fan of the show, would he enjoy it if scandal and drama would bring Eurovision back to the forefront of people's mind – regular peoples' minds that was? She mustn't let her gratitude towards the blogger blind her.

After assessing the assistants and staff of the performers who'd been on the stage in Amsterdam as well as at the Big Six party there weren't many credible suspects left. She should discount Germany, as they were a victim of an accident, too, and a not very nice one at that. Cascada looked seriously shaken following the incident and logically, if Cascada had thought of getting sympathy votes for an injury, why would she give that same advantage to her Moldovan competitor by attacking them as well? She also would have made sure that Bonnie

112

wouldn't be affected by a rolling set of stairs either. Why share the limelight that you were so desperate to get? And any serious saboteurs would have used more reliable means than this. The amateurish nature brought it all back to the five weirdos as Bebe had christened them in her head. If Tom was counted in, then it was even six.

And what about Tom's assistant and friend Giovanni?

Chapter 16

The next morning the receptionist woke her with a far too early phone call.

"Sorry to disturb you," he said. "A Tonia Carmichael instructed me to wake you and give you the Eurovision CD, so you can spend the morning listening to the songs."

"Thank you," Bebe said and stretched as well as she could while holding the receiver. "Bring it up when you can."

She had no interest in listening to the songs. She had heard them already more often than she cared about and would have to do so again this afternoon. She appreciated that studio versions often were different and could display an extra aspect of the song, which helped assess the composition further but enough was enough. She opened the door in her dressing gown, without having checked her hair or make-up, only to find Morgan and the documentary team in front of her, with a running camera.

What was worse: they had brought a portable CD player and began playing the Eurovision CD.

"I need to freshen up," she said and headed for the bathroom. Bebe's hair always was a mess in the morning. She would have to get the team to re-take that shot.

When she came out she instantly tried to persuade them but Morgan, who had to feel her pain, would have none of it.

"We need to appear very, very serious about your role as juror," he explained. "This scene was not done by accident. It's perfect because it could hardly be staged. Which 60-year-old would let us film her without makeup unless she was so engrossed in her task that she forgot? Now we're going to show you listening to the songs and making notes. The documentary is as much for Europe as it is for the UK audience."

"Even worse," Bebe said, "showing me without the make-up to the entire continent makes us appear very careless, not serious. We need to re-shoot that little segment."

"Sorry," he said and turned the volume up.

"Here are the forms for you to assess the songs," he said, with an encouraging but somewhat sarcastic grin. "Get to work and... camera roll!"

With a heavy heart Bebe sat down on the table and listened to all 42 songs, making notes and trying not to let it show when she disliked a song.

"We'll have a fifteen-minute break," Morgan said and clapped his hands quickly. "Get yourself dressed, we're expecting Peter in a minute and he'll be interviewing you about the songs and what you think of them."

"I'll need more than fifteen minutes," Bebe snapped.

"Sorry, you haven't got more than that. You need to be at Jury duty at 1pm, so you better hurry."

She rushed into the bathroom. Fifteen minutes was not enough to make herself presentable. Peter was already waiting for her as she got out, and she hadn't even decided on her outfit. He giggled when she opened her wardrobe and picked out some of the more daring dresses.

"You can't wear any of those," he said and playfully put them in front of his body. The media are going to slaughter you."

She sighed.

"Of all places I thought here I would get away with it."

"I'm afraid you won't," Peter said. He threw the lot on the floor and let her choose between a trouser suit and the velvet dress she had worn at his radio show.

"Only until we get to the arena," he said. "I'll text Nicki to let her lend you one of hers. She has so many, she can't possibly get changed that often."

Bebe picked the velvet dress and then the director made her sit next to Peter on the bed to chat about the songs.

"I signed a document that I wasn't going to discuss the songs," Bebe said, hoping to get out of this interview and get a few minutes of peace.

"You can discuss them with us," Morgan said. "This won't air until long after the competition. We're not supposed to broadcast any juror's opinion before the show, either. We would be fined if we did."

Bebe relaxed and began laying into the songs she couldn't bear.

"Cut," Morgan yelled and shook his head rigorously. "You can't say things like that. We're on a diplomatic mission to limit the damage we've done in the past."

"Bebe," Peter added. "You've got to be far more likeable in your statements. You can always side-line a question and say something about the contestant's hair, outfit or dance movements if you don't like the song. Or tell a story about the country they come from. But under no circumstances call the songs poorly arranged or the singers amateurish, even if it's the blatant truth."

"Understood," she said.

"Roll," he shouted.

"What do you make of the first song?" Peter asked Bebe.

"The Austrian girl has such a beautiful way about her," Bebe managed to say. "She seemed a little nervous, but she did well on stage."

"Is she going to make it to the final, you reckon?"

"I hope for her that she does," Bebe said.

The pair discussed all 16 songs from that day's show before they had to get to the arena for her Jury duty. Bebe realised she wouldn't get time now to meet Helena at the Euro Café and felt idiotic for promising this in the first place. After all the grief she had given Helena over not keeping her word, this was bad parenting.

At the arena, hordes of people were in the long security queues. Bebe was stunned at how many people would show up for a rehearsal. She managed to find the delegates' gate and get to the jury room in time. Tonia and her Swedish assistant, Magnus – or was he her boss really? – sat on one of the tables, sorting through documents. Every juror received a thick leather folder with forms and a pen.

"Remember not to influence each other with comments," Magnus said. "It's more professional if you keep your thoughts to yourself."

Bebe had to share the table with the white rapper. He nodded but kept to himself. This was so unlike how Bebe had expected a Jury to work. In her mind she had seen a version of 'Twelve Angry Men', with the jurors discussing each song at length before coming to a vote as to how many points might be appropriate.

Instead, everyone had their head down in their folders and only looked up when the songs came on. Nobody spoke with each other. When it was over Bebe couldn't have guessed who had voted for or liked which song.

Tonia collected the sheets and started her calculations, under scrutiny by the Swede. He pointed out two errors in her sums and when she had finished and signed the final jury voting document he sealed it in an envelope and took it away.

"Phew," said Tonia. "I'm glad that's over."

"Me, too," Bebe said. "Are we now allowed to talk about the songs and what we thought of them?"

"No," Magnus said. "All votes are kept secret until the last show is over to avoid return-the-favour or retaliation votes. Besides, it will make the entire thing so much more tense and exciting."

"Come for a coffee with me," Tonia invited Bebe. "I know just the right place."

"How about the Euro Café?" Bebe asked.

"Too far," Tonia said. "Let's go backstage and sit in the cafeteria there."

Bebe hadn't known such a place even existed. It was a shame she didn't have her camera team with her. They hadn't been allowed in the jury room and she had no idea where they were now. She texted Morgan but got no reply. Wouldn't it have been lovely to be seen mingling with the stars, chatting away with fellow juror Tonia?

"You know I specifically asked for you," Tonia told her once they had sat down in the rather unglamorous coffee corner.

"How sweet of you," Bebe said, very grateful indeed.

"I'm so jealous of you," Tonia said. "How you pulled that comeback of yours off, it's truly amazing. You wouldn't mind introducing me to your agent or manager?"

"Of course I wouldn't mind," Bebe said. "I thought you were happy with the gigs you had."

"One can always do better," Tonia said.

"Tell me," Bebe said. "What do you make of all the strange 'accidents' that have happened? You've been in the business for almost as long as I have, and doesn't it strike you as odd, too?"

"It's more than average," Tonia admitted.

"That's all?" Bebe asked.

"What else can I say?" Tonia asked.

"Maybe that you think it's a terror attack, or that someone wants to eliminate or scare the competition?" Bebe said. "There must be some motive or reason to this."

"Don't tell me you came here to play detective," Tonia said. "I thought that you had made the murder case in your village up as part of your comeback. I admired you for the originality. Now it sounds almost as if the music stuff is only secondary to you."

"I didn't make it up," Bebe assured her. "And music is never going to be secondary to me. I just have a hunch that something here doesn't add up."

"Listen," Tonia said. "I suggest you let this whole thing drop and concentrate on your singing career and duty as juror. People who try to make up conspiracies and dramas only damage the people they want to protect. If the press was going to pick up on the minor incidents and started to spread word that maybe something sinister is going on – it could ruin the competition. Police locking down rehearsals, press attention to the investigation instead of the acts and the show? The competition is an endangered species as it is. We must be united in our handling of the situation. The best way forward is to pretend everything is normal and to get on with the job at hand."

"I disagree," Bebe said. "I think we should increase security and warn everyone to be vigilant."

"And create a panic? I don't think so."

"I'd rather have a little panic than someone dead."

Tonia shook her head vehemently.

"Of course, we don't want anybody dead," she said. "But that won't happen, only damage to the competition. Security here is more than tight, if you ask me. There are so many ways to kill a person when you want to. If you can make a spotlight fall twice without being seen, then you can make it fall so that it hits the person. This is all just some stupid publicity game and could seriously ruin everything for us. Bebe, please let it drop and get on with your music."

"And I thought you'd be pleased about the publicity."

"Believe me, I'm not."

Bebe decided to let it drop, or at least, drop the subject when talking to Tonia.

"You know it strikes me as a little strange you would be here in Malmö when you have new material to record," Tonia said.

"I can't help myself," Bebe replied quickly. "Since I heard that Bonnie had decided to come here I had to see what the fuss is about. Admittedly some of it is odd, but it's great fun."

"I'll take your word for it," Tonia said and grinned.

"Don't tell me you hate it," Bebe said. "Only the other day you told me how great it is."

"Must have been a producer around when I said that," she said and grinned. "It's okay, but far from great."

Bebe was surprised by this sudden change of tone and it killed her champagne buzz.

"It's late and I better check in on my daughter at the Euro Café," she said.

"Your daughter works there?" Tonia asked.

Bebe immediately regretted she had let this slip. She preferred not to let people know about Helena.

"Yes," Bebe replied, unsure what else she could say.

"You let your daughter work as a waitress? Here?"

"Here's as good as anywhere," Bebe started to defend herself. "My daughter has her pride and wants to earn her own keep."

She knew that was a lie but the last thing Bebe wanted was to feed Tonia any more inside information about her private life. God help her if the truth about Helena's outrageous nature became public knowledge, that someone might interview her daughter and print her version of Bebe's life, career and character. She couldn't let that happen. Neither could she tell people that she had effectively cut her daughter off without that having a negative impact on her image.

The tables at the Euro Café were all full; people were even sitting outside on the floor and the stone wall surrounding the terrace. A few were dancing on the small square section of the terrace between the door and the tables, making it difficult for the serving staff to get through. There was no sign of Helena, but Bebe discovered Beth sitting inside with Lars and Ola.

Bebe ordered a bottle of champagne for the group and got herself acquainted with the two Swedes Beth had brought along.

"You made quite an impression with your version of 'Believe in Me'," said Ola, who seemed the livelier one of the two. "My friend works at the official merchandise stall at the arena and they had plenty of requests for it. Someone recorded it on their phone and uploaded it to YouTube, but it's already been taken down by Bonnie's record label. People are going mad for it."

"You must be mistaken," Bebe said in a feeble attempt to appear humble but her smile betrayed her. Her heart was overflowing with pride. The arrangement had been her idea entirely and this was a much-needed reassurance that her vision for the musical direction she should take was the right one. She had plenty of material like that from rehearsals in her own studio and this could all form part of a new album. She could be ready to record and release it in no time, and at the perfect moment, while the 'Best of Bebe Bollinger' album was still fresh in people's memory.

"He's right," Lars chipped in. "I would love to hear the song again. You must make sure you release this as soon as possible."

It was music to her ears.

"Where did you learn to be so adorable?" she asked. "You two are just what my doctor ordered."

The music changed to Abba and the two Swedes left abruptly to strut their stuff on the dancefloor.

"The Swedish police have instigated an inquiry in the high number of accidents," Beth reported when they were alone. "They don't think it's malicious, more like a negligence scenario on behalf of the organisers and they are mega cheesed off."

"How did you find out about this?" Bebe asked, pulling her chair closer so she could hear everything over the music.

"It's in the evening news," Beth replied. "Ola and Lars translated it for me. It's a big scandal. Eurovision is huge here and to be involved in it is an honour. To be criticised is a big stain on the organiser's reputation."

"The Swedes are funny," Bebe laughed.

Beth nodded.

"What are you doing here all by yourself?" Beth asked after a short pause.

"I've been looking for Helena," Bebe explained and told her friend about the sudden appearance of her daughter in Malmö.

"I wonder if her shift is already over," Bebe said.

"I'll find out," Beth said and disappeared. Bebe sat back in her chair and observed the crowd. Young or old, camp or straight faced, dark or fair – every colour of the rainbow seemed represented. Bebe had to revise her ideas about the audience's demographic. It was broader than she had anticipated and, therefore, much more attractive.

Ola and Lars returned in a huff from the unofficial dancefloor, disrupting her musings.

"I've never liked that Russian song," Ola said as he sat down, obviously referring to the one that was being played.

"I don't mind it," Lars said. "It's just that I can't dance to it. It's got an odd rhythm, which is funnily enough the most charming thing about it anyway."

What it must be like to have your life revolving around the music being played in a café, Bebe thought. She envied the boys their seemingly carefree existence.

Beth returned to the table.

"I've asked for her," she said. "Nobody has heard her name."

"God, I'm so stupid," Bebe said. "I fell for it again."

"What do you mean?" Beth asked.

"She's got no job here, she was just trying to scare me that she would encroach on my life here and scandalise my career if I didn't pay for her," Bebe said. "Pure blackmail."

"Who is this?" Ola asked.

"My naughty daughter," Bebe replied. "She told me that she started work here yesterday. You can't miss her, she's got purple hair."

"There is a new girl working in the cloakroom with purple hair," he said. "She's kind of wild. She looks like she's had a few drinks as well. If the owner finds out it could be her first and last day."

"That does sound like her," Bebe said and went in search of the cloakroom.

"Mother," Helena yelled at the sight of Bebe. "You've come."

She opened the cloakroom door and stumbled towards Bebe, falling into her arms. The boy had been right: Helena was tipsy at least, drunk or high more likely. Bebe helped her daughter to regain a fully vertical posture. There was a trace of alcohol on Helena's breath. Given the amounts of liquor that woman could consume this shouldn't have caused such an effect.

"Look at me, Helena," Bebe said and tried to make out how dilated those pupils were. They were huge, indicating that once again a dose of recreational drugs had found their way into the allegedly broke woman's possession.

"What have you taken?" she asked. "Did you smoke something?"

"It's so sweet you came," Helena said, ignoring the question. "God, I miss you, you know?"

Bebe worried exactly what type of designer chemicals were involved but the saving grace was that Helena seemed happy rather than hyper and loving instead of aggressive for once. How genuine those chemically enhanced feelings were was questionable.

"I've missed you, too," Bebe said. "I think I should take you home, don't you?"

"No, I loves it here," Helena said in an ever more slurring speech. "You knows I does."

She walked back to her cloakroom with the assumed dignity of a drunk person and closed the door, the top half of which, of course, was cut out for customers to hand their coats and jackets through.

"May I?" someone asked and pushed Bebe gently aside to hand Helena their ticket. To Bebe's amazement her daughter retrieved the requested coats within seconds.

"I love that look," Helena said to the customers as she handed them a velvet coat not unlike the one Mike Myers had worn in Austin Powers. "Groovy."

The owner beamed an appreciative smile and walked off.

"I'm having the best of times," Helena told her mother. "People here are so nice."

"What have you taken?" Bebe repeated. "I haven't seen you this high for years."

"Nothing."

"I doubt that," Bebe said.

"So sweet of you to worry about me," Helena said.

"I never stop worrying about you."

A new stream of customers arrived and Bebe left her daughter, worried but helpless.

Back at the table, Beth and her entourage made tracks to go.

"I should probably catch some sleep, too," Bebe said and went to the exit with the trio.

"Mrs Bollinger?" one of the waiters approached her.

Fully expecting a request for an autograph, she started searching for one in her handbag.

"Yes?"

"Would you awfully mind coming with me?"

"If you wouldn't mind telling me what this is about, first."

"It's about your daughter," the man said. "She's... em... not feeling too well."

Bebe followed the man and found Helena sitting slumped on a chair next to the cloakroom, now manned by one of the waiters.

"Are you alright?" Bebe asked.

Helena didn't reply. She lifted her head briefly to see who had spoken to her but then she let her head sink again.

"Where are you staying?" Bebe asked.

Again: no reply. Bebe took Helena's handbag and eventually found the business card of a B&B, luckily halfway between the café and the train station. Bebe ordered a taxi and with the help of a waiter she managed to support Helena to the rear entrance, as the kind and sensitive waiter had suggested.

At the B&B, the taxi driver and Bebe pulled the absent-minded Helena out of the car and knocked on the door.

Bebe couldn't believe her eyes when Dominic opened the door, the part-time underwear model that Helena had been seeing a fair bit of the previous year. Who had paid his ticket here?

"Good to see you," Dominic said and seemed to be aiming to give Bebe a kiss, but he turned and kissed Helena instead.

"What have you done to my girl?" he said in playful accusation. He gently lifted Helena in his arms and carried her to the bedroom.

"You should watch her," Bebe called after him. "I think she must have taken something. She was all over the shop earlier."

"I know," Dominic said and grinned. "Selfish girl didn't leave any for me."

Chapter 17

Bebe was rudely awoken by the hotel telephone long before she deemed that appropriate. She had set her alarm for midday to allow for a long overdue catch-up with her sleep. This being the day of the actual first semi-final, the documentary people would have better things to do than watch what a non-participating singer from the UK was doing in the morning.

She was wrong on that account. Her director Morgan had pulled some strings and got Bebe to be part of Peter Beatle's commentary show, live on TV. That meant the TV crew was in her hotel room by 9am, watching her getting ready and filming her without make-up yet again. She played along with it but swore under her breath. She was tired, hungover and resented that nobody had given her warning. It all didn't really matter, though. She would be part of Peter's team presenting the show on national television. She would be presenting herself to the perfect target group. Who would be watching the documentary anyway?

Nicki brought a selection of dresses for her. Bebe liked them all but Morgan insisted that Bebe wear one of her own eccentric dresses for the show. Fearing another comparison to drag queens she fiercely resisted but caved when Nicki changed her tune and agreed with the advice.

"I understand what you mean with the drag queen issue," Nicki said. "Tonight, on the other hand, is live Eurovision and people are expecting to watch weird stuff. It's good for us, too, to be memorable. If they won't let you go elegant, then be funny. The outfit he's chosen for you could be a right laugh if you know how to present it. If you're confident you can pull almost anything off, and if you are prepared to laugh about yourself then you're onto a winner. Just do it."

Reluctantly, Bebe agreed. She and Nicki were filmed talking about the chances of the various participants, about the Euro Café and all the other events that had been happening in Malmö in the run-up to the contest.

"You've been here a few days and you already made headlines," Nicki said, full of admiration, but Bebe thought she could detect a hint of jealousy.

"Oh dear," Bebe said. "What did they write about me that could have made the headlines?"

She feigned dread but obviously she was hoping for a mention of her version of 'Believe in Me'.

"It appears you're quite the dedicated mother," Nicki said and pointed at the front-page image, which depicted Bebe propping up a drunken Helena.

How could they have possibly taken the picture and written the article between last night and this morning? Bebe was as puzzled as she was furious. That devil child Helena always managed to mess things up.

Nicki continued: "The long and short of the article is this: Last night, Bebe's daughter Helena had a few too many and needed rescuing, and despite her hectic schedule Bebe left the busy Euro Café early to bring her daughter home, missing out on a late-night party with several Eurovision stars."

She looked through the paper. "There's also an interview with your daughter."

Bebe froze. She had been set up all along, and that was where the devil child had got the money for her drugs. She was steaming.

"You seem speechless," Nicki said. "You don't have to be embarrassed about this. It's not your fault what your daughter does. It's sweet that you took care of her."

Bebe didn't know what to say. She wanted the filming to stop so she could read the interview and see what her daughter had said. It could only be bad news. Who would buy a positive story in days when scandals sold so much better, and even more importantly, what positive things could Helena say about her mother?

Bebe never got a chance to read the paper. Nicki put it away as they were joined by Peter, who chatted with them in front of the rolling camera.

"We need to head to the arena," Morgan abruptly said in the middle of a conversation about the chart success of winning songs. Bebe had been listening with great interest and was annoyed at the sudden end. She hated that the director could stop you in your tracks, but if a presenter wanted to cut a scene they were almost always told off. Bebe longed for more work as a singer.

Nicki and Peter almost stormed out of the room and Bebe didn't get a chance to ask for a look at Helena's interview. The curiosity preoccupied her so much that she nearly forgot her purse. Two cars were taking the teams to the Eurovision arena. Peter and Nicki sat in the other car, leaving Bebe to listen to the banter of the camera men, who clearly weren't into that kind of music and equally clearly didn't want to talk to her.

Bebe tried to find the newspaper in question online, but she probably had got the spelling of the Swedish title wrong. By the time they got to the arena's security gate for delegates, Nicki and Peter had long disappeared. She didn't catch up with them until they were in the little commentators' box, looking down on the stage. She was wondering what Nicki was doing in here.

As if he had read her mind, Peter said: "This afternoon is a run-through for tonight. There are basically three advert breaks that we need to fill with our own material. The block between the songs and the voting is already pre-recorded. So, you and Nicki will be interviewing people. It's almost luck of the draw which artists you're going to get. We record the interviews this afternoon and then pick the best ones for tonight."

"Is there a script?"

"Of course not," Peter said. "As a juror you should know all the songs by now and you just speak about the songs and their quality and their chances in the competition, and you let Nicki do all the flirting and personal questions."

Nicki led Bebe through a labyrinth of stairs and security doors to a mezzanine between the audience levels, with a clear view of the stage. Bebe couldn't believe this part was not used for actual seating. The area was filled with TV presenters from all over Europe with their camera teams, taking test shots and recording messages to their audiences abroad.

"This is really great fun," Nicki said enthusiastically. "You know, everyone is so hyped up, these interviews are where you can sample the energy of the performers in their purest form."

"So, what exactly happens?" Bebe asked.

"People who've already performed and some who will perform on Thursday or Saturday are thrown in here and we get to interview them. Either they have something to say and you let them, or you ask questions and talk about their songs. You can't predict it because maybe something just happened on the stage and we need to discuss that instead."

"What if I don't recognise them?" Bebe asked.

"In that case let me do the talking. For now, grab a chair and make yourself comfortable," Nicki said and pointed at a stack of them. "We're going to be here for the duration."

Bebe did as she was told and brought a chair for Nicki, too.

"I thought when Peter asked me along I would be sitting in the commentators' box with him," Bebe confessed in a sudden moment of bonding with her co-presenter.

"I think we all wish we were in the box with or instead of him," Nicki said with a grin.

She opened her purse and until the show started, she was busy with her mobile phone. Bebe looked around. It reminded her of the movie 'Bodyguard', where plenty of camera teams were busy filming an Oscar's ceremony and one of the cameras was the casing for the sniper rifle. Now that was how a real terrorist would make their presence known at an event like this.

The hall was filled to the brim with spectators. An assistant came and handed Nicki and Bebe earpieces. During the brief soundcheck to verify the connection with Peter as well as with Leonard, the producer of the UK live Eurovision shows, Bebe thought she could make out Tom's new flame, Giovanni, hanging out by the balcony, a few stations to the left, looking lost. She was surprised to see him here since he was not a TV presenter. The Italian was a striking young man who stood out in almost any crowd, so she was pretty sure it was him. She had to ask Tom how he had pulled this one off when she next saw him.

The show began. By now Bebe was bored with the songs and her interest was in the gadgets and props. Most sobering was to see several backing vocalists being put on stage, as per regulation, but hidden from sight. That could have been her when she was considered as backing vocalist for Engelbert the year before. There truly was no business like show business.

The first commercial break took her almost by surprise. Ushers were taking away the chairs and stacking them out of sight and Eurovision hopefuls began to flood the mezzanine level, joining camera teams and presenters. Nicki, who had been silent all through the first five songs, sprang into action and looked as energetic as ever.

Bebe didn't recognise the people who were allocated to her interview session.

"I like the UK song," a beautiful young man from somewhere in South Eastern Europe said in a thick accent. Before she could thank him, Nicki chatted away to 'Amir', the representative from Bosnia.

"You must have a lot of female fans. Are you confident they will vote for you on Thursday?"

The man next to him translated the question and Amir laughed coyly, shook his head and said something in a foreign language.

"Amir thanks you for the compliment. We hope many people vote for him and bring victory to our wonderful country."

Nicki looked encouragingly at Bebe, who couldn't remember the first thing about the song or the country.

"Say something Bebe," she heard Peter's voice in her earpiece.

"Oh, well, I wonder what your staging is going to be like, Amir," she blurted out. It was the only thing she could think of right now.

"Great idea," Peter said into Bebe's earpiece. "We've got a clip, and it's hilarious."

The translator had to wait for Amir's lengthy answer.

"It's a very powerful and emotional song, so we have one special prop, a mirrored glass, which separates Amir from his background dancer, it represents what separates us humans from each other. The song 'Come on Over' expresses the desire to break the wall between us."

"How beautiful," Nicki said. "And Eurovision is here to bring us all together and break down the barriers between all of our many countries."

Amir agreed.

"Here we have a clip from Amir's first rehearsal," Peter said, and the producer's voice came over the earpiece: "Clip playing now, stand by."

"You can't see the clip," Peter explained to Bebe, but Amir leans against the mirror and his male vocalist mimics all his moves. It's almost erotic."

"Clip ends," the producer Leonard said.

"A really great performance," Nicki said.

"Now Finland this year is giving us a small scandal with a lesbian kiss on stage," Bebe said. "Are you playing up to the same market?" she asked.

"Bebe!" Peter hissed into her earpiece and laughed. "You're unbelievable. First drink is on me."

The translator seemed almost reluctant to relay the question but Amir smiled relaxed and answered: "Many have asked the same question. The man inside is not lover but fellow man. But we are happy for all people to be who they are, and Amir has many… em… rainbow friends."

"You're terrible Bebe," Nicki said. "Thanks for meeting with us and best of luck on Thursday, Amir. Now we must go back to the show."

The camera light went off and Amir and his translator disappeared without much fuss.

"You've got a nerve," Nicki said. "That could cause us a lot of hassle with Leonard."

"A bit of controversy is always good," Bebe defended herself.

"Only because the man is media savvy and knew how to handle it without offending anyone," Nicki said. "Don't pull that type of comment again. It's my job on the line here, too, if we sink."

On the stage the show continued with the Danish song but Bebe wasn't interested. Since she had managed the interview with Amir without having ever heard of him before, she felt confident that whoever was their guest in the next commercial break, she would be able to come up with something. Her gaze swayed around the mezzanine level. Most commentators weren't paying much attention to the stage either and instead spoke to their producers or fiddled with their head pieces or phones.

The spot where Giovanni had been standing was now occupied by a different TV team. She wondered where the Italian had disappeared to.

Nicki left to speak to Peter in the commentary box and Bebe found herself all alone in her little corner of the mezzanine balcony. Daniela was on stage next, not doing herself a favour by looking pained and not very excited to be here. What was wrong with some of these artists?

Nicki burst onto the balcony.

"It's Peter," she said, catching her breath. "Someone pushed him down the stairs. He's got to go to hospital."

She stopped and took a few deep breaths.

"You… and… I have got to do the show alone," she said. "I'm going to the commentators' box and you need to be ready for the interviews in eight minutes."

"I don't know the acts from Thursday," Bebe said. "But I know the ones from today backwards. Can't we just swap?"

Nicki shook her head and grinned.

"Sorry. They asked me and I'm not going to trade that place."

When she saw Bebe's frown she gently pushed her in the shoulder.

"Relax," she said. "It'll be good. You'll get more exposure, too. I promise I'll make it work for both of us. Trust me."

She turned on her heel and ran off without any further comment. Bebe was getting nervous and asked the cameraman and Leonard to make sure she knew when she was on and had to say things. Leonard seemed annoyed at her over this request. He was the opposite of Morgan: tall, slim, bold, cold and humourless.

The shock over Peter's fall hadn't really sunk in at first. The worry over this spontaneous gig had almost made her forget about him. Now it hit her hard. Had he really been pushed? And if so, who could have done that? The same culprit who was responsible for the spotlights crashing down? Was this unrelated or yet another of those 'accidents'?

"You're on in a second," she heard Nicki over the ear piece.

"But I haven't got a guest, yet," Bebe complained.

"Don't worry, we'll have someone shortly."

The music stopped and almost immediately all people around her started to grin into the camera and began to speak about the show. None of them had Eurovision hopefuls with them. There were no interviews.

"Unfortunately, a small accident backstage has interfered with the whole logistics, so instead of interviewing any of the participants we'll be talking about our two hostesses: Bebe Bollinger and myself, Nicki French."

"They're showing clips from you and Nicki's career now," Leonard told Bebe.

When that was over, Nicki assured the audience that Peter had now arrived in hospital and that he was as well and in as good spirits as could be expected.

"And that's all we have time for in this short break," Nicki said. "Next to Moldova, the first song of the last block."

Chapter 18

Bebe had hoped to shine in these few minutes of being the sole interviewer but she never got to say one word. She sat down and stared at the stage, her head hanging with disappointment. The show went on with the Moldovan singer being pushed onto the stage on top of those rolling stairs. She had to hand it to the woman: it had to take a lot of courage to step back on a once broken prop.

Bebe could hear Nicki telling the viewers at home the story from the prop accident during rehearsals. Leonard used the time to run Bebe through what she had to do during the next block.

She was over the moon when she saw how much time there was to cover. Admittedly, there were the pre-recorded clips Peter had mentioned but Bebe should actually have a fair amount of talking time. The topics he asked her to discuss were the same she had heard all week: the lesbian kiss, the Turkish broadcaster's reaction to it, Daniela's cast and now Peter's accident. Having spent a few days in Malmö, she felt she was an expert on all these topics as it was. She had to remind herself that the viewers at home would know so little about the dramas.

When the rehearsal was over Bebe, Nicki and Leonard met in the commentators' box.

"That was very good for a start," the producer said to her surprise. "Amir's manager has asked me not to use the interview for transmission when we do the live show, but of course we will show it and say it was an error."

He laughed.

"I never knew you had it in you, Bebe," Nicki said. "You're terrible."

"Can we show it against his will?" Bebe said.

"Of course," the producer said. "And we're actually doing him a favour. It'll earn him a few votes. He shouldn't be so uptight. Maybe the country has antiquated politics, but the people supporting them won't watch our channel."

His phone rang.

"Ah, excellent," he said, listened intensely for twenty seconds, hung up and grinned.

"Nicki, don't worry about the show tonight," Leonard said. "Bebe won't be alone on the balcony for the live show. We've got Tonia Carmichael to do it with her."

"Isn't it a bit risky to do this un-rehearsed?" Nicki asked.

"It certainly is risky but Tonia is a pro and it's only the semi-final, not the Saturday night gig. Bebe, you'll have to bring Tonia up to scratch when she arrives. What we'll do is this: We're going to show the recorded clip of you and Amir first, so we have time to edit or scrap the interviews you're doing tonight and we keep the clips we have about you and Nicki on standby for an emergency."

He didn't wait for a reply. He got onto his phone immediately and walked off.

"Break a leg," Nicki said.

"Yes," Bebe replied quietly. "Probably."

"You'll be fine," Nicki said. "That was pretty amazing for a start. Just try not to push the boat out too far."

"Thanks. I think I better go downstairs and wait for Tonia," Bebe said. "I'm sure you've got prep work to do."

"Cheers," Nicki said and buried her head in her notes.

On the corridor leading to the mezzanine balcony she bumped into Tom.

"What are you doing here?" she asked. "I didn't realise you had access to the TV crew area."

"I've got TV accreditation," he said and showed her his pass. "I want to see all aspects of the show. One day the competition will come back to Denmark and, hopefully, I'll be part of the production team then."

"I've seen your fellow Giovanni on the balcony this afternoon," Bebe said. "Did he also get a press pass from you?"

"No," Tom said. "That can't have been him. He was interviewing Daniela in her dressing room. He must have a doppelganger."

"Very odd," Bebe said. "Well, he wasn't wearing his sunglasses and it's very dark in here. So maybe I got confused."

She was not convinced, though.

"What are you doing here anyway?" Tom asked. "Isn't your jury duty over by now?"

"You'll never believe this but I'll be part of tonight's TV transmission as well," she said excitedly. "I'm working here on the balcony, interviewing participants. How I wish you and I could do that together. You would know all the things that I don't. Apparently, I almost insulted the man from Bosnia." She giggled.

"I'm so glad for you," Tom said. "Show me."

Together they passed the security check.

"Maybe you can spot Giovanni's doppelganger," Bebe said when they got to her presenting spot. Tonia was already there, chatting to the cameraman and having her earpiece fixed.

Morgan waved at her with dramatic gestures.

"I'll do just that. I'll be in your way otherwise. Catch you later," Tom said and wandered off.

"We're only allowed a few shots of you up here," Morgan said. "Then we'll take the footage from the main camera."

He made Bebe pretend to speak to Leonard and Tonia, filmed her having her earpiece fit and then walked off.

"I can't believe the news about Peter," Tonia said when she was alone with Bebe. "One of his few TV appearances a year and he gets injured. I'd be gutted if that happened to me."

"You don't think that was a deliberate push?" Bebe asked.

"I doubt it," Tonia said. "People are so nervous and rush about. Of course, I wasn't there, but I heard that Peter hasn't seen who pushed him because it was so crowded. So, my guess is that it was an accident. How could someone target him in such a chaos?"

"True, but it's very odd if you ask me," Bebe said.

"Anyway," Tonia said, trying to find a relaxed body posture against the balcony.

"Yes, anyway," Bebe agreed, who suddenly felt calm and professional by comparison. "Good luck to both of us."

In the arena, the opening act – Loreen – was ready to go, an assistant giving the artist's hair one last dose of spray, enough to blast an extra hole in the ozone layer. Child singers were eagerly waiting to join the star, while on the big screen you could see the opening scene with clips of Sweden and the last Eurovision contest, as shown to viewers at home.

The host on stage, Petra Mede, was hugely popular in the hall and, having seen the songs so many times now, Bebe was already more interested in her than anything else. Some performers were better today than they had been yesterday, and Bebe regretted some voting decisions she had made.

Tonia appeared dreadfully nervous. Bebe looked down on the stage. The Czech TV crew on Bebe's right side were preparing an interview with their entrant for the competition, Daniela, and inconsiderately kept pushing into Bebe's space. Leonard had argued with them prior to today about their reckless behaviour, but his complaints had always fallen on arrogantly deaf ears.

"Excuse me," Bebe hissed at their presenter and gently but firmly pushed him back to where he belonged. The man had a fake tan, too many blond highlights and plumped lips that had the look of plastic surgery about them. At first, he gave in to her setting of boundaries but then, as in revenge, abruptly stepped backwards, forcefully onto Bebe's foot. Losing her balance, she slumped to the floor. Feeling the filthy dust on her hands made Bebe furious. It was the last thing she needed before her big moment on national TV. She had waited so long to be in this place and if these clowns thought they could mess with her they had another think coming. Over her dead body!

Before she could get back up, though, she watched in horror as the Czech presenter stumbled too and his head slumped hard on her leg. More pain, but Bebe was determined not to let this get to her. Remembering old showbiz mantras she immediately began to compose herself for the camera while pushing and pulling hard to free herself from underneath his heavy weight. It took Bebe a while before it sank in that the man wasn't moving at all and when she finally stood upright she saw that the pale-faced Czech star, Daniela, herself with a bandaged foot, was sitting on the floor beside the presenter, checking him frantically for responsiveness and pulse. She looked terrified.

"He needs help," Daniela screamed. "Get an ambulance!"

Bebe wiped the dust off her dress and watched the events unfold with horror. Daniela pulled a slim dart-like object from the man's chest and handed it to a security guard before dragging the unconscious presenter by his feet away from the crowds by the balcony's edge. Ushers were taking charge of the situation and pushed back the reporters and camera crews who by now had turned away from the music spectacle and were trying to get a good shot of the man on the floor. The security guards scanned the crowd while speaking over their walkie-talkies.

Bebe couldn't keep up with all that was going on around her on the media balcony. A team of paramedics rushed to the scene and attended the victim lying on the floor only a few metres away.

The security guards cleared the balcony by ushering the journalists and TV crews to a large conference room on the mezzanine level.

"You may continue your coverage for now," they were told by a suited man with headsets and a clipboard. "When the police arrive they'll decide on the further course of action. To make sure they can carry out their investigation we have strict instructions to keep you all here for questioning."

Leonard grabbed her softly by the wrist.

"We're on in ten seconds," Leonard said, looking directly into her eyes. "Forget about the guy and focus on the show. Security and the police have this covered, you're not in danger. Just be professional. Can you do that for me?"

Bebe gulped and nodded. Her thoughts went to the dead presenter and she regretted her earlier irritation with him.

"What an amazing show," she could hear Nicki say over her earpiece. "The fans in the arena really loved the Danish song, didn't they? I think it's a strong contender for the crown. I'm joined today by singing legend Bebe Bollinger, one of the women that inspired me to get into show business myself. How are things in the hall, Bebe?"

"Hello Nicki," Bebe said, "and thanks for the compliment. It's chaos here. So many excitable people in one place, everyone so happy to be here, it's a total buzz. And I agree with you, that last song was an absolute knock-out performance. I was literally on the floor."

"We usually have Eurovision hopefuls with us at this stage but I had problems with my earpiece. Bebe, tell me, do you have a guest with you?" Nicki asked.

Bebe looked at the Leonard and saw that he was pointing his finger at Tonia, whom he had pulled back from watching the spectacle, holding her wrist. In the background Bebe could just about spot a paramedic attending to the Czech presenter outside the glass wall of the conference room.

"We do," Bebe said, hoping she understood Leonard's message right. "None other than the amazing Tonia Carmichael, who represented the UK in 1987, was it?"

On that cue Tonia walked up to Bebe and punched her gently in the shoulder.

"Stop it," she said and grinned. "I was still a child in 1987. I participated a few years later than that thank you very much."

She leaned forward and kissed Bebe on the cheek.

"Good to see you, darling," Bebe said. "How is it to be back after so many years?"

"Oh, I'm very excited," Tonia said. "The event has changed so much. In our days we had little fuss made about us. When we arrived at the airport nobody took any notice, the media coverage was minimal and compared to this arena we performed in someone's garden shed."

She laughed nervously. Bebe saw Leonard cringe.

"Tell us a little about your performance back then?" Bebe asked.

"It's a little embarrassing," Tonia said. "There were four of us, we all had bleach blonde hair and the worst choreography imaginable. Of course, at the time we thought it was the bees-knees but when you look at the clip today it's just cringeworthy."

"Let's have a look," Nicki said and played a clip.

Tonia looked furious and disorientated.

"I told Leonard not to use that clip and the bastard did it anyway?"

"Shut up," Leonard hissed over the earpiece.

The clip ended.

"Now that was surreal," Nicki said and laughed. "But don't worry Tonia. When I watched it back then I thought it was excellent. And you gave a very… enthusiastic… performance, didn't you."

"Yes," Tonia said and seemed to relax. "We had great fun."

"How do you fancy Bonnie's chances on Saturday?" Bebe asked.

"I try not to think about it," Tonia said. "I want her to do well and I don't want to jinx it."

"Bebe, you voiced concerns back in the UK about the presentation style of Bonnie's song. Do you still maintain that, or have you changed your mind? After all, Bonnie is still up there in the betting odds, so not everyone agrees with your harsh judgement."

Bebe hadn't been prepared for this. What was Nicki trying to do? They were meant to be uncontroversial, wasn't that why Nicki had told her off about the Amir incident?

"Oh, what do I know?" Bebe said, hoping she could laugh this off. "I'm not one to talk about success. I've always lingered in the shadows of the business. Bonnie is an excellent performer and I have no doubt she will do the UK proud."

"And that's all we have time for," Nicki interrupted them. "Next up another big favourite of the show: Russia. If a ballad takes the crown, this could be one of the strong contenders. Russia always tries extra hard to win the competition. Can they do it this year?"

Nicki's voice was replaced by that of the host on the stage.

"What happened to the Czech presenter?" Bebe asked immediately. "Is he okay?"

Leonard didn't bother replying. "What's going on down there?" Nicki asked.

"The Czech presenter," Bebe explained. "Looks like he was shot with a tranquillizer dart or something, right before we went on air. The poor thing."

"Blimey. And you didn't tell me about it? Are you mad? We're going to lose viewers if we don't report on it."

"Nicki is right," Bebe said. "Are you listening, Leonard?"

"Someone poisoned the Czech guy," Leonard said. "He's on his way to the hospital."

"Never." Bebe couldn't take it in.

"Yes," Leonard said. "Imagine the danger we've all been under, minding our business while there's a nutter on the loose."

"If it was only a tranquillizer..." Bebe started but Leonard cut her short.

"Doesn't matter," he said. "My point is that all the security is worthless these days. We're no longer looking just for guns or knives. And nobody's seen anything it seems. We're not safe here."

"I can't believe someone would have the cheek to try a stunt like that in front of all the cameras, amongst so many people," Bebe said.

"It was probably the perfect opportunity," Leonard said. "The people here are all so busy with themselves, nobody was paying any attention except the bouncers, and they wouldn't have noticed if someone stood with the back to them."

"Is he going to be alright?" Nicki asked.

"I hope so," he said. "First Peter has an accident, now that Czech guy got knocked out: not a good time to be a TV presenter."

He laughed.

"Alfie won't be here until Friday," Nicki asked. "What are we going to do with the commentary until then?"

"We'll have to cover Peter's time on the air ourselves," Leonard said. "We all better talk about our options."

Before they got a chance to do so, however, the police arrived and took everyone's details.

"I can't believe you let us carry on," Leonard said to the officer dealing with the British crew.

"The security team have already caught the culprit and found incriminating evidence on him," the officer replied. "We probably won't even need witness statements at this rate. You'll be allowed back on the balcony in due course."

When he asked her about what she had seen Bebe explained how she had been preoccupied with her injury from the Czech presenter and couldn't understand what had happened at all.

The policeman made more notes than what she thought was representative of her short answers but eventually he took his leave.

And indeed, in time for the next advert block the media teams were free to go. Leonard dragged Bebe back onto the balcony and briefed her about the kind of trivia he wanted her to tell the audience.

"We're not to mention the incident. It would be seen as a disadvantage for the performers if we distract from the music. This is a competition and all official broadcasters will have to comply with this rule. She listened like a good girl, determined not to let this chance slip through her fingers. After all, she had often hoped to be the presenter of her own TV talk show with musical guests. This could be the beginning of something bigger than a career limited to singing alone. How awful that it had to happen under such dreadful circumstances.

Leonard incessantly talked to her about how to smile, how to talk and so forth and checking that she had understood. Then he spoke to Nicki via his microphone.

Bebe's head was still spinning from all the information, but it was hardest not to think of the Czech presenter. The next advert break came so fast and Leonard had somehow knocked all confidence out of her. She wasn't ready when she saw a woman approaching her with outstretched arms who she didn't recognise. The camera was already rolling and Nicki was summing up the last song before introducing Bebe and what turned out to be Olga, the Polish representative that year.

"Bebe Bollinger," Olga called out and leaned her head back as if to present Bebe to an audience instead of hugging her as Bebe had expected. "One of my all-time favourites. How I love your music!"

"Thank you," Bebe replied curtly and took a half step back.

"My father was such a big fan of yours," Olga said. "So many of his friends love you. Well, more the ones who were around when you had the biggest hits, but the rest like your album, too."

Bebe could hear Nicki giggle.

"Thank you, but enough about me," Bebe said. "How are your rehearsals going?"

Olga laughed.

"You probably heard that Turkey isn't going to televise the show now," she said. "It's a bit of a shame but at least we now know where we stand with them. The kissing is so harmless and silly; I can't believe they are making such a fuss about it."

"I thought it was the Finnish girl who was kissing on stage?" Bebe asked, confused.

Olga frowned.

"I had the idea first," she insisted angrily. "We were going to include a variety of kisses, a man kissing a man, then a woman, then the woman kissing a woman and so on. My song is not about marriage but about full equality. 'Break All Chains' is about society's boundaries, and here we are, being censored by countries who do not even participate."

"Don't get political," Leonard whispered into Bebe's earpiece.

"With such a ménage you've got all options open now," Bebe said. "Male, female – compared to the Finnish song you doubled your market." She attempted a giggle. "Maybe I should do that, too, at my age I can't afford to be choosy."

"What are you like?" Olga said and leaned into Bebe as if to kiss her.

'What the hell,' Bebe said to herself, thinking of her street cred: 'Why not?'

So, she kissed the Polish girl on the lips.

"I bet you do that to all the presenters here," Bebe said when they came apart. "Are you trying to get your boyfriend jealous?"

"I think he likes it when I kiss other girls," Olga said and laughed.

"Here's a clip from Olga's rehearsal," Nicki stepped in and Bebe could hear the music playing.

"Throttle it down," Leonard said.

"Exactly," Nicki agreed. "You need to talk about the other songs with her, not flirt with her."

When the music clip ended, Nicki took over the interview and asked Olga all the questions the producer wanted to hear.

The interview ended abruptly as the show on the stage resumed. Olga rushed off and Leonard was having a hissy fit.

"Why do I always have to work with amateurs?" he yelled. "Absolutely useless."

He, too, stormed off, leaving her alone with the cameraman, who showed no interest in getting involved, and instead was playing with the lens.

Bebe grabbed one of the chairs and sat down. This had been a complete disaster, she knew it. She had twenty minutes before the next segment and decided to freshen up her makeup.

Out in the corridor, she thought she had seen Giovanni. She was sure he had seen her, too, and had pushed hastily onwards through the people around him.

"The audience loved you," Leonard said with unprecedented warmth when she came back to the balcony. "I don't get why, because it was all so phony and plastic, but apparently you're trending again on Twitter."

"I don't understand," Bebe said. "You said you were going to show the Amir clip on TV during the first advert break and then show the Tonia interview during the second interval."

"That was the plan but someone in the studio cocked it up and went with the live feed, and it turns out it was lucky they did."

He showed her his phone with a message from headquarters, citing a few excited tweets about the lesbian kiss between Bebe and Olga.

"It didn't work for Madonna and Britney when they kissed, so I would never have allowed you to do this live," he said.

"People tend to like me more when I'm outrageous," Bebe said. "I don't know why it's necessary, but it seems to help."

"It's fine now," he said.

She received a text from Tom who said he had found Giovanni in the auditorium and he would call Bebe the next morning as soon as he had got up – which wasn't going to be very early.

Bebe got through the evening interviewing other Eurovision hopefuls and chatting away as if nothing had happened. It was surreal. At long last they came to the part of the evening when those proceeding to the final were announced

The host took a long time with the procedure, dragging it out as much as possible to increase the tension. The audience was going mad, shouting the names of their favoured countries.

Daniela, the Irishman and the girl from Moldova all made it through to the final. Denmark had done so as well and the many Danish people in the arena were celebrating loudly.

When the show was over Bebe was exhausted. The production company's car took her back to Copenhagen where she went for a nightcap in a bar near the hotel. A news programme came on and footage of the attack on the Czech presenter was the first item.

"Excuse me," she asked the waiter. "I don't speak Danish. What is that story about?"

"A commentator has been killed at Eurovision. They don't know more details yet."

"Killed?" That thought sent shivers down her spine. So it hadn't been just a tranquilizer? And it happened right next to her. This was awful.

"Yes, that's what they said," the waiter said. "But they caught the man." With that he quickly rushed off to a different table.

Bebe couldn't get over it: an actual murder at Eurovision... why would anyone do such a thing? Thank God they had arrested the murderer. Now she could relax.

Tomorrow, the rehearsals for the second semi-final would begin. Bebe went to her hotel to listen to the Eurovision channel, hoping for some news about the Czech presenter in English but the only thing being discussed was who had qualified and who hadn't. Bebe was beside herself how such a murderous incident could not be the top story but then again, none of the scandals so far had really made an impact in the media coverage.

Chapter 19

The next morning Beth woke Bebe up by knocking noisily on the door.

"I've been wondering where you've been," Bebe complained and opened the door wide to let her friend in. "Are you alright?"

"Of course I am," Beth said and walked in. "It's taken me a while to find my feet in this investigation. I kind of assumed that Tom would have a sense of direction but he's easily confused or distracted and doesn't follow up on all the leads."

Bebe put the kettle on and sat down on her bed.

"Isn't it all over?" she asked. "They arrested a man, I'm sure given time they can link everything that's been happening to him."

"I was hoping that would be the case," Beth said, "but I doubt that very much."

"Why?"

"Their suspect isn't our man."

"That can't be," Bebe said. "The police said they found incriminating evidence. Enough to continue with the show, too."

"So they did," Beth said. "Tom heard it from one of his sources in the police force. They found a tranquillizer blow gun near the suspect but without his fingerprints on it. They didn't know that at the time. They suspected him because he's a diabetic. There was a misunderstanding amongst the security guards about what type of weapon had been used and it all snowballed from there. The security guard in question had never seen the rare injection device the suspect had in his hand. The man ran away when approached, had no diabetic bracelet on but had what was deemed the murder weapon on his person. And the actual blow gun was right next to him, too."

"If he wiped off his fingerprints it could be him." Bebe pointed out.

"The suspect ran because he saw the Czech presenter fall and thought there was a killer running amok. He's from Belarus and doesn't speak English. This is his first trip abroad, his passport is brand new, so he's never been to Amsterdam and he wasn't here for the Big Six party."

"If they found the dart stuff near him then I wouldn't dismiss him completely, but maybe we have several criminals at work," Bebe said.

"That's right," Beth said. "So you see, the investigation is still ongoing. Tom asked me to continue with it anyway."

"If we discount the murder on the balcony and just think about the other incidents: none of our first lot of suspects could have pushed Peter down the stairs, apart from Peter himself."

"I better have that checked out, too," Beth said. "I know that the Dutch cousins have performer or press passes for that documentary they're shooting."

"How do you know?"

"Lars managed to get me an audience with Anouk's producer. He revealed to me that he took both the de Poel cousins under contract. By talking to him I also solved the mystery why they were here before Marcha got her documentary gig: She's dating a guy on Anouk's team and Claudia was allowed to come since her ticket and room had already been paid."

"Excellent," Bebe said. "About time someone picked up some of our loose ends."

"The real question is whether the two strands of attacks are related or separate," Bebe carried on.

"Is one culprit after the singers while someone else has got it in for the press?"

"That would be a hell of a coincidence," Beth said.

"Exactly," Bebe agreed. "Could there be such a coincidence, that two attackers are at work at the same time, with two different motives and techniques?"

"My gut feeling tells me that they're one and the same," Beth said. "Just look at all this work backstage. Maybe it's more than one person but I bet they're working together."

"But why?" Bebe wondered. "Why were they picking on those artists?"

"It's either random or very carefully chosen," Beth ventured a guess. "The spotlights both fell when people were near them, which implies the culprit knew who they were meant to hit, unless it wasn't important who, as long as someone got hit. Your position on the balcony is near the exit, so the Czech presenter could also have been a mere chance target."

"It doesn't sound like an elaborate plan," Bebe observed.

"Exactly," Beth said. "I think it's all about Daniela."

"The Czech girl?"

143

"Yes. She was the first person to be almost hit by the spotlight. Okay, the next spotlight crash was nowhere near her, but that might have been a diversion, so the police wouldn't focus on Daniela exclusively."

"Interesting."

Beth smiled.

"The tranquillizer shot might have been meant for Daniela, too," she said. "The presenter was talking to Daniela at the time. Maybe he made a sudden movement and got into the line of fire."

"I was wondering about that," Bebe said, and then realised that it was she herself who had pushed the guy just seconds before the dart had hit him? A wave of guilt washed over her.

"I've also found out something really fascinating about Giovanni. He lives in Scotland of all places and his mother performed in Eurovision in the 1970s, so that explains his obsession with the competition."

"I always felt he was a dark horse," Bebe said. The kettle had boiled and she got up to make coffee for her visitor and herself. "Is that why Tom is so obsessed with him?"

"Tom didn't know until I told him. Can you believe it? I googled the name and 'Eurovision' and suddenly there are all these European articles with a picture of a woman who is clearly his mother. Sometimes you can be the greatest expert in a field and still not see what's right in front of you."

"How did he react to your news?" Bebe asked, handing Beth her cup.

"Of course he's over the moon and adores Giovanni even more. I'm not sure exactly how much is going on between the two of them but obviously Tom is smitten and now he's got another reason, as if he needed one. Our Italian friend on the other hand was all coy. It turns out that his mother didn't get the final ranking she had hoped for and withdrew from the music business ever since."

"Well I for one am glad Tom found Giovanni," she said. "The two boys are made for each other."

Beth's phone rang. "I've got to take this."

Bebe nodded, picked up her clothes for the day and went into the bathroom.

She was glad for Nicki's donations to her wardrobe. Those dresses somehow always hit the right tone effortlessly, Bebe couldn't put her finger on exactly why. Maybe it was the age difference, Nicki hadn't lost touch with current trends.

Dressed for success and feeling refreshed from her shower, Bebe re-joined Beth and the two went down to the hotel restaurant for breakfast.

"What was that phone call about?" Bebe asked once they had settled with coffee and pastries.

"That was Leonard. He said that we've got to expect increased security today and make sure we get to the stadium in time. We better hurry up."

Bebe sighed and washed down her croissant with a glass of orange juice.

"I still think all of this has something to do with Daniela," Beth said. "I remember she said something about being bisexual in her interview. The Polish singer Olga is on a vendetta against the Finnish girl over the lesbian kiss that should have been part of Olga's stage show."

"I don't follow."

"Daniela had hits in Poland and Russia," Beth continued. "So, Daniela competes with Olga not only here but at home. And both could be using an ambiguous sexuality as publicity device."

"What about the assistants to the singers?" Bebe asked. "Have any of them flagged as suspects?"

"No," Beth said. "The police have naturally considered the possibility but it turns out the only two likely candidates each have a solid alibi for one of the attacks. Which brings us to another possibility. What if you had been the target on the balcony? You stood right next to the man and had he not stomped on your foot, you wouldn't have doubled over and you could have been hit."

"I was thinking that at some point, but I'm not competing in this show. Why would anyone go after me?"

"The spotlight at the Euro Café might have been meant for you, too," Beth said. "And with Peter having had a mysterious accident, the theory of presenters rather than singers being targeted is back on the agenda."

"That would make Nicki and Alfie the next people on the hit list," Bebe pointed out.

"And you. I better not let you out of my sight until then."

They finished their breakfast and took the train to the arena in Malmö. The queues were tremendous and it took them a long time to get through security. All bags were hand searched, no liquids allowed, people were frisked and anything metal, from rings to belts, all had to be taken off and put into the screening machines.

By the time they sat in the auditorium reserved for press and watched the next seventeen contestants perform Bebe felt exhausted, but far from reassured. She needed not to think about the case for a little while.

"The songs in this semi-final are much better," she told Beth, who didn't seem impressed.

The morning went by without incident – no attack, no dropped tool, spotlight or rolling gadgets.

"I had another thought," said Bebe. "The girl from Finland. She seems to be the most ambitious, throwing everything she can at the show: her private life, her sexuality, she's perfectly styled, dressed and has this stunning figure. Yet, there's something so desperate about her, I wonder whether she could be part of this."

"It's difficult to tell," Beth said. "Usually murderers try to keep a low profile, but here they can't afford that. We could suspect any of the contestants. They're all in competition with each other and want to win so badly."

"Didn't you notice that none of the performers from the second semi-final got attacked? It's all people from the first semi-final and from the Big Six group. That could be deliberate to make the competition nervous, and also, maybe the attacker is busy performing during that semi-final?"

"Was Krista in Amsterdam?"

"I would be very surprised if she wasn't," Bebe said. "As I said, she's so eager and wouldn't stop at anything."

The second run-through of the songs went smoothly as well. Bebe was beginning to see the logic in her theory about Krista from Finland. She recalled the interview with the woman on Eurovision TV where the Finnish singer had even specifically mentioned Bonnie and Daniela as main competitors. Currently, the favourite was the girl from Denmark and the couple from Georgia, with Krista being still only an outside chance.

"We should consider Tom a suspect, too," Bebe said. "I love him to bits, but he was at all those shows and he was on the balcony for a while. And so was his Giovanni."

"That seems a definite possibility," Beth said. "I'm not sure of the motive, though."

"People don't always need an obvious motive," Bebe said. "He's a rich kid who might have a penchant for drama."

"I thought you were talking about a friend of yours for a second," Beth pointed out.

"He is my friend," Bebe insisted. "I'm just being realistic."

They had arranged to meet Tom after the show at the south gate of the arena. Giovanni was still with him. The Italian hid his eyes behind his dark sunglasses, the face frozen in an undefinable expression that could be arrogance or shyness. Bebe couldn't decide between the two.

"God, that woman from Georgia sang out of tune," Tom said. "Absolutely vile. To think they are favourites to win the semi-final. I can't imagine that happening. I can't wait to see how that performance affected her betting odds."

"Yes, let's find a café with Wi-Fi," Bebe said.

"I've got an early start," Giovanni said. "I'll take the train home."

He kissed Tom then turned towards Bebe and Beth.

"Ciao bellas."

"Wait," Beth said. "I need to call it a night, too. I'll come with you to the train station.

"Please," Giovanni said and led the way. If he was uncomfortable with it, he and his sunglasses hid it well.

Bebe and Tom found a nearby café where the Danish man was pleased to learn that in the official betting the out of tune Georgian song now had slipped into fourth position, behind Finland.

"Now about that man of yours," Bebe said. "What is this between you? I mean you employed him just because he's cute without even knowing his mother performed at Eurovision once? Beth said she did a simple Google search with his name, and you didn't figure it out yourself?"

"I only ever watched the show from the Eighties onwards. The name of his mother never rang a bell with me." He paused and took a sip from his coffee. "You're right, of course" Tom said. "I should have checked him out more thoroughly. He left a series of really impressive comments on my blog, so we got chatting and he said he would meet me at Eurovision. I do need an assistant during that time and asked him if he fancied becoming an assistant reporter for me."

"If he's such a fan, does he go to the other Eurovision shows, you know, Amsterdam, Riga, Moscow and Tel Aviv?"

"He went to Riga," Tom said, "but not to the others. It's a shame I didn't go to Riga."

"You did well enough to meet here and fall in love," Bebe said.

"He's not as keen as I am," Tom said. "Normally, I have people fall over me because of the blog but with him I have to do all the work."

"Treat them mean, keep them keen," Bebe said. "Looks like he knows how to keep you interested."

They ordered a bottle of champagne and then Tom talked her through the ins and outs of Eurovision betting, the background for each singer and how well the various countries did at the competition traditionally.

Many drinks, speeches and hours later they took a train back into town. Bebe had texted Beth and had arranged to meet her at a bar in the town centre. She dropped Tom off at his hotel and walked through the beautiful town, loving the relatively mild spring air.

Over a few cocktails in the surprisingly empty bar, Bebe told Beth how Tom had met Giovanni."

"I'm highly suspicious of that man," Beth replied. "Giovanni is such an odd character. He more or less ignored me throughout the entire journey home, playing with his phone," Beth reported from her evening. "When we left the train, he walked with me for a bit, then he suddenly stopped and said he had forgotten something and left me, walking in the opposite direction. I played along but managed to catch up with him later and tailed him back to the Plaza, which is not the hotel he is staying in. However, he had a key card in his hand and took the elevator to the 11th floor."

"And?" Bebe asked, impatiently. "Who stays there?"

"Unfortunately, quite a lot of interesting parties: The floor seems home to the Finnish and the Dutch delegations and the press teams from Italy and the UK."

"Mother of God," Bebe said.

"Indeed," Beth said, "The possibility that he knows Krista or Nicki would support your theory that there are several culprits working together as a team."

"Nicki?" Bebe asked.

"Of course," Beth said. "With Peter and you out of the way, the shows is all hers. She counts as prime suspect as far as I'm concerned."

Bebe laughed out loud.

"She nearly got hit by a spotlight, too, remember?" Bebe pointed out. "I was there."

"Exactly," Beth pointed out. "She was there, so she could have been the one to lay the trap in the first place, and was unlucky you moved."

"Going back to Giovanni," Bebe said, "he could have an Italian friend?"

"And he may also have known that I was tailing him and so he took the 11th floor to throw me off course. It happened to me once on a case."

"Oh darn," Bebe swore. "So many possibilities; we're stabbing in the dark again."

"I'm afraid so," Beth said. "But I feel we're a lot closer than we were."

"In that case we should keep more of an eye on Giovanni to see if the pattern repeats," Bebe suggested. "I have a feeling what we're looking for is on the 11th floor of that hotel and we'll get to it sooner or later. There are really only two suspects on that floor: Nicki and Krista."

"If we consider individual personal assistants then the Dutch assistant is coming back into the radar," Beth added. "Remember that De Poel girl who was singing the backing vocals at the Dutch song presentation? She lives on that floor, too."

Chapter 20

It was very late when Bebe got to her hotel. Back in her room, Eurovision TV had no interesting or relevant news for her either. Helena had left her several messages, thanking her for taking her home that night and asking her mother to meet her at the Euro Café again. That reminded Bebe of the newspaper article Nicki had mentioned, the one with Helena giving an interview about Bebe as mother. How could she have forgot about this? All those years she had managed to keep her daughter away from the press. Helena had always threatened to ruin her mother's reputation yet had never crossed that line. Now one drunken evening in Denmark had wrecked that record and god knows whether the UK press would get wind of this and spin it in a less favourable way.

Googling herself on the internet she found the Swedish newspaper article, which was terrifying and useful at the same time. She would be able to track the article down and have it translated, but so could plenty of journalists.

Bebe was in luck. Her hotel stocked the newspaper in its café area and the receptionist on duty brought her a copy up and even translated it for her.

She couldn't believe it: Helena had made up a lot of lies, but not the ones Bebe had been expecting from her rebellious daughter. Helena had painted a picture of Bebe as a feminist heroine who had battled hard all her life for the good of her daughter. The wild child owned up to being difficult and ungrateful and sung her mother's praises in a way that Bebe never had heard once from the child's mouth. Bebe remembered how Nicki had said words to a similar effect during the interview, but she had never believed that to be actually true.

It was too late to call the number Helena had left for Bebe, so she would have to defer it to tomorrow. When her head hit the pillow Bebe couldn't suppress a hopeful smile. Could mother and daughter move forward on a different footing? Could a leopard really change her spots? She was eager to find out.

Far too soon her documentary team woke Bebe and subjected her to the same routine of filming without make-up.

"I thought we didn't need to film during the second semi-final," Bebe protested once she was dressed and in the hotel restaurant for breakfast. "I'm not voting in this one."

"We need as much material to pick from as possible," Morgan explained. "How about we take you shopping and come with you to the rehearsal this afternoon?"

"I could actually do with a new dress," Bebe admitted.

The task proved harder than she had anticipated. Insecure form the many derogatory comments about her dress sense, she couldn't decide what to get and ended up not buying anything. Nothing she had seen was better than the trouser suit Nicki had lent her. It was frustrating, though. Now, that she had been filmed in this costume, she would need something new to wear tomorrow. She couldn't possibly wear the same thing twice on TV.

Because of the documentary crew following her around, Bebe thought it was pointless to meet up with Beth. They wouldn't be able to talk properly, so it was better to divide and conquer.

Beth spent the morning tailing Giovanni and sent Bebe frequent updates via texts. Giovanni had gone home to his own hotel at some point in the night apparently. Beth had rung his room at the hotel and he had picked up.

From there she had followed him that morning to the arena, where he'd met up with Tom and watched the show from the press room. So, nothing exciting was happening there.

Bebe headed for the media balcony. Leonard pushed an earpiece into her hand and asked the cameraman to do light tests around her head.

Tonia was there, too, nervous as ever.

"Can you hear me?" Nicki's voice came over the earpiece.

"Loud and clear," Bebe said. "I miss you," she continued. "Leonard is so rude to me and Tonia so nervous."

"Come on," Nicki said abruptly. "It took me years to get to that place in my career and it's not a bad one. Count yourself lucky to be here."

Bebe did understand, but she was affected all the same.

"Bebe, we can talk about this some other time," Nicki said. "I'd really love to but we're on in half an hour and I really need to get my act together."

Between Leonard's instructions, the extra make-up and shooting a few segments with Morgan for the documentary, the time until the show started ran through her fingers like sand. Tonia stood there like a lemon, so Bebe gave her a big hug.

"You'll be fine," Bebe said. "I've done my homework for this. Now let's show them what we're made of."

Bebe delighted the camera crew with all the insider information she had picked up from the night before, listening to Tom. She may have gotten the odd detail wrong but probably all presenters did. There just were too many countries and performers in the competition and its 60-year-old history.

The dress rehearsal had started and TV presenters on the balcony were busy addressing their audiences at home. Nicki did all this from the commentators' box without linking to Bebe or Tonia. Given the number of different hats Bebe metaphorically wore, she was almost relieved. And then there was the stage to observe, where anything could happen. Literally. Would there be any more attacks? If this was all nothing but a prank or tactic to scare people, the actual presenter's death would have made the people behind it stop in their track. On the other hand, if the criminals were serious, who would be next? Bebe watched with great tension as act after act performed without incident.

There was Amir and his mirror, now rehearsed not just with a man but with a woman dancing as well. She had to laugh at the immediate knee-jerk reaction of the Bosnian team to the 'misinterpretations'.

Next was Finland, the last song before the commercial break. Krista seemed assured of victory, her performance confident and sassy and the kiss at the end came as a real surprise to large parts of the audience. Where had they been all this time?

"Now that *has* to be a strong contender," Tonia said. "All week I've been on the same hotel floor as Krista and she couldn't be nicer or more energetic. You have to love her and wish her well. Bebe, what do you say?"

"Oh, I agree," Bebe replied, "and that's such a sweet thing, to dedicate the song to the rainbow community; especially right after Amir's entry, who has added a woman to his choreography so nobody can accuse him of any rainbow vibes."

"Oh yes," Nicki said and giggled. "Can we show that clip between Amir and Bebe on Tuesday please?" she asked, and as if on cue the interview replayed.

"Krista on the other hand can't get enough of her gay friends," Tonia said.

"That's right," Nicki said. "We have a clip of her performing at the Euro Café last week where she showed just how comfortable she is with that community."

Bebe of course never got to see the clip, but as it was playing the Irish boy and his muscular drummers joined her and Tonia on the balcony.

"Nicki, you won't believe who I've got here," Bebe said. "I know I'm old enough to be their mother but Holy Mary look at these men. I want to take them home with me."

"Hello Ryan," Tonia said. "You must be so pleased that you qualified for the final after Ireland missing out so many years in a row."

"Of course I am," the young lad said. "We've worked really hard for it and it's great that the effort paid off."

"You've gone up in the betting odds," Bebe said. "How do you rate your chances for Saturday?"

"We'll just have to wait and see," Ryan said.

"I saw one of the large drums on stage fell onto your dancers," Bebe said. "Were you nervous that would happen again? Did you double and triple check it before going on stage?"

"Of course we did," Ryan said. "The stage team here are doing a marvellous job, with so little time between acts to set everything up. Really impressive, but of course, small mistakes can be made and we were lucky nothing serious happened."

"How do you rate the UK entry?" Nicki asked him. "Will the Irish jury give us any points, you reckon?"

"I hope so," Ryan said diplomatically. "The song took a while to grow on me but now I can't get enough of it."

He looked at Bebe.

"Your version of it really rocks, by the way."

"Thanks," Nicki said. "That's all we have time for. Next is Gianluca for Malta, another highly respected contender for the competition. Best of luck Ryan and thanks for joining us."

Ryan asked for Bebe's autograph and then left the balcony.

Morgan and his team replaced the TV crew and quickly asked Bebe a few more questions about the competition and the entries she liked. Then she was free to watch with eager interest how the participants got on. She half expected more accidents, but none came.

The next commercial break was not far off. Bebe checked her phone for more information from Beth, who had joined Tom and

Giovanni in the media room. 'Giovanni is missing', Beth's last text read. She had sent it only ten minutes ago. 'I think he's on the balcony.'

"How long before the next break?" she asked the cameraman. "I want to stretch my legs."

"You're kidding, right?" the man said. "Stretching your legs during Eurovision? You can go to the ladies' room, but we need you back here in five minutes at the latest. Can't you wait until the next block is over?"

"Sorry," she said and quickly ran off. She craned her neck to check the area outside the balcony for signs of Giovanni. When she hadn't spotted him, she went back to see if he was lingering around any of the TV crews. To no avail. She made it back to her team in time.

"You've got a nerve," Leonard said. Next to him stood Loreen, last year's winner, chatting away to Tonia.

"Sorry to keep you waiting," Bebe said and kissed Loreen on the cheek.

"No problem," Loreen said with a warm, broad smile. Bebe could see why people liked her so much.

"How does it feel to be back at the competition without the pressure to win?" Nicki asked.

"It's lovely," Loreen replied. "I had a wonderful time last year. Not everything here is about competition and you can feel the warmth and positive vibe from everyone. It's not about winning but about being here."

"Winning can transform careers," Tonia said. "Who of the other 40 participants from last year are here today? It's only you, so it's a lot about the winning."

"What Tonia means is whether your career has taken off the way you hoped for?" Nicki interrupted.

Loreen laughed.

"I had the most fantastic year and I can't wait to crown the next winner and have them enjoy a year like mine."

"Do you have a favourite song in the competition tonight?" Tonia asked.

"Of course," Loreen said. "Almost too many. The quality of the songs is really high again."

"Who do you want to win?" Bebe asked.

"Sweden, of course," Loreen said and grinned. "Robin's so adorable."

"That he is," Bebe said. "And he won your national heat as a complete outsider, right?"

"Yes," Loreen replied. "He stunned us all with his win. So good on him."

"Well thank you very much, Loreen," Nicki said. "It's all we have time for. Next up in the arena is Armenia."

Chapter 21

Loreen gave Bebe a big hug. "Your song was amazing," she said to Bebe. "Maybe you can do a version of 'Euphoria' like you did for 'Believe in Me' and we can sing it together. You're such a talented artist."

"Aww thank you," Bebe said. At that moment she spotted Giovanni in the door to the balcony. It felt as if their eyes had locked for a brief second – he took an instant step back and disappeared out of sight.

"Excuse me," Bebe said and pushed past Loreen, who struggled to keep her balance but looked highly amused and cheerful all the same.

Bebe ran as fast as she could on her high heels. By the time she got to the entrance she couldn't spot Giovanni anywhere. She searched the corridor up and down and just as she was about to give up she saw him coming out of one of the interview rooms. She hid behind a pillar and watched him walking back to the balcony. He stopped in the doorway and after probably assuring himself that Bebe wasn't around he stepped out onto it.

She shot out of her hiding and rushed to the balcony herself, eager to find out what he was up to. Who was he going to kill? Was he after a journalist or a singer, the balcony was full of both. She systematically searched the area to the left of the entrance and then looked for him on the right. She couldn't find him anywhere. As she walked back to her team, Bebe heard a big bang and then Tonia let out a mighty scream. When she got there, the Polish cameraman – one of Bebe's 'neighbours' on the balcony – was lying on the floor. As he'd fallen he'd evidently taken the camera equipment down with him with a resounding crash. He was not moving. People stood around him without seeming to know what to do. Bebe knelt beside him and saw that he had a tranquillizer dart in his thigh.

She pulled the dart out and got Tonia to call the emergency services. She stayed with the victim while scanning the area for Giovanni.

Within a minute a paramedic was on the scene and the man was removed from the balcony. Bebe managed to tell the paramedics about the poison from two days ago before they left. Then everything happened so fast. Bebe went back to her team and tried to calm herself in anticipation of yet another improvised chat session. Her heart was still racing. Out of nowhere a bouncer and a Swedish policeman came up to her and asked her to come with them.

"I can't," she pleaded. "I'm on the air in a minute. When the show is done I'll assist you with all I can."

"You can forget about that," the policeman said. "You're a suspect in the attack on Karel Novak and Michal Wolonski. I need you to come with me this very instant."

She waved apologetic at the cameraman and went with the police.

"It's not me you're after," she explained. "The person you want is a Giovanni Genuardo. I saw him at the scene of both incidents. He's the one who blew the blow gun, not me."

"They say it takes one to know one," the bouncer said drily. "You were also there both times."

The policeman, a Detective Svartman, fortunately, didn't drag her to the police station but led her into one of the many small interview rooms not far from the balcony. There was hope she would be back with her team in no time, once all misunderstandings had been cleared up.

"I didn't do anything," Bebe assured him. "I was busy presenting a show when the dart was shot."

"That's exactly true," Svartman said. He was an overweight, middle-aged man with slightly unwashed greying red hair – exactly as she pictured Wallander from the books, not the TV show.

"On Tuesday, you bent down at the very moment when the dart flew, else it would have hit you. Today, you arrived on the scene just seconds after the dart flew and you pulled it out, so your fingerprints are all over it now. We find your behaviour and the circumstances naturally very suspect. You might not have operated the blow gun on Tuesday, but you knew it was going to be fired and you made sure you went down to give the culprit the opportunity to shoot Karel."

"I don't know Karel from Adam," Bebe said. "He stomped on my foot, else I wouldn't have gone down."

"But couldn't it be said that you were benefitting from the accident by achieving notoriety for yourself? This is the first time you get a shot at being a presenter and any drama around it can only bring more notoriety and higher viewing figures. It seems an obvious motive."

"I didn't deliberately bend down," Bebe said calmly but the policeman would have none of it. His face didn't move once.

"Mrs Bollinger, there are a lot of questions unanswered but they all revolve around you."

She took a deep breath and told herself to be calm.

"Giovanni Genuardo is a friend of a friend," she began. "I saw him both times in the restricted area. He shouldn't have been here. Today, I heard from my friend that Giovanni had left them in the auditorium and when I saw him I concluded that he is the blow-gun murderer. I found him and followed him but then I lost him and only got to see his nasty deed when it was done."

Still no movement from the Swedish policeman who sat on his chair like a stone statue.

"You would have us believe in a phantom murderer instead of the suspect that we have right in front of us? That's not all too convincing, I must say. They teach us at police school in our first few days that the easiest solution is often the right one."

Svartman scribbled in his notebook.

"What do you assume the motive of this Giovanni person is?" he asked.

"It must be professional envy, rivalry... I don't know."

"Then you would agree that his motives could be anything?"

She nodded: "Yes, of course."

"And wouldn't you agree that an elusive murderer, only seen by a suspect themselves – a murderer without a known motive – is of less interest to the police than someone who was seen on both occasions and had a motive for both?"

Bebe shrugged her shoulders.

"I guess I would have to agree with you," she admitted. "From your perspective that is a valid assessment. But I can assure you that I'm not interested in a career as presenter. I've been a singer for decades and I would never risk my career by murdering someone in front of hundreds of potential witnesses."

"That could be your alibi," Svartman said.

"Of course," she said.

"Would you mind if we had a look in your purse?" he asked.

"Of course, I don't mind," Bebe said. "The sooner we clear this drama up the better for all of us. And please note how calm I am. If I wanted to be on TV so badly, then wouldn't I be much more annoyed at you for keeping me from being on TV?"

"I'd call that overplaying your hand," he said. "This afternoon is only the rehearsal for tonight. The next run-through is the one televised. You have hours before actually missing anything worthwhile."

Darn, she hadn't thought this through.

The policeman put on rubber gloves, took her purse and emptied it on the table. And there in plain sight was a small wooden blow gun and a dart, exactly like the one she had seen in the Czech cameraman's thigh.

"That's not mine," she said with assumed authority, as the real thing was slipping away from her grasp. "Someone could have planted that in there while I was giving first-aid to the shot man."

"I have to take you to the station for an official statement – at least," Svartman said. He put the dart and blow gun into a clear plastic bag and labelled it, then stuffed everything else back into the purse.

"It isn't mine," she assured him.

"Let's see if we can find DNA or fingerprints," the policeman said. He seemed to have sympathy for her and softened a little. "I want to believe you," he added. "The sooner we get you to the station the sooner we can return you if your name is cleared."

"Thank you," she said. "Let's go."

She followed him out of the building. People were staring and taking pictures. Bebe wanted to sink into a hole in the floor for shame. She could be all over the news with this. She tried to stay as dignified as she could and smiled rigorously. Whether she could fool anyone with this was questionable. But she could hope.

In the police station, she decided to come clean with the police officer and told him about her role as hobby detective here in Malmö. She told him about the death threats, the accidents and Peter's injury.

"You see," she concluded. "Nicki or Tonia would benefit far more from this than me. I never would have had a shot at being the commentator. For Nicki, that's a great breakthrough, and Tonia told me she needs the job to pay her bills. If you look for motive, go there."

He noted it down.

"I'll check their alibis," he said. "Now to the DNA swab, so we can compare our findings on the blow gun. Fortunately, even without

159

fingerprints, there's always a bit of saliva and DNA in those tools. Very amateurish of your assassin, if he planted it in your purse."

"Indeed," she agreed.

She was made to wait in a small empty room while the lab sorted out the DNA.

"It will be four hours," the policeman had said. They still had her phone. Bebe thought it wise to look cooperative and didn't ask for it back. She was furious and frustrated, though. This was all a formality – the DNA test would clear her name and she would be able to go back to work. By then, of course, the show was over and her TV gig with it.

Who was Giovanni working for, she wondered. Was it Nicki, Tonia, Claudia De Poel or Krista? Then she returned to the other possibility: What if she herself had been the intended target and her bending down had been her lucky star and Karel's demise? But that didn't explain the attack on the Polish man. Was that also meant for her, even though she wasn't standing next to the victim at this occasion? Was it meant for Tonia? Maybe Bebe had to see the incidents in isolation: What if the spotlight in Amsterdam really was an accident which had then inspired the real killer? Then all recent victims or targets were presenters. Those hit on the balcony were standing right next to the UK team, so maybe the UK presenters were the target: Peter, Nicki, Bebe and Tonia, and from Saturday onwards: Alfie. Who would fancy their chances of replacing the commentators, and who believed that the combined TV audience was worth such a risk?

Precious time was being wasted here while the police were going through the motions. Were they even looking for Giovanni? She doubted it. Were they considering the possibility that Nicki might be behind all this? Nicki admittedly had never been on the balcony where the blow-gun incidents had occurred, she had been near Peter's 'accident', she could have been behind the spotlight crash in the Euro Café and she had so far benefitted the most. If she worked with Giovanni, then all angles seemed covered. Did the police take anything Bebe had said seriously at all? If only she could at least warn Beth and Tom. The waiting was so frustrating.

She hadn't been charged with anything, so she should be free to go. After what seemed an eternity but according to her watch had only been forty minutes, the policeman came back into the room.

"I'm sorry to keep you," he said. "I can bring you some magazines and food if you like?"

She put all her effort into sounding polite, grateful and agreeable.

"That would be very kind," she said.

A few minutes later he came in with a plateful of meatballs and a stack of magazines. Sadly, most of them were in Swedish, so she could only look at the pictures. A fair amount of the articles were about Eurovision, and given the amount of time she had to kill, Bebe studied each of the pictures long and hard. Maybe she could spot something in the background that would give her a clue. An hour later she was beginning to go mad with boredom. She gave up on the magazines, there had been nothing of relevance.

Svartman came back in again to check in on her.

"We've received a phone call from your TV station about your situation," he said. "They were pressuring us to let you go so you could carry on working. I was willing to let you go back to the arena, under my supervision, if you surrendered your passport and purse. We have strict instructions not to interfere with the contest and wouldn't want to disrupt the UK's transmission of the competition. Unfortunately for you that's no longer possible. Some of your friends showed at the police station to look for you. We took statements from them which worsen your case. The chief is no longer willing to take that risk."

"Worsen my case? How can that be?" she asked, more confused than worried, still.

"A Tom Rønnenfelt, or Tom Pillibi as you know him, provided Giovanni with a solid alibi for both events and when we checked the security list for the balcony access, Giovanni's name isn't on there once."

"But I saw him, he must have used a different name," Bebe insisted. She couldn't believe how quickly the man seemed to have given up on this possibility.

"I want to believe you, but the evidence points towards you," the policeman said.

"Can you check Nicki French and whether she has a connection to Giovanni, then? Please, she's the one benefitting most from all of this."

"How would she benefit from the death of a Czech TV man? It would make sense for her to get rid of you and Tonia, but not him. That points at you more than anyone else, regardless of how slim a motive that were. Are you sure you don't have anything to tell us? Lighten your mind?"

"No," she said and crossed her hands over her chest. "Is it time to ring a lawyer, yet?"

"If you're that sure about the DNA test I suggest it could wait another two hours before you do so. You won't get charged until then. For now, you're only assisting us."

She threw him daggers.

"I take that as a no then," he said and left the room.

Chapter 22

There was plenty of DNA on the blow gun, but none of it Bebe's. At midnight, she was released and escorted back to her hotel in Copenhagen. She was tired and drained from all the waiting and aggravation. Under normal circumstances she would have taken to the phone and given that Tom a piece of her mind. How could he possibly give Giovanni an alibi when he knew himself that the Italian had been on the balcony? Could Tom be in on this with the object of his affection? Was he some kind of nerd who wanted extra drama at his favourite show? Before the blow gun everything had been mere speculation. It had been Tom who was talking it all up and who had pushed Bebe to come to Malmö. She googled the Czech and Polish victims, wondering if there was something about them she had missed.

It turned out that the Czech presenter was a singer, though without the international glory. Who had stood near them when the shots had been made? Both times it had been Bebe and Tonia. And she scolded herself for her detective skills this afternoon. The second she had arrived at the scene of the murder she had focused almost entirely on the man on the floor and his wellbeing. Little good that it did to the man – she couldn't get the poison out of him. If the Czech presenter was anything to go by, then the poor man was probably dead by now. Instead, Bebe should have looked for the culprit and left the victim to other first-aiders.

She woke up at 6am, having fallen asleep dressed, on the bed with the TV on. Eurovision TV was showing the highlights of last night's semi-final. The result of the qualifiers and non-qualifiers from the second semi-final were more or less as predicted. It shot to Bebe's mind how Nicki and Leonard had handled the show without her being there. Tonia had been so nervous, Bebe doubted that Leonard would let her do the gig alone. Maybe the show had already been uploaded onto YouTube. She switched on her laptop and fired up the website. Indeed, the show coverage with Nicki French was available to view.

Bebe ordered room service and started watching the show. The producers had got a Swedish pop group who had some minor chart success in the UK in the past, to do the backstage interviewing, with Tonia. They were a fun bunch and probably a much better fit than Bebe, if she was being honest; although she hated to acknowledge that.

Nicki had found her match, though, which greatly satisfied Bebe. Against the three over-the-top enthusiastic presenters, Nicki had no chance of getting a word in edge ways.

At 7am, the phone went. It was the documentary crew giving her advance notice. Gratefully, she stopped the YouTube video and got herself ready for their arrival.

The team filmed her having breakfast and watching the YouTube clip, asked her a few questions about the incident with the Polish cameraman but then spoke at length about the group who had stood in for her. Then it was the usual questions about the songs that qualified and who would she put money on as the overall winner of Friday night's final.

There was no mention of her time at the police station.

"Aren't you going to talk about that in your programme?" she asked Morgan. She couldn't believe it.

"We decided to make a separate documentary on that issue," he replied. "The producers want a different team to look into that, so for now we're leaving these attacks out. It's all over the news anyway. Now we need to get you to the arena early for your jury duty. Expect even more security measures."

She was relieved to hear that this task hadn't been taken away from her. She had wondered if they would replace her after the arrest.

On the way to the arena, Bebe realised that she hadn't had a call from Beth. That was odd, to say the least. Hopefully, she'd be able to meet her during the rehearsals and catch up between the morning and the evening sessions.

Since today was the first rehearsal for the grand final with 26 instead of 17 songs and with more show blocks and voting simulations, this was going to be a long day. She'd be forced to watch all two run-throughs back to back.

The room for the UK jury was still empty when she got there but filled up pretty quick.

"Tonia has had a nervous breakdown," the tenor told Bebe. "I got a call from Magnus yesterday, panicking if I would be jury chair."

"It's such a shame she's not here, though. I liked having her around."

"I don't," the tenor said.

She didn't like his attitude. She waited for him to pick his seat and then chose a different one. The rapper and the businesswoman sat on the sofa, apparently now very chummy. They would have been the last people Bebe would have guessed to become friends.

The rehearsal had already started, but there were considerable preliminaries and introductions to go through before any of the songs would be played. There were a good fifteen minutes to go, and strictly speaking, the jurors didn't have to watch the first run-through if they so wished. It was an unwritten rule that everyone did, though.

While she was wondering who would be replacing Tonia as juror, Nicki walked through the door, came up to Bebe and hugged her.

"I'm so glad you're back," Nicki said. "I missed you yesterday."

"Thank you," Bebe said, unconvinced. "You had a great replacement for me, it hurts me to say. I'm sure the younger audience loved them."

"Not according to the opinion polls and ratings," Nicki said. "The viewers rated you much higher than them. So much so, that the producers are thinking of using you as replacement for Peter on Saturday night. He was meant to be interviewing guests in the ad breaks but he's still not well enough they reckon."

"What about you?" Bebe asked.

"I'm standby for Alfie should anything happen to him," she said. "God help me, but I secretly pray that his plane is delayed or something. I know I shouldn't be thinking this, but can you blame me?"

"Of course not. If Alfie doesn't come to harm, why wouldn't you hope for the opportunity," Bebe said, wondering if she could lure Nicki into a sense of companionship and get her to confess more.

"I'm only kidding," Nicki said. "People would hate me for doing it. They want Alfie for this but thanks for the support."

"Are you going to be jury spokesperson?" Bebe asked.

"No," Nicki said and laughed. "They asked, but my cousin co-wrote the Irish song, so I couldn't do it. They've got someone else now." She lowered her voice. "I'm sorry about that. They said you wouldn't be pleased."

Bebe's heart went racing. Which industry rival had they dug up now? Alison Moyet?

That moment the door opened. Bebe didn't turn around. She didn't even want to look at her.

165

"Bebe," she heard one of the few voices she would never forget in her lifetime. She froze. It wasn't Alison but equally bad: her ex-husband Richard Karajan.

The producer who had made Bebe's career, who had given her the beautiful name, had a child with her but then had traded her for a younger model the moment the record sales were dwindling: the love rat. She took a deep breath and forced a smile, then she turned around.

"Richard, my love," she said and got up to kiss him on the cheek. "So good to see you."

He kissed her back and roared with laughter.

"You can't possibly mean that," he said, "but thanks for being nice." He winked at her and grinned – far more benign than he usually did. It was confusing. They'd always bickered, mostly about Helena, the wild daughter that neither of them was able to tame. Bebe was grateful that Richard had chosen to be civil around her, at least for today. For a man almost 70 years old he looked amazing. He had lost the weight around his midriff, was blessed with few wrinkles and a moderate tan, rather than the overdone ones that men his age often sported. The grey suited him and made him far more distinguished than she knew to be the case.

"How's the wife?" came out faster than she had time to suppress.

"We're getting a divorce," Richard said. "That's why I'm so cheerful," he added and roared over his own joke.

"I take it from your happy demeanour that she hasn't left you for a younger model?" she asked and winked. She remembered that when they had been an item, they enjoyed a bit of banter like this. It was refreshing to see him smile and play along.

"You're right," he said. "Amicable separation this time."

"So, what are you doing here?" she asked. "I mean, how come you're in Sweden?"

"Well, what else than our delightful daughter and her troubles," he said and sat down next to Bebe. "Helena tried to fly back to the UK yesterday morning but was detained at Malmö airport for possession of small amounts of illicit drugs. They let her off with a warning but she had missed her plane and the airline wouldn't accept the old ticket. Her spineless boyfriend abandoned her at the airport and flew home without her. She tried to get hold of you but you wouldn't answer her calls, so I got on a plane and sorted her out."

"Thanks," Bebe said. "I'm not sure, though, that we should keep bailing her out."

"Absolutely right," Richard said. "I've picked her up and let her stay with me in my hotel, but I told her she'd have to earn the money for the flight home herself, exactly as you always told her, too. I thought it was worthwhile keeping her here for a few days to make her think about how that man abandoned her. She's back working at the Euro Café. Despite her wildness, they love her there."

Bebe was so pleased to hear this. She had been fighting with Richard over Helena ever since the girl was old enough to understand the concept of money and what it could do for her.

"Thank you," she said and sank back in her chair.

He squeezed her hand and gave her one of his intense puppy-eyed looks.

"We're gonna be good friends from now on," he said. "I promise."

She'd believe it when she saw it. Decades of fighting couldn't come to an end like that. She knew him too well to have great illusions.

Richard had been a businessman and a playboy too long for this to be convincing and somehow, that was okay... all they had to do was get through the next two days and then they could take it from there. It was sweet of him to do what he had done. For him that was plenty.

She explained to him the voting procedure and how he would have to add all the scores and make a top ten jury vote out of the figures.

"Sounds like you should be the one doing this, not me," he said.

"No, you're not getting out of the hard work," she said and put the pile of papers onto his lap. "Enjoy!"

The first song of the rehearsal – France – came onto the TV screen, so Bebe sat back down at her table and the businesswoman joined her and started making notes.

"You've got to hand it to the Swedes," the woman said after about the third song. "Since Tuesday there hasn't been one single hiccup onstage. Have you noticed?"

That was true, Bebe realised. It raised the question whether Giovanni would be striking once again. She texted Beth again to find out where she was and to suggest a meeting. Her friend had still not replied; her phone was switched off.

Act after act preformed without any issues: Moldova, Finland and Germany, suggesting that the focus of Giovanni's action had shifted to press or former contestants. Bebe had no doubt now that Alfie, Nicki and she were the only likely targets left and that tomorrow's dress rehearsal was odds-on favourite for Giovanni's next strike. She had to speak to the police again and warn them.

"Do you fancy grabbing a bite to eat?" Richard asked her when the final song had been performed on stage.

"Thank you but I have things to do," she said. She had two hours before the next run-through, the one she couldn't miss as juror. That was enough time to get to the police station and back. In the taxi, she remembered all the things she hadn't told the police the previous night: How Giovanni had been spotted in the Plaza, going to the 11th floor; where his official hotel was and so on. How could she have been so preoccupied to miss out all this information? It showed that she wasn't really cut out for the life of a detective. They should speak to Beth, instead of her.

Detective Svartman took note of her statement and thanked her for her patience the night before.

"I'll make sure we look into all this," he said.

"I'm not sure if I'm overreacting but my friend Beth Cooper, who was assisting me with the amateur detective work we were conducting, she seems to be missing. I've not been able to get hold of her and she was one of the people who shadowed Giovanni. I worry that he's done something to her."

Svartman nodded. She wasn't sure if it was to himself or whether he was agreeing with her theory. It was clear he felt still somewhat guilty over his treatment of her the previous day and tried not to upset her under any circumstances, and she was willing to use that to her full advantage. She gave him all of Beth's details – the address where she stayed, her phone number, described the Swedish boys who had kept her company and then emphasised how Tom's alibi for Giovanni might be tainted.

"I've got to run to go back to my jury duty," she said and stood up.

"Thank you, Mrs Bollinger," he said. "We appreciate your help."

Back at the arena she found Richard chatting intently with the other jury members, particularly the middle-aged businesswoman. So,

168

the leopard hasn't changed his spots and was already working on the next feast for his high sexual appetite.

"Bebe," Richard said. "I think you should meet this fine lady here."

He pointed at the woman. "This is Cora Messenger," he said. "She runs an event company and specialises in pop concert tours. I've been telling her about your recent comeback and she's very interested."

"So nice to meet you," Bebe said and offered her hand for a shake.

Cora took the hand but remained quiet.

"I apologise for Richard," Bebe said. "He seems to think that if he can hook me up with one of your tours he can get out of paying alimony. Fat chance for that."

Richard laughed.

"Anyway, I'll give you my agent's card, but let's not talk about this here."

Cora seemed relieved to hear that. Her body relaxed.

"So, Richard," she said. "Where on the Riviera is your house? We must be practically neighbours."

"The show's already started," Bebe said. "Why don't you sit here, Richard? Then you two can carry on chatting?"

"Thanks."

Bebe sat down on the desk next to the tenor and carried on with her assessment of the songs. This time it was much easier to concentrate. She felt good about Richard flirting with the businesswoman. She didn't want him back for herself, of course she could never trust him, and was more than content with the idea of her and him being good old friends. Something she had never thought would be possible.

Time went by rather quickly this time round. Again, there were no hiccups during the show and she composed what she thought was a fair scoring for all 26 songs. Bebe handed the sheet to Richard, who, together with the Swedish overseer, compiled the UK jury vote.

"That is now top secret," Magnus reminded them, before they were dismissed. The documentary team got her to chat about the experience. In the background Bebe could see that Cora had hung around, waiting for Richard. Eventually, the two wandered off together.

When the filming was over Bebe got her phone out to check for messages. Still no word from Tom or Beth, which was very worrying, but there was a voice message from Detective Svartman, asking her to come to the police station. It didn't sound very urgent, so she was tempted to ignore the call. Tonight was her last night in Sweden before the contest. The Euro Café and the entire town had to be awash with celebrities, producers and songwriters. She should be mingling with them and furthering her career prospects. She should speak to Leonard again and make sure she was the person to interview people during the big final live show the next day. If she didn't, they'd most likely get the Swedish trio to do it again, or Nicki. As if that woman hadn't gotten enough chances already...

Bebe took a taxi into town. When it stopped outside the Euro Café she suddenly felt a pang of guilt and asked the driver to turn around and take her to the police station instead.

"I've got some amazing news," Svartman said when she was led into his office. He pointed at the seat next to him. "Sit down."

She did as she was told and listened to Svartman's report.

"We found your friends Beth and Tom," he said.

"Where?" she asked, trying to process the information but feeling she failed.

"They were locked in a room on the 11th floor in the Plaza," he said. "They're both unharmed and in our recovery cells, waiting for the effects of a date rape drug to wear off, most likely administered by Giovanni Genuardo."

"I knew Giovanni was behind all this," she hissed under her breath.

"We don't know that for sure," Svartman pointed out. "Both victims can't remember anything at all. The room they were found in, however, was hired by the Italian press agency and occupied by a Fabio Nannini. Neither of those names are checking out with the Italian authorities and the press agency. Unfortunately, Mr Genuardo or however we want to call him for now, is still at large," Svartman said.

"How did you find my friends?" she asked.

"The roaming signals of Tom and Beth's phone both implied that they had last been close to the Plaza before their phones were switched off. We checked the hotel lobby security cameras during the time Beth's phone had been near the Plaza that night and checking the computer for the key card record on the 11th floor we could narrow our search to two rooms: 1104 and 1127. One room is occupied by Nicki French, the other by an Italian cameraman by the name of Fabio Nannini. You can guess where we found the victims."

"That's unbelievable," she said.

"What's even more incredible is that Fabio's or Giovanni's description fits that of the 'Tom' that came into the police station and gave 'Giovanni' the alibi. The man's got balls, I give him that. He walked in here with a fake press pass to give himself an alibi by pretending to be someone he had just locked into a hotel room."

"Poor Tom and Beth," Bebe said. "Are they both fine? Can I see them?"

"Give them some time," Svartman suggested. "Our plan of action is to lay a trap for Giovanni. Obviously, if he returns to the Plaza or his other hotel we'll have him arrested. It turns out though that he hasn't been to either of the hotels since he drugged and locked his victims in the Plaza. There must be a third place from which he operates."

"Do you think it's likely that he will carry out another attack?" Bebe asked.

"Highly," Svartman said. "If Thursday's was the last one he had planned, then he wouldn't have had to bother with drugging Beth and Tom. That move only bought him time. At some point he knew we would find them and the suspicion would fall onto him. We would have found video camera evidence somewhere to link him to the abductions. So, he must be after someone else, one last strike at least."

Bebe felt a shiver running down her spine.

"He's coming after me, isn't he?" she said.

"That's one of the possibilities," Svartman admitted.

"What are you going to do?" she asked.

"We would very much like you to help us laying a trap for him," Svartman said.

"What do you mean?"

"We want you to be on that balcony tomorrow, broadcasting live, which seems to be what Giovanni tried to stop you from doing."

"I think I agree," Bebe said. "And I'm concerned that it might be all Nicki's doing."

"Maybe," Svartman said. "However, there's also the remote possibility that Nicki was the target. She was scheduled to be on the balcony that day, but Peter's accident put her into a different location, something that hadn't been foreseen. Alfie Armstrong could also be a target. So, we have put police protection on all of you."

"Have you spoken to the producer about this?" Bebe asked. "He hasn't asked me yet whether I'd be willing to do the show, so I guess he's got someone else in mind for that."

"Leonard Wilson has been very cooperative," Svartman said. "In fact, he seemed relieved. Reading between the lines, he didn't think you'd be interested in being cast in the role of a presenter. Especially not after all the lip he gave you."

"What about police protection for tonight?" Bebe asked. "It's one of the most important nights of the Eurovision season and I would very much like to take advantage of it."

"I don't think that would be a good idea," Svartman said. "We can plant undercover officers on the balcony of the arena, but we couldn't guarantee your safety in the open streets. Not without giving away what we're doing."

"That's a shame," she said. "What if I was willing to take that risk?"

"We strongly advise you to control your urges," Svartman said. "You probably want to be rested for tomorrow's event in any case. You'll have to start early. There are plenty of after Eurovision parties tomorrow and by then it won't be too late to mingle and be seen. Hopefully, by then we'll have caught Giovanni and it will be a lot safer for you."

She gave in. Svartman was right, and she was terribly tired out from the long day. The entire week had been very taxing. She took a cab to her hotel and enjoyed her last evening in with Eurovision TV and champagne in the bath tub. Tomorrow was going to be a very long day. A message from her documentary team let her know that they would meet her at the arena at 9am. That meant an even earlier start for her. Leonard had also left a message, confirming her involvement and directing her to be at the arena at 8:30 for a briefing, costume and make-up.

Chapter 23

Bebe found herself in the make-up room allocated to the UK team at 8am. She'd tossed and turned all night, finally throwing in the towel as far as sleeping was concerned well before 6am. She wasn't worried about being tired today. There was too much excitement in every possible way waiting for her.

Bebe was more concerned about looking good for the huge TV audience. She spent a long time having her make-up done and then was told to try on various dresses Leonard had suggested. Bebe guessed they were Nicki's, who now had become a disembodied voice and didn't need them.

At 8.30am sharp, Bebe walked through the door of the commentators' box for the scheduled meeting with the directors and producers. She had settled for a dark red evening dress, reminiscent of the ankle-length style and colour schemes of the Seventies, although the cut was updated to fit contemporary, more body-tight norms. Nicki was in deep conversation with a very handsome young man with stunning strawberry-blond hair, fantastic bone structure in his face and even through his loose clothes it was obvious that he had an athletic body.

"That's Tristram," one of the producers explained in a low voice. "He's Tonia's husband… come to collect her belongings. She couldn't face coming here herself and he's a little emotional, too. It's very awkward."

Bebe sat down quietly and let Nicki do all the talking.

"I can see you have work to do," Tristram finally said and prised himself from Nicki's clutching hand.

"Thanks for letting me come here," he said.

"Take care," Nicki said, trying to hug him.

He escaped her arms and briefly caught Bebe's glance.

"Thanks, Bebe," he said. "Tonia always praised your genial spirit. I know she had a good friend in you."

Bebe gave him a long, heartfelt hug.

"Tonia is a special lady. When this is over, tell her we've got to catch up and go for dinner or something."

"Thank you, Bebe. She'd love that."

He looked awkwardly at Leonard.

"Would you mind terribly if Bebe went downstairs with me to the balcony to let me see where the attacks happened? Just so I can maybe understand Tonia's mental state better?"

Bebe looked at the producer for permission.

"If you can give her half an hour, Tristram," he said. "It's very unfortunate but we have to have this briefing now. I'm sure after that Bebe can find a few minutes to grant your wish. It's the least we can do."

Tristram nodded.

"I'll wait outside," he said and left.

Nicki closed the door shut.

"Poor guy," she said. "But talk about bad timing for a guided tour..."

"The police were questioning him and Tonia forever," the producer said, "talk about adding insult to injury. I feel so sorry for them."

"Of course," Nicki said. "We all do."

"Where's Alfie?" Bebe asked.

"He's doing interviews," Nicki explained. He briefed me on the show, as I'm his stand-in and asked me to brief you."

She sat down and shuffled her papers.

"So, let's start."

The instructions were simple, so much so that Bebe wondered why such a fuss had been made about them. Nicki and she had been doing the routine of interviewing and chatting plenty of times by now, only this time it was easier as they knew who they would be speaking to and had a ready set of questions.

"This is the real thing," Leonard said to Bebe. "No sudden disappearing acts and chatting away. You need to be watching the show and be ready to pick up what's happening on the stage at all times."

She looked at him and pulled her eyebrows together.

"You do know about the police, do you?" she asked. "I understand I'm here more at their suggestion, not because I was your first choice?"

"Yes," he said, holding her gaze. "And we both need to make the most out of that awkward situation and not mess it up."

Bebe was glad to get out of there, even though dealing with an emotional Tristram and showing him around was far from pleasant either.

"I know this isn't easy for you," Tristram said as they walked down the stairs.

"That's alright," she replied. "I know how important closure can be."

"It's not just that," he said. "I know she always moans about it, but Tonia loves the show."

On the balcony the documentary crew was waiting for Bebe already, as was the Live TV team.

"Guys, can you give us some privacy please?" Bebe asked them. "This is important. I promise we won't be long."

Both groups reluctantly granted her wish and left the balcony.

"So, we were standing right here," she said and pointed at the spot. "She was just telling me how nervous she was and how happy. The Czech TV crew kept moving into our space and there almost was a fight over this. Tonia was texting someone when their presenter stomped onto my foot. It was so painful, I tumbled to the floor and seconds later the presenter did the same. I assumed he had lost balance but then I noticed that he didn't move. We immediately got an ambulance and he was taken to hospital as fast as humanly possible. If he hadn't been so slim he might have withstood the dose. It probably wasn't meant to kill him."

"I wish Tonia would believe that," Tristram said. "She's in complete hysterics."

"So sad," Bebe said and squeezed his hand.

"Thanks," he said and built himself back up. "I better let you get on with the job. I've taken up far too much of your time as it is. Tonia would hate for me to get in the way of the show."

"Take care," she said and watched him leave.

He hadn't even reached the door when both of her camera teams stormed back onto the balcony and overran Bebe with instructions and preparations for the final dress rehearsal.

The arena was starting to fill with viewers and an atmosphere of excitable showbiz anticipation settled over the entire hall, not just in her little corner of it. Her professional instincts kicked in and Tristram was soon forgotten

When she had recorded a little snippet for the documentary and run through a fake interview with a stand-in to get the lighting ready for the real thing later, she even had a few minutes to spare and checked her phone.

Beth and Tom had both sent her lovely texts. They had recovered and were on their way over to the arena. Her ex- Richard had also sent her a text. That was new. He hardly ever even replied to hers. He had invited Helena to the show that afternoon, so they could watch Bebe on TV live tonight when the real thing was being transmitted. Svartman had also sent her a little message reassuring her that the undercover team was in place and watching her every move. That was an unsettling reminder of the danger she might be in, but she could tell herself that at least the suspects were known: Giovanni and Nicki; as were the likely victims: likely winners for the competition, and Alfie and Bebe.

Time passed far too quickly and the show began before Bebe felt ready for it. Alfie Armstrong, the official presenter for the final, briefly introduced Bebe to an imaginary audience, since the rehearsal wasn't seen by anyone but the producers. They chatted amicably about Bonnie and her chances and how Bebe had found the experience during the semi-finals. Bebe loved Alfie and his warm wit and had to be reined in by the producer to give shorter answers and let Alfie do more of the talking.

Bebe was impressed by the opening act the Swedish TV station had produced, the smooth transition from one act to the next and by how the audience loved the presenter, Petra Mede. Bebe made a mental note that her future public persona should contain some of Petra's cheeky wit; it would complement the naughty image she was now nurturing, yet it might take the edge off it.

Bebe's first guest was the Irish boy, who wasn't performing until much later in the show. He was nervous and Bebe feared for him and his results. The next time she was on, she spoke to a couple from Azerbaijan, who had won the contest two years previously. That was cut short for a brief tribute to previous UK winners.

The last person she was hosting was Daniela, from the Czech Republic, who was outrageously flirtatious.

"I heard about you and Olga," Daniela asked. "Is she a good kisser?"

"I'm not one to kiss and tell," Bebe said and laughed nervously. "Try kissing her yourself if you want to find out."

"Talk about the music," Leonard reminded her via the earpiece.

"How do you feel the rehearsal went for you?" Bebe asked. "Are you happy with your performance?"

"Yes," Daniela replied. "I couldn't really do much on the stage with my cast but the background dancers did a great job."

"Krista must be fuming that you had such a sexy show," Bebe said. "She probably hoped she'd be the only act to be so provocative."

"Well, it is what it is," Daniela said. "Sexy, prude, artistic – we all have a limited amount of staging options and there'll always be unintended similarities and overlaps."

Alfie took over the interview, confessing that he had bought and loved Daniela's album. He was a very fast talker and left Bebe with little to say. Her nerves started to play up. Daniela's presence reminded Bebe that there was going to be another attack, the time for it was coming rapidly. Giovanni had not much time left to do the deed. It would have to be done this afternoon if the prize for Nicki was being commentator for the live show tonight. Alfie was safe in his commentator's box, which could be locked. Bebe on the other hand was fair game and she could only hope that the undercover team was capable enough to protect her. Thank God they knew who to look out for.

"You're doing such a grand job," Nicki said to Bebe when the segment was over and the show on the stage behind them had resumed with the last set of songs.

"I'm not so sure about that," Bebe confessed. "I'm more comfortable doing a gig and talking about what I know. I don't care for many of the songs and find it hard to keep faking interest. Doing it once is fine, but two, three, four times on the trot... Next time I come here it will be as performer or not at all."

"Darling," Nicki said. "When you reach our age, you have to be grateful for what you get. Eurovision isn't anyone's first choice – compared to the Grammys for example, but it pays the bills and can lead to more in the future. Let's both make the most of it."

"Of course you're right," Bebe admitted and looked around the balcony as if to assess whether this world could be a new direction in her career. She spotted Daniela, talking to the Czech team next to her. They had a new presenter, she noticed: taller, younger and with dark

177

curly hair. Something about him looked familiar but with the camera in the way it was hard to make out where she knew him from.

"I was talking to Tonia's husband earlier," Nicki said. "Tonia would have loved to be here."

"Yes, I got that impression from her, too," Bebe said. "Poor girl."

Daniela seemed to have finished filming. Flashbacks of the falling spotlight that nearly had killed her and Nicki came flooding to Bebe's mind. If Giovanni was here that would be the perfect moment to kill a few birds with one stone, she thought. She scanned the area round her for policemen or Giovanni. Didn't the new Czech presenter stand a bit like Giovanni did, always swinging his hip to the left? The man stood with his back to her and hiding behind the camera, so she couldn't see properly, but she was becoming convinced that this was him. It was a good place from which to discreetly use a blow gun. The camera shielded him from one side, and people on his other side would mistake the weapon for a microphone, if they saw it in his hand at all. Nobody would notice, nobody would recognise his face with the wig and most importantly, once he had done his deed, organisers, security and police would not want the media around. Whenever a security incident occurred press were shoed away, so Giovanni could disappear from the scene easily. And there he stood, a few metres from his potential targets. Bebe had to do something, but what? Did she have time to call Svartman and wait for him to alert the undercover agents? Daniela was chatting away to the Polish team now – flirting with their star Olga right at the edge of the balcony. All it would take for Giovanni were two shots from the blow gun and the competition would be two favourites down.

Or, one shot from him and the UK would be one more presenter down, if that were the target.

She couldn't just stand there and wait for something to happen. She knew that there were people watching her every move, which suddenly gave her unexpected courage. It should be possible for her to challenge the man. If he was Giovanni, then the police would be able to arrest him before he could harm anyone. She would have the element of surprise on her side, wouldn't she? Anything was better than to do nothing.

Bebe walked up to the man and tapped him on the shoulder.

"Excuse me," she said. "You look awfully familiar. What's your name?"

He turned around. She scrutinised his features. It could be him, but she couldn't be sure. She rarely had seen Giovanni's eyes as he had always worn sunglasses, and the man in front of her also wore a thick beard, which Giovanni never had.

All she noticed was that the cameraman turned with him and the lens was pointed at her. Was the blow gun hidden in the camera? She had a sense of foreboding and quickly stepped forward to get out of the line of fire. She leaned into the cameraman a bit too hard, lost balance and stumbled, falling forward into his arms. The man struggled but then lost his balance and toppled over, crashing to the floor. He had managed to hold the camera up, saving it from harm but it hit Bebe hard on the forehead.

"Ouch," she screamed and held the spot to ease the pain.

"Are you crazy?" the cameraman shouted.

Lying next to him she noticed that his hair and beard were genuine. It wasn't Giovanni after all.

She was lucky not to have caused damage to the equipment. People came to their rescue and helped them up.

Bebe was so embarrassed. As she brushed the dust from her dress she thought she had spotted Giovanni in the crowd, but his head disappeared before she had been able to see clearly. She had lost one of her contact lenses when she hit her head on the camera and her vision was blurred. Maybe her mind was blurring, too.

"My contact lens," she shouted and went back to the floor searching, pushing people around her out of the way the best she could. The Czech team had made a point of stepping away from her as if she was crazy, while the documentary team was too busy filming the scene. She didn't care. She'd make sure that this would never air.

"I'll help you," she suddenly heard a familiar voice. Tristram bent down next to her and illuminated the floor with the torch on his mobile phone.

She sat back and let him get on with the search.

"Thanks," she said. "I'm a complete mess today."

"That makes two of us," he said and gave her one of his sad puppy smiles.

He found the lens and handed it to her.

"Do you have a cleaning solution for it with you?" he asked.

She nodded and grabbed her handbag. A true gentleman, he opened it for her and helped her sorting out her vision.

"Bonnie and her manager were kind enough to take me backstage and show me around," he explained. "I can understand a bit better now what motivated Tonia."

"I think I saw the murderer," Bebe blurted out. Tristram's eyes narrowed.

"What did you say?" he asked.

"The suspect," she said. "The police have a suspect and I thought I've just seen him."

"Where?" Tristram said. "You've got to tell the police."

"I was going to," she said. "I got distracted by the fall."

"I'll call the police right away," he said. "Do they know the suspect, so they know what he looks like?"

"Yes," she said. "They know him well. His name is Giovanni."

"You be careful," Tristram said and then he rushed off.

"What's the matter with you?" Leonard asked Bebe. "Are you alright? Did you have a dizzy spell or something?"

It was too much to explain and too embarrassing. The man hated her already.

"Old age," Bebe said and tried a convincing laugh.

Chapter 24

When the last song had been performed Alfie and Bebe were on air again, chatting about the show's highlights. Bebe found it hard to concentrate after all that had happened. Leonard gave her a serious telling off when it was done, threatening to replace her with the next best thing that came his way if she didn't get her act together.

She apologised and walked off. She had an hour-and-a-half before the live final was going to be shown. The police still hadn't turned up, but then again, some of them were already here and maybe the sighting of Giovanni was nothing new to them. Beth and Tom were unable to visit her on the balcony, due to increased security restrictions for the final. She was alone with her worries.

She tried Svartman's phone to get some reassurance that the police were taking this still seriously.

"We've found Giovanni," Svartman said.

"You did?" she yelled. "And you didn't bother to tell me?"

"You were busy making TV," Svartman said. "We had to wait until the show was over. I expected a debriefing from one of our agents any minute and was going to call you then."

"Never mind," she said. "What about Giovanni? Has he confessed?"

"Unfortunately, he's not in a condition to confess," Svartman said. "The idiot either shot himself with the blow gun or got silenced by his accomplice. To me, it looks like a stupid accident. We found him on the mezzanine level, inside a cubicle, lying on the floor; the blow gun in his hand and a dart in his thigh. Hopefully, not a lethal dose but it will take a while before he comes round."

"That means we can't be sure who he was working for or with," Bebe said.

"No," Svartman said. "Now that we got him he's sure to talk when he comes round. All of our suspects are accounted for and can't get anywhere near you or any of the singers."

"All suspects?" she asked. "Are you quite sure? What about the crazy fans I mentioned to you?"

"Those suspects are being strictly shadowed tonight. They have tickets to watch the show over in the Euro Café, courtesy of the broadcasters. You can relax now."

She couldn't relax, though.

"What about Nicki?" she said. "You never regarded her as a serious suspect. If something were to happen to Alfie, she'd be quids in?"

"Not quite," Svartman said. "If it was her, her accomplice has just been immobilised. Of course, we will be watching her."

Bebe wasn't entirely convinced but she had to accept the situation as it was. The auditorium was filling for the last time. This was the real show, this was where the alleged billion people tuned in to watch. Only now did most UK viewers follow the competition on TV, which meant that she had to give it her best shot possible. One more time pretending, just the one more time.

The show began and she could hear Alfie welcoming the UK viewers via her earpiece.

"I've also got former contender Nicki French with me today," he said. "Here is a brief clip from her performance thirteen years ago."

Bebe's heart was racing. Nicki was in the commentators' box?

"We also have singing legend Bebe Bollinger backstage," Alfie continued. "Not everyone will remember her but those who do, remember her so fondly."

"Welcome Bebe," Alfie said, the camera showing it was recording. She was shaking.

"Hello Alfie, hello Nicki," she said. "And hello everyone. I wish I could make you all feel the tension and excitement we have had this last week here in Malmö. Every shop, every street, every corner of this beautiful city is breathing Eurovision. It's such a buzz."

She was sweating.

"Some countries need to break for TV adverts," Alfie explained. "We're not showing the adverts on UK TV so when that happens Bebe will be interviewing a few guests for us. We'll have Bonnie Tyler and many others to talk to, so don't switch off."

Behind her Bebe could hear the famous "Hello Europe", the traditional greeting for the show.

"Watch out for Nicki," Bebe said, hoping that Alfie was still able to hear her. "She's after your job and we're already one presenter down."

Leonard made a cutthroat gesture towards her. Had she still been live?

"Haha," Alfie said. "I will watch her closely."

"And Bebe, after Alfie you're my next target," Nicki said and joined him laughing.

"Anyway," Alfie said. "Over to the lovely Petra Mede."

"What on Earth are you playing at?" the producer said.

"I'm sorry, but I didn't know we were still on air. I'm genuinely worried that Nicki had something to do with all this."

"That's ridiculous," Leonard said. "What a pathetic excuse for a blunder, too. I know I shouldn't have agreed to all this. You don't have what it takes. This was the last time I'm working with an amateur."

During the second interval things picked up again. Bonnie's manager was there to speak about how they had come to accept the UK's offer to perform and how the journey had been.

"The only downside to this gig is Bebe," the manager joked.

She tried to look surprised but her beaming smile gave her hopes away and she wasn't disappointed.

"Yes," Alfie said. "Bebe has given a stunning performance earlier this week at the Big Six party. Traditionally the prequalified countries host a big gig and they often cross borders and sing their songs together or even produce competing versions of each other's songs. Bonnie was foolish enough to let Bebe perform her song, and look what it got her.

He played the clip.

"Are you going to sue her or take her under contract?" Alfie joked.

"We're still undecided," the manager said.

"And Bebe I'd like to thank you for the warning. Nicki spilled drinks over my notes, nearly pushed me off my chair and probably has spiked my drink. You were absolutely right, it's murder in the commentators' box."

"I told you," Bebe played along.

"Well, we'll let you two negotiate a record deal and go back to the show," Alfie said.

"Thank you," Bebe said to the manager when the camera was switched off.

"Don't thank me. Thank Bonnie," the manager said. "I didn't want to do this, but she persuaded the producers to do it and I didn't have a choice. The record label will sue you for your last penny if you release that song, you understand?"

"Of course," she said. "The thought never occurred to me. Give my love to Bonnie and Tristram."

"Who's Tristram?"

"Tonia Carmichael's husband," she explained. "I thought he was backstage with you."

"Oh him," the manager said and rolled his eyes. "Yes, he's with us."

He turned and left the balcony without a goodbye. Bebe couldn't believe the discrepancy between his charming public persona live on TV and the rudeness off screen.

"I need a comfort break," she said to Leonard and made her way to the commentators' box. She had to find a way to warn Alfie about Nicki. She should have done so long ago. Svartman had been wrong for proposing that they focus on Giovanni alone. Now that he had been captured, the mastermind would have to act on her own and every minute of the show passing was more of an incentive for Nicki to act and to get Alfie out of the way. Bebe doubled her pace: she hoped she wasn't too late.

When she got to the commentators' box security staff made her wait. Alfie was currently on air and only when the next song had begun was she allowed in. He looked displeased to see her but the thing Bebe noticed was that Nicki wasn't there.

"She's popped to the ladies," Alfie explained. "Maybe you can wait for her outside?"

"You've got to be careful with Nicki," Bebe said and sat down. "I truly mean it. There have been a lot of accidents lately. Look at Peter's ominous fall, and Tonia turned hysterical over the 'fainting presenters'. That wasn't an accident but murder."

"Nicki told me all that," he replied. "Bebe we're in the middle of a live show. There's no time for this."

"Aren't you worried that Nicki's behind all this to get your job?"

"Absolutely not," he said and laughed. "You watch too much TV. Nicki and I are good friends. I got her this gig."

"There are no reliable friendships in the show business," Bebe warned him. "You must know that."

"Of course I do," he said. "But I can put your mind at rest anyway. Nicki has been really unwell all evening."

"What do you mean?"

He looked nervously at his watch and on the stage.

"I think it's food poisoning. If anyone is going off air tonight, it will be her. Now go and let me get on with it, okay? I'll speak to you on air after Bonnie's song."

Bebe left the box and hung around to wait for Nicki. The security guards kept an eye on her, making the waiting very uncomfortable. When Nicki didn't appear after a few minutes Bebe went to the ladies to see if she was indeed ill or maybe was only making this up so that she could continue her evil deeds.

The ladies room was empty. Nicki was nowhere to be seen. Did that mean that Alfie wasn't her target? Maybe Nicki really thought she could benefit from being on air with the well-liked chat show host more than doing so on her own. Was Nicki downstairs, waiting for an opportune moment to do away with Bebe instead? That way she would replace Bebe and be seen on TV, not just heard.

Her phone went.

"Where on Earth are you?" Leonard shouted at her. "Come back immediately!"

"I'm on my way," she said but first she dialled Svartman's number to tell him all about her suspicions.

"Nicki is not behind all this," the police officer told her. "She's collapsed and is in the lobby, waiting to be taken to hospital."

"Oh." Bebe said. "That's awful."

"We've got some new information that might clear up the case anyway," he said. "We found a room key on Giovanni and linked it to his actual hotel room, not the ones Tom and Beth knew about. He had a Swedish pay-as-you-go phone which we've had a good look at. The number he most frequently called is another Swedish pay-as-you-go phone, which is active right now at the Eurovision arena area. It's someone backstage. All of our men have moved there to find the person owning it."

"Tristram Carmichael." The words left her mouth before she was thinking them. "It all makes sense now."

"No, it doesn't," Svartman said. "His wife wouldn't benefit, she's at home on sedatives."

"I don't know about that part but the blow gun was meant for me," Bebe explained. "It must be him, avenging her or continuing her game. He's with Bonnie and her team."

"I'll send someone to check him out," Svartman said, "and I'll send someone back to the balcony in case he's coming for you. You be careful."

He didn't have to tell her that.

She rushed back downstairs, got to her position and looked around the balcony. Was she safe? Could she trust the police to protect her if she was under threat? What if Tristram was working with someone else? Or, if Tristram wasn't the person they were looking for? Than it could be anyone. Daniela's performance was due in a few minutes. The Dutch song had just finished and soon it would be Bonnie's turn. Bebe's phone rang.

"We've detained Tristram," Svartman said. "He doesn't have the phone on him. That's still live."

"Then watch the stage," Bebe said. "It all started with Daniela and she's on next."

"Yes, we've got it covered," Svartman said.

"And watch Bonnie," she added. "She was the other credible target."

"I know," Svartman said. "We're sending you more people, plus Beth and Tom as backup. It looks more and more likely that this is a general vendetta against the UK. If I were you, I'd consider asking the producer to let someone else do your job. It really isn't safe."

"Over my dead body," Bebe said. "I've missed one TV opportunity because of this and I won't miss another. At my age these chances don't come around so often. You just make sure your men are in place and together we'll get the culprit and present the show."

"I thought you might say that," Svartman said. "Good luck."

Bebe had another look around, but she couldn't see anything or anyone suspicious. Every person was busy with the job at hand. So, she watched Daniela's performance, constantly scanning the stage for something that looked suspicious. From her position she could see further than the TV cameras did and every time she saw a technician move she nearly jumped. Where were all those policemen Svartman had assured her would protect the Czech singer?

"There you are," she heard Beth's voice behind her.

She turned around and hugged her friend. Tom was also there.

"Hello darling," he said.

"God, I've missed you," Bebe said. "And I'm so sorry about Giovanni," she added, directed at Tom.

He shrugged. "He was too good to be true," Tom said. "There's no faster cure than a date rape drug from the person you thought you loved. Don't worry. I'm over it. After all, we've only been going out for a week."

"I'm glad you see it that way," she said.

She turned to Beth.

"How are you feeling?" she asked.

"Bit like a bad hangover," Beth said. "Dazed and slow."

"They shouldn't have let you out then," Bebe said. "You two should go home and rest."

"And miss all the action? I wouldn't dream of it," Beth said. "I came to Malmö to do a job and I intend to finish it."

"It's no longer necessary," Bebe said. "The police are finally taking things seriously."

"I don't think so," Beth said. "Svartman talks about the many men he's got behind the stage but it's only four altogether, including him. That's not the number you need for a comprehensive coverage. The stage is not safe, you're not safe. The show shouldn't go on with a murderer on the loose."

"I thought they had a trace on the phone Giovanni was calling?" Bebe said. "Why hasn't that helped them to catch the culprit?"

"The phone was found backstage," Tom said. "No fingerprints. We're back to square one as far as that is concerned."

"Then you two need to go backstage and help the police," Bebe said.

"No, we need to stay here with you," Beth said.

"Nonsense," Bebe insisted. "I'm perfectly safe with the two policemen assigned to me. The phone being found backstage means that's where the attack will happen. Go!"

"Okay," Beth agreed and took Tom downstairs.

Daniela had finished her song by then and Bebe switched on her earpiece in preparation for the interview to come.

"Next up is Romania," Alfie said. "An interesting performance, to say the least."

"Yes," Bebe heard Nicki's voice. "The performance as well as the staging. I'm curious to find out what people say about this. Please use our hashtag on Twitter to let us know your thoughts."

How had Nicki recovered so quickly? Hadn't she collapsed? What was going on here?

187

"All I'll say is: He's got a talent," Alfie said. "Whether or not it's a winner, see for yourself."

The music started playing but Bebe could still hear Alfie and Nicki talking in the commentators' box.

"I'm glad you're feeling better," Alfie said. "It wasn't quite the same without you."

"I wouldn't have missed it for the world," Nicki said. "I'll just go and freshen up. I'll be back for Bonnie's song."

Bebe panicked and called Svartman, but he didn't pick up. She was on her own.

"Enough of this," Leonard said and took the phone off her. "You're here for a job, not to chat with your friends."

She protested but to no avail. She had to speak to one of the undercover agents.

"Like it or not, I need to go to the rest room," Bebe said and headed for the door. As she looked around the corridor she saw Tonia coming towards her, arms wide open.

"I don't want to be rude, but what are you doing here?" Bebe asked.

"I couldn't stay away," Tonia said. "I missed it so much, and I got cabin fever in my room, so I came here to be with Tristram."

"Isn't he downstairs with Bonnie?" Bebe asked.

"I think you're right. I can't get hold of him, maybe his phone conked out. I just came to wish you good luck," Tonia said, hugging Bebe and patting her back cordially.

"When I spoke to him earlier, Tristram told me what you said about me. I wanted to thank you personally and wish you luck."

"Really?" Bebe asked.

"Yes," Tonia said. "I was so upset about everything. I must confess when I was thinking about the whole thing, I had my suspicions about you, you know, that maybe you ducked on purpose and all that."

"I see."

"I feel much calmer now," Tonia said. "They've given me lovely sedatives, so I came to wish you good luck."

"Well enjoy," Bebe said, anxious to warn the security men of Nicki. "I've got to go back to the balcony."

"I've got to dash back to the commentators' box," Tonia said, "I want to say hi to Alfie."

Bebe heard the Romanian song approach its end with the traditional key change for the last chorus. She rushed back to her position on the balcony.

"Leonard, tell the police to watch out for Nicki," she said. "She's left the box again. This would be her moment."

Leonard nodded and made a phone call. Whether he was humouring her or actually believed her she couldn't tell; probably the former.

"The last two slots are the most important ones. Don't mess them up, okay?" he said when he returned.

"Okay."

In her earpiece Bebe could hear Nicki talking to Alfie. What a relief. She actually liked Nicki and hated that someone she respected had to be considered a murderer.

"Now the moment you've all been waiting for has come," she heard Alfie say. "The UK's very own entry, our wonderful Bonnie Tyler."

"Bonnie is amazing," Nicki said. "Her song tonight should change our recent poor luck on the scoreboard."

Bebe's vision started to blur and she was feeling dizzy.

"I remember how it felt to go on that huge stage with a TV audience that big," Nicki said. "I was so excited but also so nervous. Of course, for Bonnie that's nothing new at all."

Bebe held on to the balcony but her feet were giving way and she sank to the floor. Leonard was coming over to her and tried to speak to her, but she could hardly make out what he was saying. Then everything went black around her.

Chapter 25

When Bebe came around she was on the floor in the corridor, Beth, Tom and a paramedic beside her.

"What happened?" Bebe asked.

"You fainted," Beth explained. "You were out for a few minutes."

She tried to get up.

"I'm meant to do an interview," she said.

"Too late," Beth told her. "Tonia did that for you. I'm sorry you missed that chance, but you can relax now."

"And Bonnie?" Bebe asked. "Is she okay?"

"Yes," Tom said. "And she gave a brilliant performance with no problems at all. The attacks and death threats have all been cleared up."

"How so?" Bebe asked.

"Remember Jan Ola, the rude Norwegian?"

"Yes?"

"He split from his lover in a very unamicable way. In revenge, the dumped guy spoke to the police and produced diaries as evidence that Jan Ola had planned to get publicity and notoriety for the show. He was behind the spotlight crashes and death threats. He wanted the contest to become the focus of a criminal investigation with huge media attention. He was worried that the contest might die away."

"So who was Giovanni working with then?" Bebe asked. "It's a UK presenter thing, it must be. And I just thought that Nicki was innocent."

"She is," Beth said. "Svartman's team found several suspicious substances in Giovanni's hotel room. One of them was pulverized beta-blocker. If ingested, it can cause fainting and the symptoms that Nicki experienced earlier. The same symptoms you are experiencing right now. We suspect that the water bottles left in the commentators' box were laced with it. Some of the bottle tops show signs of tampering and you and Nicki both have been drinking from that water."

"What about Alfie?"

"He hasn't consumed any soft drinks."

"Well we'll see about that when Giovanni has recovered. How is he?"

"He's dead," Tom said. "He died an hour ago."

"Then how do we know who he worked with? How did Giovanni manage to get into the commentators' box? And why do we think he did all of this? You must know, Tom. You spent more time with him than any of us."

"I once took him to the commentators' box with me," Tom admitted

"And what about his motive?"

"I can only assume it's to do with his mother," Tom said. "I've asked a few friends of mine about her story at Eurovision. She missed out on victory to the UK and received no points from the UK jury either, which she always considered a deliberate and tactical move.

"But he lives in Scotland. Why move to a country he hates?"

"After his mother's death his father remarried and they moved to Inverness. Much to Giovanni's chagrin."

"So, this is it?" Bebe asked. "Everything's over?

"Yes," Beth said. "Everything that Giovanni did was aimed at the UK and its representatives, singers or presenters, to get back at us for his mother's heartache."

"He hated Alfie and his commentary of the show as much as he hated how back in the UK everyone is poking fun at the competition. We had a few heated arguments about that," Tom confessed. "I never thought much off it, because it's such a well-worn argument. Little did I know he had such personal grief with the country.

"Case closed," Beth said. "I think you owe Nicki a huge apology, Bebe."

"I guess I do."

Bebe made a fast recovery, just like Nicki had earlier. When she felt well enough to get up she joined Nicki and Alfie in the commentators' box. The Europe-wide voting process had started and the TV was showing a re-run of all the songs with the numbers to call to vote."

"I'm so sorry," Bebe said and hugged Nicki.

Nicki hugged her back.

"You've got something on your back," Nicki said, pulled a small piece of sticky tape from Bebe's back and handed it to her.

Bebe looked at it and let it fall to the ground.

"I've been recovering on the corridor outside," Bebe said. "I must have picked it up when I was lying on the floor there."

"Anyway, don't worry," Nicki said. "We were all thrown off course by the confusion between attacks on singers and presenters. I don't blame you."

"Indeed," Bebe said.

"I'm sorry you missed out," Nicki said. "It was fun working together."

"Maybe we can do it again next year," Bebe said. "Now, I better get out of your way."

"Yes," Nicki replied.

Bebe said a mental goodbye to the show and reunited with Beth and Tom on the mezzanine level.

"You've got something stuck to your foot," Tom observed and bent down to get it off.

"A nicotine patch," he said.

"Let me see," Bebe said. He handed it to her.

"Oh that? Nicki just pulled that off my back," she said. "I thought it was just some sticky tape that I've been lying on when you put me to recovery here in the corridor."

Beth put a plastic glove on and put the sticker in an evidence bag.

"I'll have that analysed," she said.

"You know it's funny," Bebe said. "I'm not altogether sure I did drink any water in the commentator's box. But if I remember correctly, before I collapsed I spoke to Tonia and she patted my back when we were hugging."

Beth got her phone out.

"Svartman?" she asked. "Could you please check the security records and find out all of Tonia and Tristram Carmichael's movements backstage tonight?"

She told him about the nicotine patch and the possible implications.

"He'll find out for us," she said when she had hung up.

"What would that prove?" Bebe asked.

"Only what we already know," Beth said. "Between Tristram and Tonia they had ample opportunity to spike the water in the commentators' box. Both were in there. Tristram might even have done it right under our noses. By planting the beta blockers in Giovanni's flat and killing him off, suspicion wouldn't have fallen on anyone else. Tristram was able to plant the accomplice phone

192

backstage, diverting our attention to the stage, so Tonia could come in and stick the nicotine patch on you, once she realised that you hadn't drank any of the poisoned water. You fainted, and she could sweep in and rescue the show, despite her illness. So Giovanni had an accomplice after all, right under our noses."

"But why did Tonia do it?" Bebe asked. "She could have simply taken the job when it was offered to her."

"And pale in comparison to you and Nicki? Leonard said himself that the two of you had incredibly good approval ratings," Beth said. "You two were too much of a competition for her. Beta blockers can be lethal. Had either of you drank higher doses it could have been the end of you."

"How cunning."

"I can't believe I'm saying this, but I really enjoyed this case," Beth admitted. "Maybe my days at crime solving aren't quite over yet, after all."

"Good," Bebe said and gave her a hug. "I'm sure with all his connections Tom can hook you up with a job or two."

A few minutes later, Svartman appeared on the scene.

"Where's Tonia?" he asked.

"She's still on the balcony, chatting with the producer," Beth said. "I haven't let her out of my sight."

"I think we're ready to make an arrest," he said. "Tristram was backstage at the precise moment we can link the accomplice phone there, not a moment before."

Beth handed him the evidence bag with the nicotine patch.

"That's the patch she put on Bebe's back before Bebe collapsed. We only need to check it for her DNA."

"Let's close this case."

Tonia was on a complete high when the four of them approached her on the balcony.

"What a fantastic night this has been," she said. "I'm so glad we got this all sorted in the end."

Svartman held up the evidence bag with one hand and got his handcuffs ready with the other.

Tonia's face gave her game away immediately once she recognised the nicotine patch.

"And I thought we were friends," Bebe said. "Shame on you."

"I'm arresting you on suspicion of conspiracy to murder, possession and illegal administering of controlled drugs, obstructing the course of justice and probably a few more charges when I have time to think about it," Svartman said.

"No, no, no!" Tonia yelled. "No!"

"Oh yes," Bebe said. "Do you really think you were going to get a career out of this?"

"Why not?" Tonia said defiantly. "Nicki does, and I was well on my way when you came along. Damn you Bebe. You ruined it all."

"You did that all yourself," Bebe said.

"Let's go," Svartman said and led her off. Beth went along with him to assist.

"So, you did it again," Tom said.

"I guess," Bebe replied. "Although I had a lot more useful help than last time."

"Let's go to the Euro Café and celebrate," Beth said.

Bebe sipped from a glass of champagne in the VIP section of the Euro Café.

"I hope you're not disappointed about your 19th place," Bebe said to Bonnie, who shared the bottle with her.

"Oh don't be silly," Bonnie laughed. "It's an over-used phrase here but Eurovision is an extraordinary experience and it's a privilege to get a chance to be part of it. I don't regret a minute of it."

"That's my girl," Bebe said.

"Next year it's you turn," Bonnie said.

"Who knows?" Bebe replied and laughed. She looked around the room full of musical ambition and talent. She felt lucky to be part of it. Tom seemed already recovered from his heartache and had a great time with Nicki and Peter Beatle, knocking back shots by the bar and making plans with them for future journalistic Eurovision projects. If Bebe wasn't mistaken Beth had left with Olga after hours of intense flirtatious conversations. The Polish singer had not made the final but seemed to have taken it in her stride. From her lively demeanour you wouldn't have known.

Richard was also here with Cora, keeping an eye on Helena, who not only appeared to be relatively sober but also genuinely to be enjoying herself.

194

"Excuse me," a tall beefy man around her own age said to Bebe in a Scandinavian accent.

"Yes?" she asked. "Can I help you?"

"That you most certainly can," he said. "My name is Thomas and I'm a composer."

"And?"

"I heard your version of 'Believe in Me' and think it's marvellous."

"Thank you."

"I actually write rock music," Thomas said. "Rock doesn't sell that well. I need to work with people like you who can transform my melodies into other genres as it were. I compose them as rock and in a few years, when the more popular versions of my songs have ceased to sell, I get rock bands to release 'their rock version' of 'my' songs on their albums."

"Brilliant!"

"So, what do you say? Would you like me to produce your next album?"

From the London Herald:

Brave British Singer Brings down Murderous Trio at Eurovision

Singing legend Bebe Bollinger became an overnight hero in Europe for solving a murder mystery that has puzzled authorities for weeks. While a worldwide audience of one billion viewers were deciding on who should take home the crown at this years' song contest in Malmo, UK TV presenter Tonia Carmichael, her husband and an accomplice attempted a series of deadly attacks on the journalists reporting for the UK network in a move to revive Carmichael's stagnated career. Earlier in the week she pushed commentator Peter Beatle down a flight of stairs. He was admitted to hospital and has been out of work since. Their somewhat clumsy accomplice, however, missed his target twice and in the run-up to Saturday night's final accidentally killed a Czech TV presenter and a

195

Polish cameraman, before the Carmichaels managed to poison Nicki French and Bebe Bollinger on Saturday. While in the actual competition UK entrant Bonnie Tyler sadly was beaten into a mid-field ranking on the leader board, Bebe Bollinger proved resilient to the attack on her person and managed to outsmart her scheming rival Carmichael and even helped with the arrest.

This is not the first time Ms Bollinger has been involved in crime solving. Last spring, she assisted the police in solving a murder in Carmarthenshire, in Wales.

Ms Bollinger has recently enjoyed revived public interest after a clip of her appearance on the Peter Beatle show went viral and even entered the charts. She attended the European song competition with her daughter to support British interest at the event and both of them are still in Sweden. Bollinger has been regularly spotted at Swedish recording studios ever since.

Rumours of a romantic reunion with her ex-husband and producer Richard Karajan, also still in Sweden, are not true according to Karajan's spokesperson. Karajan has been linked to a string of media celebrities since his recent split from his second wife but denies there's substance to any of the rumours.

Whatever might be going on in Bebe Bollinger's private life, there's no doubt that we haven't heard the last from her in terms of her musical career.

The End

Did you like the book?

Please take a moment and let everyone know by posting a review on Goodreads, Amazon.com or Amazon.co.uk to tell others about it. Reviews – however short - and word of mouth are the best way to support an author. Thank you…

… or read on. Here is the first chapter from THE HEALER

The Healer - Chapter 1

The tired, small hatchback hit a rock next to the edge of the road and came to an unexpected and abrupt stop. Erica had not seen the bulky thing hidden underneath the uncut grass. She switched off the engine and got out. There seemed no significant damage to her old banger but she couldn't care less right now, to be honest, and decided she would leave it parked here anyway. She must be close.

Quite frankly, she considered herself lucky to have made it this far; the roads had been bumpy and her car was in a dire condition, too. It wouldn't be much longer before it would have to be scrapped. Living in London she rarely needed it and had often been tempted to sell it anyway.

This was deepest Wales, the countryside - something that the Londoner in her had not seen for years and certainly hadn't missed. Poor phone reception, miles to the nearest supermarket with its supplies of cigarettes and bubbly: that's what the countryside meant to her.

She guessed the car was sufficiently off the road and out of the way. Who would come here, anyway? It was unlikely that two cars would find this remote corner of Wales at the same time, she reckoned. Erica looked around: not a living soul in sight, no houses or vehicles; she was totally off the beaten track. She could see no significant landmarks; all views were blocked by large trees and hedges. It was drizzling a little and although it was past lunchtime, there was mist that reminded her of early mornings. The wind had made the spring temperatures drop more than she had anticipated and she was chilly in her inadequate city clothing.

She searched her purse for the map, which her assistant Hilda had drawn for her. It seemed as if she was in the right place; there was the small path at the foot of the hill, and the two opposing gates leading to fields with horses and sheep. Since leaving her nearby B&B, all the road junctions she had come to had been easy to recognise and here was the little shoulder by the side of the road, where Hilda had recommended she should park the car.

She assured herself once more that it was the right path and then she psyched herself up for the walk up the steep hill. The tricky part, Hilda had explained, was finding the hidden gate, which would lead her to the man himself. However, Hilda didn't have pancreatic cancer and was not recovering from a course of chemo and so she had no idea how difficult it would be for Erica to walk up that hill. It seemed by no means the easy climb her assistant had called it. For all her recent goodness, that woman could drive her mad.

Erica looked at herself in the outside mirror of her car before getting ready to face the man. Her hair had not fallen out from the chemo but it had turned grey and made her look much older than she was. There were still crow's feet and wrinkles despite being facially bloated – it really wasn't fair; the worst of both worlds. People used to think of Erica as at least five years younger than she actually was, but now people thought she was five years older. Overnight it seemed, she had aged from 40 to 50 but given her current situation she would be lucky to reach 45. Additionally, she had lost a lot of weight, despite the effect that the steroids had had on her. With her mere 5' 4" frame, she looked tiny and felt thin and weak.

Only this man might be able to improve her chances and she desperately hoped the trip here would be worth it. If the man really was who Hilda thought, there was a slight chance for her. If she could make him speak to her, then she was sure she could persuade him to help - if he still possessed *those* powers. There suddenly seemed a lot of ifs.

She locked the car and began the climb up the tree-covered hill. Her trainers slid on the moist moss, her jeans too tight for some of the big steps she had to take. There was only a tiny trodden path, which seemed easy to lose sight of, curving its way upwardly through the trees. She was glad she had the map. Hilda deserved an award for organising this; if Erica ever made it back to her position at work she would make sure to find a way of compensating her, if she had anything left after she had paid the man.

Her assistant had come here a few days ago and had scouted the place out in the manner of a gifted detective. Hilda had been an angel the last few months with an uncalled for loyalty and devotion which Erica felt she didn't deserve. Erica cringed when she thought of the numerous times she had blown a fuse in the office and let out her life's frustrations on this woman: she had complained about the coffee being too milky, the memos being too floral or the diary too busy. If only she had known how her life would play out, she would have made many decisions in different ways and definitely would have treated Hilda with more respect and humanity. Well, it was too late for regrets, she could only hope to make it right in the future, if she had one. For now it was time to keep going and move forward and rescue whatever she could.

A chicken wire ran parallel to the path, then some strong wooden fence panels replaced it that were so thickly overgrown with ivy that Erica would have missed seeing the gate itself, had it not been for the directions on the map.

To her surprise the gate was unlocked. A dog barked and howled from afar but it stayed at a safe distance. The noise was not very aggressive anyway and her guess was that this was a companion rather than a guard dog; a further indication that she was at the right place. She doubted that this spiritual guru called Arpan would have aggressive attack dogs around for protection: that would not be the style of someone so ostentatiously non-violent and serious. What she remembered about the man was admittedly extremely vague and distorted by what Hilda had told her.

He had made some headlines a long time ago and at the time, Erica had often seen his picture; if only she had paid more attention to current affairs. Her personal circumstances at the time had kept her pre-occupied and now she was unsure how the press had handled him. Hilda was of the opinion that this was a good thing, since Erica should meet him and find out for herself anyway. Arpan would probably not like to give such an unfavourable impression; Erica thought she remembered him as being very image orientated. He'd either maintain a soft and gentle outward image or would be far too cocky and confident; since the beginning of mankind, gurus had behaved as if they were invincible.

She reminded herself that she had to keep an open mind about this and that it was better to think the best of the man. After all, she had nothing more to lose.

Erica had to navigate between some very overgrown bushes until she came to a small clearing at last. A dome structure was at the other end of the clearing, made of wood and concrete and what looked like parts of camping tents. Solar panels, vegetable beds and free range animals populated the clearing: goats, chicken and sheep. She should have expected that. Green and new age living, she supposed.

"Arpan?" she called out. "Hello?"

An Alsatian came jumping out of the dome full of excitement and began to sniff and lick Erica's hand. He did not look like a puppy but he certainly behaved like one. She knelt down to stroke him gently. The dog wagged his tail excitedly and lay down on the ground, inviting her to rub his belly, and Erica happily obliged. What a happy little dog. She'd forgot how much fun dogs could be.

"Ashank, come back here!" a male voice called from inside the dome. "Come here!"

"Arpan?" Erica repeated shyly. "Hello, is that you, Arpan? I need to speak to you... please."

A young man, maybe 20 years old, slim, spotty and dressed in baggy, red and pink clothes, came briefly out of the dome and called the dog back. Ashank rolled on his side, jumped up and ran to his master. Before Erica could engage with him, the man had zipped the entrance to the dome shut. From what she had seen, his was not the voice she had heard, Erica was sure of it. The person who had called the dog from inside the tent sounded mature and older, much more like that of the Arpan she had heard about. Exactly how she had imagined him to be.

"I need to speak to you, Arpan. It's urgent," Erica called out again, unsure how best to proceed. She wished he would come out of the dome, so she could read his body language and figure out how to best 'work' him. Years in the advertising business had taught her how to handle these situations and she prided herself for her skills in that department. Him not coming out of the dwelling was its own kind of body language and dictated the rules of engagement; she would have to change them, break him down and transform this into a more intimate conversation.

"Go away. You're in the wrong place," the voice called out, sounding tired and slightly annoyed.

"Arpan, I need your help. Please talk to me!" she pleaded. "Hear me out. A few minutes of your time is all I ask of you. Please listen, and then I will go away."

"Who are you anyway?" the man asked, still not showing himself, but she thought she had seen a piece of the tent move. Perhaps he had seen her now and in her current fragile state that had to work in her favour. She looked positively ill and maybe this would appeal to his charitable side. To have done all the good things that he did in youth, he had to have some feelings and a heart. Even if he was a changed man now – as the abrupt stop to his healing practice implied - there had to be a little of his old self beneath the icy exterior, and she would try her damnedest to get to it.

"I'm very ill. You are my only hope now," she said calmly, eager not to overplay for sympathy.

"As I said: you've come to the wrong place," was the curt reply. "I can't help you."

"You have a gift, Arpan, I know you do. And I know you cannot let me die like this. You have a good heart, don't you? They once said that you were an 'Offering' to the world, that is the meaning of your name Arpan, isn't it? Even if you hide yourself away now, you have a responsibility to the world to share this gift. Save me, please!"

"I have responsibilities alright, but they are not to you or anybody else out there," Arpan replied in the manner of a sulky child. "You need to leave now."

"I beg you," Erica said, and sank to her knees. The sudden plunge hurt not only her knees but every other of her joints too. The muddy floor drenched her jeans, but she hardly cared.

"You seem familiar. You're not some journalist, are you? What did you say your name was?"

"Maria Miller," Erica lied. "So you really are Arpan," she added relieved and hopeful. She had found the right man, or rather, her assistant Hilda had. If she were religious, she would bless the Lord.

"I said no such thing," the man shouted back angrily. "I call myself Amesh. A different name altogether, a different man and a different life. One more suited to me. Please get up and leave."

"It doesn't matter what name you have. I'm dying, Amesh, so I don't have much time left to persuade you to help me."

"The man you're looking for is no more. I wish I could help you, but I simply can't. He disappeared with the name. Go home and do the only thing you can do: make peace with your enemies, tell your loved ones how much they mean to you and sort out all of your affairs in a manner that will make you proud. If it is your time to die, you should not waste the gift of time by looking for miracles that didn't find you on their own. Not many have the opportunity to right their wrongs. Use it wisely."

"Maybe you're right," Erica said, after a few seconds of deliberation. "If it really is my time to die, I will. I have already begun the process of righting my wrongs, as you call it. I had given up all hope and had resigned myself to die. But then I found you and I seriously believe that found you for a good reason. Many others must have tried to find you and didn't succeed. If things are meant to be, then this meeting between us now might not be a coincidence, so please let's talk. Let me at least look at you. Let us stand face to face. Maybe it will help me so I can bury the illusion that you would have been the one man left on the planet able to save me."

She heard a whisper in the tent, then the young boy came out from under the dome and looked her up and down. He was slim but more muscled than what she had initially thought, not as tall as he had looked just moments earlier, blond dreadlocks and a beard hiding some of his spots, piercings, tattoos and a cocky walk. Although he had a young face, he carried himself like someone who had been through a lot and knew how to handle life. He was focused but not quite calm enough to carry it off completely convincingly.

"You don't have a microphone or anything, do you?" He asked and frisked her. He was not shy touching her. "Let me look into your backpack," he said and rummaged through it when Erica offered it to him without hesitation. All Erica had brought with her were pen and paper, some snacks and her purse.

"She's clean," he called out to the man still hiding inside.

"What does Amesh mean?" Erica asked. "If Arpan meant 'Offering', then surely Amesh must have a meaning. What is it?"

"Coward Boy," said the old voice.

She was shocked at that and fell silent.

At last the man himself stepped out of the tent, with the Alsatian dancing around him. "The name represents what I have become."

202

Amesh looked nothing like she had expected. He had shaved his beard off and also his long, dark, Jesus-like hair. Bold and haggard he was a shadow of his former self. At least 60 and looking every bit of it, his face seemed deflated, his shoulders were hunched and there was nothing left of the charismatic persona Arpan had once been. She could see why he had chosen Amesh as his new name, there was something timid about him. It suited him better than Arpan, 'the Offering', as he had been known.

"You see," Amesh said shrugging his shoulders. "Stripped off all the glamour and of all power! I'm just your regular woodland hermit, growing vegetables and talking to the trees."

A hint of recognition slipped across his face.

"You remind me of someone," he said, but Erica shook her head. "Well, maybe it is the disease you have that makes me think I know you," he added. "I spent years with it and have seen it in all of its shapes and forms. Are you sure we haven't met before?"

"I know we haven't," she said quickly.

"How did you even find me?" he asked, looking intensely at her as if scanning her thoughts while he was doing it. "It's quite worrying," he added. "I'll finally have to succumb to necessity and install security again. Can't you people simply leave me alone? It's been years since anyone has taken notice of me. I thought I was at peace at last."

"I'm sorry," she replied sheepishly. "I guess it was the right amount of desperation and luck. For what it's worth, I can assure you that the people who helped me wouldn't give out your secret easily."

"I should hope so. Not many have any clue as to where I live these days. Trust me, I will silence them myself as soon as I can," he said forcefully, but Erica didn't think he meant it.

"Well, now that you've seen me in my new earthly incarnation I hope you can go back to your life in peace, knowing that you didn't miss out on some miracle that was meant for you. You can tell that I'm not the man you're looking for." He opened his arms in a gesture of disclosure and even turned around for her to have a good look.

"What happened to Arpan?" she asked, hoping to play up to his vanity. As long as she kept him talking, she was building a rapport. The more he knew about her, the more likely he was to feel sorry and change his mind. If he ever had the powers to heal pancreatic cancer with his hands, then that ability had to have stayed with him. As long a shot as this was, if he had done it once he had to be able to do it once more for her.

He shook his head. "As I've said, Arpan is no more. The world has transformed him and his gift, and it put me in his place."

"That's very cryptic. What's that actually supposed to mean?"

"You know, you sound just like a journalist," he said with a grin. "If I didn't see the disease in your face I would say you're here only looking for a scoop. Either way, what I said means simply that I don't have the powers that you seek."

"You healed hundreds of people," Erica insisted.

"That wasn't me; it was Arpan, 'the Offering'. He was something else, entirely. I cannot heal you, however much I wish I could," Amesh said resigned.

"You could at least try."

"Maria, you know nothing about me, about Arpan or about the so-called miracles. I indulged you by letting you see me, as you requested but I beg of you to leave now and to keep my location a secret. Arpan has given enough to the world, now it is time for Amesh to live his life to suit his needs."

"You can't give up on a calling like yours," Erica said with growing desperation.

"Amesh can and Arpan did, too. If you knew more you would probably understand."

"I have money, plenty of it, and I can get more, if that's what it takes," Erica blabbered in panic. She knew it was the wrong approach but she just couldn't help herself.

"Do I look like I need money?" Amesh said, shaking his head and pointing around him. "This is not the life of someone who wants lots of money - that should be very obvious to anyone."

"Actually, if I'm honest, it looks like the property of someone who could do with quite a lot of money." Erica contradicted. "It could buy you more living space, better isolation against rain and wind, to say the least, and security or a receptionist to help you out."

"I don't want any of that," Amesh said dismissively, "and I really don't need or want your money, thank you very much."

"Arpan took 50% of everything his patients owned," Erica said accusingly. "How does that fit in with what you are saying? For all his spirituality, Arpan did like the cash. Has it all gone? Looks like Amesh could do with a topping up his bank accounts to improve this place. At least get it safe for the next winter. I can help you if you help me."

"Arpan didn't 'like' the money, but the payment was an important and a very necessary part of the process," Amesh replied. "If the people who came to him weren't prepared to give this much for their life, then Arpan wasn't able to help them, just as western medicine couldn't help them. You need to value your life and the cost of keeping it."

Erica had to bite her tongue. Her natural distrust for miracle healers and un-scientific claims was ever-present but she mustn't alienate Amesh with her critical thoughts.

"If someone values their wealth above their health, then western medicine or *any* alternative measures can only slightly prolong their life," Amesh lectured her. "They are doomed, and nobody can stop the course of their destiny. People cheated Arpan and paid him only a fraction of what they were worth. When the disease then indeed didn't go away they asked for their money back, and Arpan returned all of those monies, without even charging them for his time, which they wasted. Every single person who didn't get cured was reimbursed. Many brought it onto themselves, I hasten to add."

"I get that you are retired for some reason or another and bitter with the world about something it did to you, but that doesn't necessarily mean that you're suddenly incapable of healing," Erica said. "Whatever it was that stopped you practicing at the height of your fame doesn't justify throwing away your gift. You mustn't let the newspapers and their hate campaigns get to you. You must at least try. Try on me to see if your powers are back. Please."

"You are so naïve," Amesh replied and sneered. "The work Arpan did was more complex than you will ever be able to comprehend. The newspapers and their treatment of him were not what stopped him; they were simply a symptom of the all underlying evil that stopped him: human nature and society. I don't want to get into the whole thing. As Amesh, I'm happy now and I lead a life that suits me just fine. I have a right to enjoy it."

"But…" she began, but he interrupted.

"Enough said. I have asked you to leave on numerous occasions and you have refused to comply. You are trespassing on my property and I wish for you to leave now. Anuj will escort you of the premises," he said and, as if on command, the young man came towards her, followed by the excitable Alsatian; he took her by the elbow and led her away.

"Please, Anuj," Erica pleaded on their way to the gate. "Put in a good word with him for me. I'm desperate and I don't have much time. Here is my card. I'm staying at Woodlands B&B, which is not far from here."

Anuj took the card and put it in his pocket.

"Don't get your hopes up," he warned. "As Amesh, he is hurting and as Arpan, he hasn't seen a client since he retreated from the limelight years ago. We also don't have a phone or computer and I doubt that you will hear from him. Do as he says and get on with your life, or what is left of it. He doesn't play games and this is not a case of 'playing hard to get'. I agree with him, that your time is a gift to get your life in order. I can tell there is a lot for you to do. Trying to be saved is a selfish use of the little time you have left when there are many things you should be doing instead. Think of the things you have to do before your time is up. Think of the people around you and what they need: goodbyes, sorting of affairs… there is so much. When you come to think of it, I doubt that you really have time for us, don't waste it by holding out for an unobtainable miracle. Think of the things you need to do and the people that need you."

"Those people need me alive," Erica said. "If they care, they need me alive."

"You need to trust what he said. Amesh might only be a shadow of what Arpan was but he can still see into people's souls. It's like a psychic X-ray; he gets people with only one look. I'm only his apprentice but I too can see the disorder in your life that needs to be rectified. You carry hurt and anger with you. Your disease has prompted you to fast track those issues and requires you to sort them out. Look into your heart and you will find this to be true."

"Tell him I'll be waiting for your call," Erica said stubbornly, "Amesh must have seen my determination," she added just before Anuj closed the gate behind her.

Angrily she walked down the hill, slipped twice and fell over the root of a tree. She had a few scratches and skinned one of her knees. Since the chemo, her skin was so fragile and seemed to rip open at the slightest touch. She got into her car and tried to start it, but the engine would not spring to life. She tried and tried but gradually realised that she was stuck. Here, of all places. This couldn't have happened anywhere worse. There was nobody, no sign of civilisation, people, houses or even mobile phone reception. For a brief moment she contemplated going back up the hill but she feared Arpan and Anuj would see it as a fake excuse and that would in no way help her cause with those two, of that she was sure. They would help her with the car but it might put them off for good and then he would never agree to help her with her illness.

Her body was aching badly and her painkillers made her terribly tired, so she decided to take a little rest before making any further plans. She quickly nodded off in the driver's seat and slept for several hours. It was late afternoon when a knocking on her car window woke her. It was Anuj with the Alsatian.

"Nice try," Anuj said dismissively when she explained her predicament to him. "Don't think we'll be changing our mind because of a broken down car."

"I wouldn't dream of such a thing," she said. "Just tell me what you suggest I should do."

He nodded and said with a hint of sarcasm: "It's only a two mile walk from here to the next farm. I'm sure they'll let you call the rescue services. I'll draw you a map how to find them."

"Thank you," Erica said as gracefully as she could. "I'll do that then."

She took her backpack and followed his directions. The walk was definitely much longer than the two miles Anuj had promised. The thought occurred to her that she mustn't get lost or she would never get out of here alive. The lush green Welsh countryside here started to grow on her a little: the constant rain had at least one upside. She had heard her fanatic hiking colleagues say that one could go days without meeting anyone else in some of these 'off the beaten track' locations. Obviously that was what Arpan or Amesh had gone for and what had brought her into trouble. She had tempted fate by driving here in such an old banger, she knew that.

She had to sit down and rest several times as she kept running out of breath. The farm was abandoned when she got there. After what seemed like an eternity of resting on a garden bench, she was getting concerned. At this time of the year, the sun would set soon and she had to consider all of her options. She began to worry that no-one would come home to the farm and she had to make use of the little daylight that was left to get back to her car. She would rather sleep in her car than somewhere here as an intruder in a farm outbuilding. At least, she had some food and a blanket in her car, here she would be nothing but a trespasser again. When she got back to her Fiesta it was already pitch dark. It didn't take much for her to fall asleep again and despite the wildlife noises that she was unaccustomed to, she slept all the way through to sunrise...

More books by Christoph Fischer:

The Healer

When advertising executive Erica Whittaker is diagnosed with terminal cancer, western medicine fails her. The only hope left for her to survive is controversial healer Arpan. She locates the man whose touch could heal her but finds he has retired from the limelight and refuses to treat her. Erica, consumed by stage four pancreatic cancer, is desperate and desperate people are no longer logical nor are they willing to take no for an answer. Arpan has retired for good reasons, casting more than the shadow of a doubt over his abilities. So begins a journey that will challenge them both as the past threatens to catch up with him as much as with her. Can he really heal her? Can she trust him with her life? And will they both achieve what they set out to do before running out of time?

Amazon: http://ow.ly/J4Wt6
Facebook: http://ow.ly/J4Wun
Goodreads: http://ow.ly/J4Ww4
Book-likes: http://ow.ly/J4WxU
Rifflebooks: http://ow.ly/J4WzY

The Gamblers

Ben is an insecure accountant obsessed with statistics, gambling and beating the odds. When he wins sixty-four million in the lottery he finds himself challenged by the possibilities that his new wealth brings.

He soon falls under the influence of charismatic Russian gambler Mirco, whom he meets on a holiday in New York. He also falls in love with a stewardess, Wendy, but now that Ben's rich he finds it hard to trust anyone. As both relationships become more dubious, Ben needs to make some difficult decisions and figure out who's really his friend and who's just in it for the money.

Amazon: http://ow.ly/S5tJC
Facebook: http://ow.ly/S5tcQ
Goodreads: http://ow.ly/S5tmE
Booklikes: http://ow.ly/S5sU9
Rifflebooks.com http://ow.ly/S5t2W
Createspace: http://ow.ly/S5txM

Ludwika:
A Polish Woman's Struggle To Survive In Nazi Germany

It's World War II and Ludwika Gierz, a young Polish woman, is forced to leave her family and go to Nazi Germany to work for an SS officer. There, she must walk a tightrope, learning to live as a second-class citizen in a world where one wrong word could spell disaster and every day could be her last. Based on real events, this is a story of hope amid despair, of love amid loss . . . ultimately, it's one woman's story of survival.

Editorial Review:

"This is the best kind of fiction—it's based on the real life. Ludwika's story highlights the magnitude of human suffering caused by WWII, transcending multiple generations and many nations.

WWII left no one unscarred, and Ludwika's life illustrates this tragic fact. But she also reminds us how bright the human spirit can shine when darkness falls in that unrelenting way it does during wartime.

This book was a rollercoaster ride of action and emotion, skilfully told by Mr. Fischer, who brought something fresh and new to a topic about which thousands of stories have already been told."

http://www.audible.com/pd/Mysteries-Thrillers/The-Healer-Audiobook/B01G62A7MQ/
http://bookShow.me/B018UTHX7A
http://smarturl.it/Ludwika
https://www.goodreads.com/book/show/28111001-ludwika
https://www.facebook.com/LudwikaNovel/
http://www.barnesandnoble.com/w/ludwika-mr-christoph-fischer/1123093504?can=9781519539113

The Luck of the Weissensteiners
(Three Nations Trilogy: Book 1)

In the sleepy town of Bratislava in 1933 the daughter of a Jewish weaver falls for a bookseller from Berlin, Wilhelm Winkelmeier. Greta Weissensteiner seemingly settles in with her in-laws but the developments in Germany start to make waves in Europe and re-draw the visible and invisible borders. The political climate, the multi-cultural jigsaw puzzle of the disintegrating Czechoslovakian state and personal conflicts make relations between the couple and the families more and more complex. The story follows the families through the war with its predictable and also its unexpected turns and events and the equally hard times after. What makes The Luck of the Weissensteiners so extraordinary is the chance to consider the many different people who were never in concentration camps, never in the military, yet who nonetheless had their own indelible Holocaust experiences. This is a wide-ranging, historically accurate exploration of the connections between social status, personal integrity and, as the title says, luck.

Amazon: http://smarturl.it/Weissensteiners
Goodreads: http://bit.ly/12Rnup8
Facebook: http://on.fb.me/1bua395
B&N: http://ow.ly/Btvas
Book-Likes: http://ow.ly/J4X2q
Rifflebooks: http://ow.ly/J4WY0
Trailer: http://studio.stupeflix.com/v/OtmyZh4Dmc

Time to Let Go

Time to Let Go is a contemporary family drama set in Britain. Following a traumatic incident at work stewardess Hanna Korhonen decides to take a break from work and leaves her home in London to stay with her elderly parents in rural England. There she finds that neither can she run away from her problems, nor does her family provide the easy getaway place that she has hoped for. Her mother suffers from Alzheimer's disease and, while being confronted with the consequences of her issues at work, she and her entire family are forced to reassess their lives.

The book takes a close look at family dynamics and at human nature in a time of a crisis. Their challenges, individual and shared, take the Korhonens on a journey of self-discovery and redemption.

Amazon: http://smarturl.it/TTLG
Goodreads: http://ow.ly/BtKs7
Facebook: http://ow.ly/BtKtQ
Book-Likes: http://ow.ly/J4Xu0
Rifflebooks: http://ow.ly/J4XvR

Thanks

A big thank you to 'crime fiction junkie' Ryan, without whose enthusiasm I would never have fallen in love with the genre and written the book.

A huge thanks to my editor David Lawlor for his invaluable contributions and suggestions, his honesty and diplomacy in the process, and to my excellent beta readers Noelle Granger, Patricia Zick, Susan Tarr, Lucinda E. Clarke, Olga Nunez Miret and Anna Belfrage.

Thanks to my amazing friend and cover designer Daz Smith for getting it right once again and for pushing me into publishing in the first place.

Last, but not least, to Celeste Burke and Dianne Harman, two professionals in the genre, for their inspiring body of work and lending support.

Disclaimer

This book is a work of fiction, even though it is set during an event that really happened and includes some public figures. I have transcribed what Bonnie Tyler or other participants have said about the contest to be able to make them part of the book, but everything else about them in my book is purely fictional.

I used some actual participants of the contest as side figures. All their actions are totally fictional, too.

I have met Nicki French at some Eurovision events and had friendly permission by her agent to use her as a real character.

Although my story playfully involves some public figures (such as Adele and Alison Moyet) their interactions with my fictitious characters are naturally made up. Any similarities with their actions in the real world are coincidental. All other characters in this novel are fictitious.

I have deepest respect for all artists mentioned in the book and have not intended to portray them in any negative or dubious light.

This book is a work of fiction. Except for some real singers and TV personalities, the characters of this novel are all fictitious.

A Short Biography

Christoph Fischer was born in Germany, near the Austrian border, as the son of a Sudeten-German father and a Bavarian mother. Not a full local in the eyes and ears of his peers he developed an ambiguous sense of belonging and moved to Hamburg in pursuit of his studies and to lead a life of literary indulgence. In 1993 he moved to the UK and now lives in Llandeilo in west Wales. He and his partner have several Labradoodles to complete their family.

Christoph worked for the British Film Institute, in Libraries, Museums and for an airline. His first historical novel, 'The Luck of The Weissensteiners', was published in November 2012 and downloaded over 60,000 times on Amazon. He has released several more historical novels, including 'In Search of A Revolution' and 'Ludwika'. He also wrote some contemporary family dramas and thrillers, most notably 'Time to Let Go' and 'The Healer'.

For further information you can follow him on:

Twitter:
https://twitter.com/CFFBooks
Pinterest:
http://www.pinterest.com/christophffisch/
Google +:
https://plus.google.com/u/0/106213860775307052243
LinkedIn:
https://www.linkedin.com/profile/view?id=241333846
Blog:
http://writerchristophfischer.wordpress.com
Website:
www.christophfischerbooks.com
Facebook:
www.facebook.com/WriterChristophFischer

Printed in Great Britain
by Amazon

81889946R00129